Forerunner
The Last Cities Series, Vol. 1

‒

Brandon List

Printed in the United States of America

First Printing, 2016
Second Printing, 2019

ISBN 0-9981579-1-0

A special thanks to those who helped this story along its journey

Kevin, Le, Rachel, Kevin, Sarah, Jason, & Amy

Much love

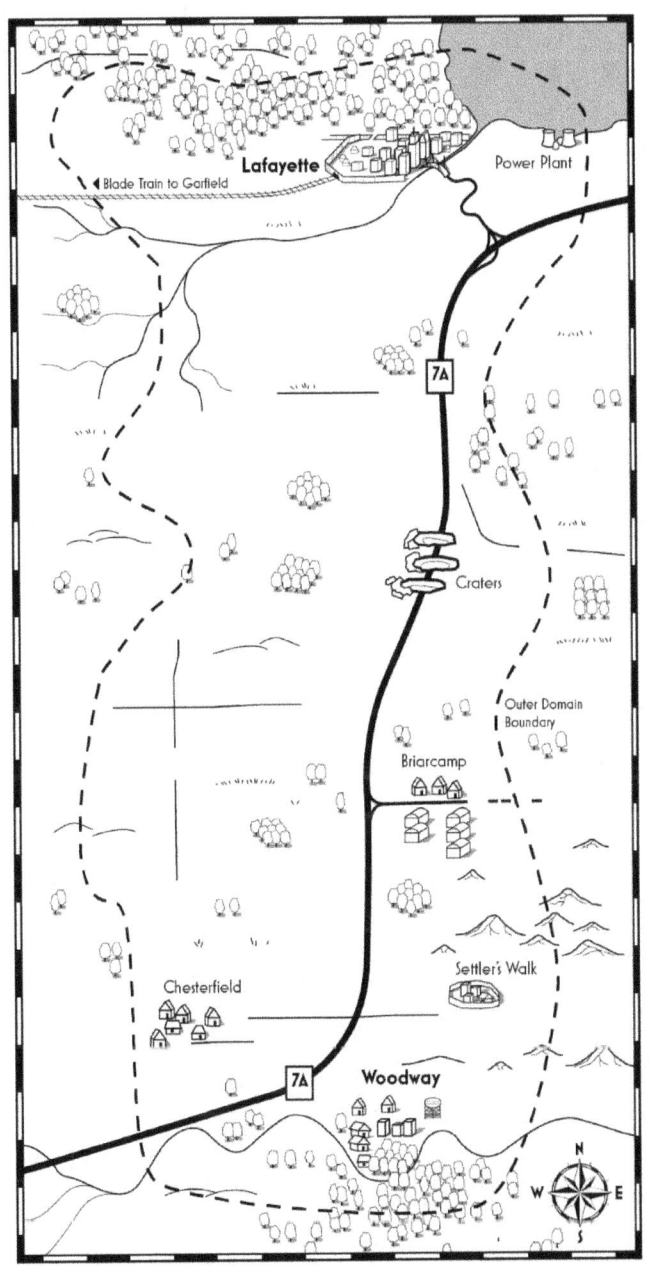

Prologue

So the story goes that the first generation of Fenders seized control of three Last Cities shortly after Leveling had waned. Each possessing impressive powers of mind or body, they banded together and encountered little resistance in establishing a kingdom of sorts. They called it The Chancellery, three sovereign cities in a loose coalition:

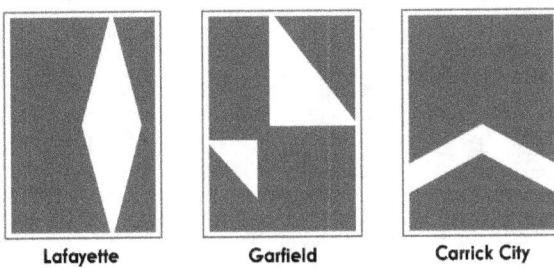

Lafayette   Garfield   Carrick City

For most, the Fender's Articles of Protocol provided a welcome structure in tattered and desperate times. Walls provided defense from bandits. Protocol checks provided security among their own. The Blade train provided transportation that didn't involve scrounging for gasoline. A steady flow of food and other resources provided assurance of a future.

And other Ables found a special place in the Last Cities. The three Fenders welcomed the use of their mysteriously unlocked powers toward maintaining order. So there was more calm than not in the beginning years of the Chancellery. The system worked, despite whispers of terrible attacks, missing family members, and worse. The Fenders prospered, titans in their own right.

This particular story starts in the midst of their third generation. Kenyon Hubbard, Fender of Lafayette, was the oldest. He had taken control of Lafayette at the age of twenty-one when his father died. Most Fenders were sons or daughters of the generation before. Dell Ashburn was a spitting image of his father, and ruled Garfield in a fast and loose manner that made his fellow Fenders anxious. And Groa Stanton's father seized control of Carrick City in a vicious military coup that had left more than half the city dead. His origins were still a mystery.

Avery Jackson lived outside the direct control of these three cities, at the fringes of The Chancellery known as the Outer Domain.

Section 1

A Witness Tree.

Chapter 1

With the World

Early morning gave the crumbled bits of civilization an anonymity that Avery liked. He rode hard and loud along the faded and potholed road, clamoring through a scattered grey forest blanketed in pre-dawn fog. The rusted motorcycle vibrated rhythmically. He wore a tattered leather riding jacket, a helmet cinched under his chin, faded jeans, and steel-toed boots.

The asphalt strip rose gradually from a steep river valley behind him. Long abandoned subdivisions dotted the landscape. Blurred by the moist air, rectangular structures sulked behind barricaded residential streets. He was still inside the fenced zone, minimal risk of bandits rolling out of a sagging split-level to give him trouble.

It was two days before Avery's nineteenth birthday, and all he wanted was to put distance between himself and home. His mother hated the bike. Gasoline was expensive and the vehicle was a dangerous possession in a world with many watchful eyes. Nevertheless, he had spent more than half of his annual earnings last year on the decrepit old thing and he loved it.

Arriving at a large misty intersection, he slowed. Doublewide turn lanes, designed for traffic that had gone silent eons before, reached out in each direction. Weed-invaded gas stations sat on the corners. None of the underground tanks held even a drop of gasoline.

The bike's first gear was ground to the bone and liked to slip out of place, which it did. This would stall the engine, which it did, sputtering and spitting angrily. *Crap.* He kicked out both legs. His compact frame handled the tipping weight with confidence, trim and agile from years spent tending a grove of massive

Sentinel oak trees with his uncle. Croaking insects filled the silence as he instinctively checked over both shoulders. With words of encouragement, he urged the engine back to life and pulled a wide arc to the north.

Two miles from the intersection, the tree line broke open and Avery turned into the narrow parking lot of what once was an elementary school. A covered walkway connected the driveway to a low tan building. Grass and weeds grew shoulder high against the dark windows. He parked and pulled off his helmet to the smell of vaporizing oil. His sweaty hair was dark and trimmed close on the sides. His eyes were deep set and attentive, a rounded chin and broad jaw sitting above wide wiry shoulders. With fingers pressed between his narrow lips, he blew a shrill two-tone whistle before walking up to the school entrance and pulling off his canvas pack.

A distant bark echoed through the surrounding woods. Avery whistled again. Two empty bowls sat on the concrete slab. He filled one with water from a canteen and waited. A minute later the tangled weeds parted, an orange and grey spotted dog romped toward him.

"Hey Wink!" Avery exclaimed, kneeling down to pat the shaggy mutt, "Hey buddy."

Wink was missing his left eye, burrs stuck to his undercarriage, and he emitted a dreadful stink. Regardless, Avery scratched behind both ears and was thrilled to see his old pal.

"How you been? Hungry?" he asked, checking for ticks. "Spending your days chasing girls out there in the woods?"

Wink wagged his tail in circles, tongue flapping happily.

"Home is super boring these days. And my mom, she's been getting on my nerves lately. Thanks for asking," Avery said.

Wink nosed him in the chest and he finally pulled out what the dog had been waiting for: a cracked plastic bag filled with vegetable bits and dried squirrel meat. This got dumped in the second bowl. Wink then munched urgently, pushing the bowl along the dimpled pavement. Avery sat on the step as he ate.

When the bowl was empty and with his snout dripping after a long drink, Wink padded over, circled, and laid his head on

Avery's knee. Together they watched the fog stroll past as it slowly turned orange with morning sun.

After some time, Avery reassured his companion that he would be back soon and returned to his bike. With his riding jacket zipped and pack tightened on his shoulders, Avery said goodbye to Wink who sat back on his haunches with a forlorn expression.

"I'll be back in a few days, K?" Avery said as he fired up the bike and pulled away with an ache in his heart for a friendship that was something more than a stray dog in an abandoned schoolyard.

As the climbing sun burned off any last pockets of fog, Avery headed north from the school. At another anonymous intersection, he turned west. The forest soon thinned. Canopy gave way to a patchwork of fallow fields. Regular plots had long since given way to swaths of mustard grass and thistle. The bike's power gave him a sense of freedom. At a heart-quickening pace, he wove a smooth path through piles of debris that dotted the road. Morning scented air rushed across his face.

The land eventually rolled up toward a flattened hilltop where a lone Oak stood. It was quite different from the organized variety of his grove, this was what they called a Witness Tree. With gnarled bark and tightly twisted branches, this tree had been standing in this field long before Leveling pulled civilization to pieces. He had watched a hundred plus years pass, the world changing several times over. And in the last few summers, he had become a favorite spot for Avery Jackson, the young Oak Keeper.

Avery parked in the driveway of what remained of a farmhouse near the Witness Tree. Bits of the foundation stuck up in places. Through rustling leaves, Avery looked up at the narrow clouds painted with yellow and ran his hand along the deep cords of bark.

From the canvas pack he pulled his climbing harness and a coil of rope. Even with a few tattered edges, it fit him like a pair of old running shoes. He stepped into the straps and tightened them around his waist.

He then coiled half of his rope in a loose figure-eight pattern, pulled several loops around this length and flung the bundle overhead. It arched just over the top of the lowest branch and came uncoiling down to him. He fastened the rope into the harness rigging and stepped toward the trunk. With a second, shorter length pulled around the circumference of the trunk. Avery scaled the tree with speed. He kept his weight pushed back onto his hips and pulled higher in a steady rhythm. Soon he stood on a familiar branch and unhooked.

Swinging from branch to branch, he climbed until his head popped from the very top branches. A hundred yards from the tree, dilapidated border fence ran in each direction. Numerous holes dotted the mesh and Avery could never understand how it kept even the foxes from getting through. The world beyond lay out before him. More fallow fields, abandoned boxes of a Wal-Mart and a Walgreens, and decaying infrastructure were overtaken by nature engaged in its task of reclamation. Smoke rose from a few scattered bandit encampments, all of which were situated near the cleared lanes of Fender toll road 7A.

A line of military-style cargo trucks chugged along the road, trailed by a pair of sleek grey escort vehicles. Avery had seen only two of these impressive escort machines before. The nose was pointed. The back end squared off just behind the tires. Even from a distance the vehicle looked fast and mean - probably driven by a highly trained soldier from the City of Lafayette, which was located several hundred miles north. The convoy moved along at a deliberate pace, with the escort vehicles following close behind.

But as Avery watched, strange movements popped up along the road. A hoard of rusted out vehicles stumbled into view and cut in front of the lead cargo truck. The convoy screeched to a halt as the bandits, dressed in tattered clothes and holding a hodge podge of weapons, advanced with limping steps. Distant hoots and jeers echoed from the approaching bandits. Avery clutched to the branch tightly, eyes glued to the attack.

Out of the escort machines came two soldiers dressed in slate grey uniforms with green details along the seams. They flew toward the bandits, who fired their rifles recklessly. Avery expected the soldiers to draw their own weapons but they stopped short of the attackers. The first uniformed man produced a glowing green spear in his hand and vaulted it square into the chest of a bandit. Avery was convinced he was hallucinating. He squeezed his eyes closed for a second.

But when he opened them again, another spear glowed to life in the soldier's outstretched hand and was quickly released. Then another. And another. Each took down their target with perfect precision.

Meanwhile, a pair of bandits had ducked around the convoy and scaled onto one of the trucks. They slammed spikes into the cargo roof. The second soldier catapulted an impossible height, landing directly on the bandits, and flinging them off the roof with a violent strength.

These must have been Lancers, Ables who had been conscripted by the Fenders to use their powers to maintain "protocol and order throughout The Chancellery". Their powers were overwhelming and in short order the last of the bandits made a desperate retreat for the trees. Soon enough, the abandoned vehicles had been cleared and the convoy moved on.

The mysterious soldiers captivated Avery. His mother had always warned him about how dangerous they were. How Lafayette's Fender, Kenyon Hubbard, had his men on such a tight leash that they could snap at any time. But Avery disagreed. They were amazing. Had she seen them do that type of stuff?

Avery went back to watching the stillness as the convoy faded away. For a long while, he watched as a gentle breeze pushed waves through the tangled fields, sun easing higher in the sky. He cherished these moments with the world. When he seemed to float above the bounds of his gnawing one-towned, samething-ed life, which was nothing like that of a soldier. His imagination could accelerate into the vast and disordered openness laid out before him.

In due time he descended, reattached the rope, and repelled back to the ground. With the climbing gear neatly packed, he pulled away with a roar. He retraced the route back into the protected cocoon of his hometown - past the school, past the ramshackle homes, and into the deeper woods.

What Avery did not know was when he rode by a nondescript telephone pole, a series of sensors flanking the road were activated. A small camera came to life, focused and quickly snapped three high-resolution photos. These images were packaged together and broadcast to a receiving station hundreds of miles away. The camera received a confirmation code in return and quickly powered off.

Woodway sat in its own elbow of the world. A quiet enclave nestled in a tight river bend and Avery's home for the last eighteen years and three hundred and sixty-three days. It consisted of two intersecting streets lined with a few time-beaten storefronts and townhomes. Scattered around the periphery were secluded homes among the trees. Several blocks from Main Street sat a school building, a library, a rusted water tower and a cluster of green houses. A geothermal vent powered two turbines that provided half the town with electricity. Avery had never ventured more than ten miles from the town's edge on account of dangers that lingered beyond the fence.

He turned at the main intersection and slowed. The bike regularly caught folk's attention. They stuck their heads out of windows, scowling while trying to identify the face under that helmet. He paused at the central intersection and the engine stalled. Damn. Both pistons slugged back and forth, unwilling to catch.

In the midst of his third attempt, Jasper appeared around corner. Avery squinted up at his tall Uncle who wore a similar outfit of jeans and work boots. A greying five-o'clock shadow covering his wrinkled neck.

"Hey Uncle Jasper," Avery said.

"Glad I found you," Jasper said with an unusual urgency in his deep voice. He was normally a stoic, quite guy. Avery decided to wait to tell him about the bandit attack he had just seen.

"What's up?" Avery asked, aborting the engine restart.

"Water tower's sprung a leak," Jasper said rapidly.

"That's neat."

The rust eaten tower was a constant source of dispute in Woodway. Every council meeting included debate on reinforcing the ancient storage tank. Now they had a problem.

"Come on," Jasper waved.

Avery pushed his bike to the curb and joined his uncle in an urgent jog to the other side of town. The deteriorating tower stood on the far end of the schoolyard and a group of small children gathered in the playground. They giggled and pointed at the rust colored water spitting from a split in a lower seam.

Avery and Jasper discussed the leak from the tower's shadow when a barrel chested man with a white beard arrived carrying several metal panels and a toolbox.

"Clarence, good to see you," Jasper said, shaking his hand.

"Had this coming, didn't we," Clearance grumbled. "You get the honor of climbing up there?" He asked.

"Avery's gonna do it," Jasper said.

Avery's face contorted, "What...Me? Why me?"

Clarence dropped the materials in the dirt and waddled off, "Back in a few."

"I can't fix that leak," Avery protested. "It's frickin' impossible."

"No it's not," Jasper said with a grin. "Just like climbing in the grove. You can anchor to the cross bracing right there next to the bust. Screw the panels in fast to the sidewall. It'll be good for ya."

"No way."

Jasper checked the charge on a drill and handed it to Avery, "Clarence will be back soon with some tar. You can seal the edges with that."

"This is literally the worst plan ever."

"Service to the town kiddo. Strap up."

After several more minutes of protest, Avery was back in his climbing harness and scaling the tower. He was going to have to suck it up and get the job done. It was dumb and stupid, but there was no getting around his uncle on this one.

He methodically worked his way upward, the metal panels and bucket of tar hanging from a second cord, drill and metal screws in his pack. The height did not faze him, but the extra weight and rough metal girders threw off his typical climbing rhythm.

Water hissed as he secured himself near the under belly of the tank. He looked at the baseball-sized hole, then at the panels and bucket hanging from his hip and then down at his uncle who gave him a grinning thumbs up.

Sun baked him as he bent the first metal panel to the curve of the tank. He tested his hand against the high-pressure water stream with a sting. He then tested the panel against the water and it nearly flew from his grip.

How the hell was he going to do this? For a while he just hung in place and stewed. Stupid water tower, stupid Woodway. A small audience of residents had gathered below. He dripped with sweat from the heat and their scrutiny.

"Go for it kid," Jasper called up.

He dropped the panel against his knees, cocked the screwdriver in his right hand and swung perilously toward the leak.

In a surge of force that surprised even himself, he slammed against the side, sending a deep vibration through the tank. Water spurted from around the edge, but the panel held. An unfamiliar energy surged through his limbs. In that moment, he felt like he could produce his own set of green death spears like the Lancers on 7A.

But instead, he frantically drove in the first of a hundred and thirty-seven screws. Once the first panel was fastened, water only dripped slowly at the new seam. The second panel got modeled and similarly fastened in the opposite direction, making a cross shaped patch. He then lathered a thick coat of smelly black sealant along the edges. The sticky goop clung to his hands and stung his nose.

It was well after midday when he checked the newly patched water tower from top to bottom and lowered himself.

Before he could even touch down, a pack of residents rushed over to congratulate him.

"You saved our water young man."

"Strong work, son. Strong work."

"Hey Avery, Avery!" A small child squealed, "Can I get your autograph?"

He bashfully played off the daring repair. Saying that he was just doing his job, that's all. Though he privately welled with pride.

They hurried him over to the shade and pushed a water bottle in his hands from which he drank in long gulps. At some point his mother arrived, rushing through the crowd to balk at his rust and tar covered condition.

"Mr. Jackson. What on earth have you been doing?"

He just grinned and pecked her on check. Jasper explained the situation.

"He did what?!" she exclaimed, pushing strands of greying blond hair away from her piercing eyes.

"And you let him!"

With her jaw set, she checked him thoroughly, ensuring all limbs were attached and that he hadn't swallowed any tar. This thoroughly embarrassed him, of course. His mom didn't know when to shut up sometimes. Though he still enjoyed the thrill from all of the public attention.

Then Quincy Pratt arrived. Lafayette Outer Domain Council Representative Pratt, as he preferred to be called, was a wiener of a man. He consisted of a wide belly, hanging chin, and boney arms. He took his appointed position as liaison to the distant City of Lafayette very, very seriously.

Looking indignant, he shouldered his way over to Avery and the crowd started to disperse.

"Fill out this 3B-67 Incident Response Form, please."

Avery swallowed, "But I just…"

Quincy continued to present report form, "Lafayette officials like to be fully informed of incidents like these, including the parties involved and materials utilized."

Avery took the paper with a strike of panic. Syllables and phrases spun around in his brain without organizing into complete sentences. He struggled with reading, he always had. And the surrounding bustle made things a thousand times worse. Quincy glared down his long nose. Avery's mother stood talking loudly with the other women. The overexcited child was still bouncing around with a pen in his hand, waiting for an autograph. Avery's stomach felt like it was growing to a bursting point.

"For the records. Very simple, Avery," Quincy absconded. His term as Woodway representative was close to running out and in recent months had been keen to follow every item of Protocol as precisely as possible.

Avery felt stupid. He wanted to disappear, rocket back to the quiet forests outside town. But he wasn't stupid, he just couldn't freaking read sometimes.

"Here, I'll take care of that," Jasper said knowingly. His uncle took the paper from Avery's sweaty hand and steered Quincy away from the group. This gave Avery a chance to slip away. With his pack slung over one shoulder he hurried back to his parked bike. The engine mercifully started on the first turn and he peeled away in a tight loop. Any glimmer of satisfaction was now completely overwhelmed by gnawing embarrassment.

At a narrow gravel driveway several blocks north of town, he turned toward home. The small bungalow, no more than a kitchen and two bedrooms under a sagging roof and faded cedar siding, sat in a small clearing facing a metal paneled barn. A barrel filled with rainwater sat alongside the house. Throwing his pack onto the porch, he ripped off the barrel top. Then dunked his head in the cool water and tried to clear his mind as he scrubbed the dried tar from his arms.

Stupid paperwork. Stupid monitoring Protocol.

Little did he know, paperwork not much different from that protocol report, would soon change the course of his life forever.

Chapter 2

Signed and Sealed

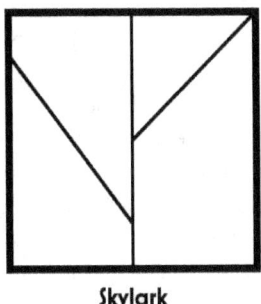

Skylark

The next morning Avery arrived for work at the Skylark Grove twenty minutes late. His shoulders sagged as he walked down an overgrown path to his uncle's cabin. Tar still clung in patches to his forearms and under his fingernails. He wasn't sure exactly where his funk had come from. Quincy was a dweeb. After all, he wasn't the one who'd fixed the water tower. Regardless, Avery felt like pond sludge.

Jasper was filling a bucket from a hand pump outside the cabin.

"You're late," Jasper said without turning.

"Sorry."

Jasper was an Able. His powers didn't allow him to jump high or throw energy spears. He could, however, identify people simply by hearing their personalities. It was an ability he had possessed since a young boy when his older brother had given Jasper his key, which was a hatchet.

The exchange of a meaningful item, the key, was what unlocked an Able's power. Jasper kept his status as an Able a closely guarded secret. The Fenders often searched for new Lancers throughout The Chancellery. Avery himself hadn't known until he started working alongside Jasper five years prior, and at times found himself fiercely jealous of his uncle's Able-ness.

"Lots to get done today," Jasper said. He shuffled inside with the bucket hefted onto his shoulder, the hatchet hanging from his belt.

"Yeah, lots to do," Avery said just audibly.

Jasper crossed his arms and leaned against the counter.

"Don't let that Quincy stuff get to you," he said. "The guy's a munt, a fraud."

"Yeah," Avery repeated, he squared his shoulders even though he still felt dumb. The act of not letting it get to you was not something he had yet mastered. Was it something anyone ever mastered? And he knew Jasper was hearing this whole emotional whirlpool in full stereo sound across the room.

"That council spot comes open soon anyways," Jasper said as he walked back outside. Avery followed him around to the far side of the house where the northernmost line of Sentinel Oaks arched high overhead.

As part of Lafayette's control structure, the city forcibly installed representatives in many of the loosely formed town councils that dotted the Outer Domain. These representatives were selected from local residents, but in a secretive process held every six years. They then became the eyes and ears of the Fenders beyond the walls of their three cities. And in true form, Quincy Pratt had turned into a puppet for Hubbard, the Fender of Lafayette. But a puppet that could soon be replaced. Who could take his spot? And in a town more organized than most, that was cause for concern.

"Should be you," Avery stated confidently. Any connection to one of the Last Cities seemed like such an honor to him. He didn't share his uncle's doubt in the system.

Jasper chuckled, "They'd never pick me. Too old, no way I'd pass the exams. But someone like you..."

"Written exams?" Avery interrupted, not hearing that last part.

Jasper pointed to a pile of tools. A sledgehammer, thick canvas gloves, extra coils of rope, "Let's get moving," he said.

Avery knew all too well that when Jasper changed the subject, any further attempts on the matter would go nowhere. He shouldered the hammer, grabbed the other supplies, and followed Jasper into the grove. A narrow path wound through the rows of neatly spaced trees. Their bark was woven in a tighter pattern than the Witness Oaks, but they stood equal in stature. The scalloped leaves were a deep blue-green, held together in a dense canopy.

For a while they walked without words, as they often did. The two Keepers checked their trees instinctively. The Skylark grove was located on the south end of Woodway. Four hundred Oaks stood in rows. Over a century ago they overtook a cornfield and a strip of large houses along the steep riverbank. As all Sentinel groves had, the trees of Skylark had mysteriously found an abandoned spot and taken root. Not planned or planted by anyone, geometric forests similar to Skylark lay scattered throughout the empty and renaturing places of the post-Leveling world.

The path was second nature to both. They turned at the fork near the middle of grove, heading toward the river and what was going to be nearly a week's worth of labor. One of the remaining houses had recently collapsed, crushing a Sentinel Oaks. As caretakers of the grove, their first charge was to clear the tree. The loss had hit Jasper hard. He had been a Keeper in this grove for more than thirty years.

Avery found the cleanup tedious, but the work brought them closer to the Watson's house. They were the richest family in Woodway and lived in one of the only habitable structures left along the river. Rebecca Watson was two years older than Avery and he always hoped to catch her attention as they broke up moldy sheetrock and rotted framing.

The Watson's house peaked through forest not far from the work site. A generator hummed, they were too far from the geothermal turbines to receive town power. Avery kept an eye on the back deck while they canvassed the walls slated for demolition. Oak branches hung low over the disintegrating house. They scaled the closest tree together and cinched back branches in danger of damage from their work.

Becky often appeared on the deck wearing a bikini top and shorts. She never looked directly down at them working below, that would have made the game too easy.

She had dated Beck West once. Beck had been Avery's one and only friend in Woodway before moving off to Garfield when he was sixteen. She claimed they broke up because she couldn't handle being... 'Beck and Becky', it just didn't have a good ring to it. But years later, after his best friend had moved away, she had confided in Avery the actual truth: she was looking for a Lafayette man. Her family had visited the Last City three hundred miles to the north when she was fourteen - a trip that must have cost thousands in toll road fees. Within the city walls she met a young lieutenant trainee and he was going to wait for her. That was the story anyway.

Regardless of her breeziness, Keepers were well respected, and she came and went strategically as they worked. The groves provided an indispensable food source. Avery and Jasper, part farmers and part arborists, watched over the grove and provided bushels of acorns from the Skylark to every family in Woodway, even the Watsons. For every community and settlement in The Chancellary, Keepers were played a key role.

Jasper caught Avery distracted by Becky's presence and barked in his trademark baritone, "Hey. Keeper. Eyes over here, remember what pays your salary."

By Tuesday, his birthday, they had dissected the fallen Sentinel, and dropped the most dangerous walls of the decaying house into ragged piles. Jasper was not one for celebration and left Avery to the drudgery of shoveling, hauling, and brick stacking on his birthday. When he returned home that evening, not having seen Becky a single time that day, he found his mother waiting with two cupcakes each with a candle glowing on top. Somehow she had scrounged up enough flour and cocoa. They sat on the porch and celebrated year nineteen with a rare chocolate treat.

The next day Avery anticipated more of the same. But Jasper started him in a curious direction.

"Why don't you head over to the saplings this morning. They could use some water in this heat and I've got work to do around here."

"What's that?" Avery asked.

"Just paperwork," Jasper said spreading thick layers of acorn butter on slices of dark bread.

Odd. Jasper was a studious Keeper, he knew each tree by name almost. But most of that knowledge was in the man's head, not in any records. Or paperwork.

"We gonna try to sell bushels to that creepy little town to the south?" Avery asked.

Jasper shook his head. His eyes darted across the floor and over to the back window. Avery dropped the subject. His uncle looked uncomfortable. Whatever. They ate breakfast while sitting on wide freshly cut cylinders of oak. The fallen Oak had been more than three feet in diameter at chest height. The slow growing, iron-hard timber would soon enough be put to good use somewhere in Woodway.

Avery then pumped two buckets full of water and made his way east. Jasper stayed at the cabin, doing paperwork.

The Keepers of the Skylark Grove had managed a rare feat. The trees were well adapted to erratic climate patterns and degraded soils. But outside of the mysterious groves, growing Sentinel Oaks from seed was troublesome.

The trick to success was something Jasper called *setting*. The trees were vulnerable in the first three growing seasons as roots explored the surroundings. Near the end of the third year, the trees shot roots deep into the soil. Once a Sentinel set, it was hard to kill. Two of these young trees, still in their delicate phase, grew on the eastern fringes of their grove. They hoped one could survive to be replanted in place of their fallen tree.

Avery moved at a brisk pace to cover ground quickly, shifting the water buckets as he went. Visiting the small nursery was always a prideful event. Two gangly saplings poked through a small plot in the last bits of the shade thrown by their older siblings. Narrow branches reached up toward the available light, sagging from the weight of thick clumps of leaves. Avery placed the buckets in the grass and squeezed his fingers where the handle had dug into his knuckles.

The young trees looked healthy. Their growth rate was three times that of a mature oak. But they would still need close tending for the next three years before transplant. He pulled weeds from rings of dark soil and checked the bark for signs of insects. Then slowly tipped the first bucket in a ring around each. The water soaked in quickly. He had just finished when a mechanical buzz filled the air.

A four-rotor W Series 150 drone sliced over the horizon. Lights blinked in rapid succession from under the nose. It approached at great speed, passing Avery's position no more than a few seconds after coming into view. He made out the Lafayette symbol on a side panel: a white diamond set in a green rectangle. It zipped low across the trees. Avery bounded toward the clearing, tripped over the water bucket, and tumbled with the half the contents soaking his pant legs.

He pushed up just in time to see the drone gain elevation quickly along the northern end of the grove, rotating several times and then dropping ominously. Down toward the cabin. Panic flooded his chest. He kicked the empty bucket and ran. When the path bent back toward the river, he broke off, knees driving high through the dense underbrush. He could hear the rotators spinning along with a rapid succession of electronic tones.

As Avery broke through the grove, drone engines surged and the machine pulled up and away. His heart raced. He burst through the door to find Jasper turning off an ancient radio that had sat on his shelf forever.

"Hey," Avery said panting and holding his knees with relief.

Jasper grinned. He looked relaxed. Avery then noticed the crisp white envelope sitting on table. The green and white symbol was embossed in the corn and a name was printed in the center: Avery Jackson.

"What's that?" he asked. His heartbeat still pulsing in his neck.

"You got a letter."

Other than notes passed in the single classroom in town, this was a first.

"That drone. It delivered this?" Avery asked.

Jasper nodded, his grin lingered.

"What is it?" Avery pushed his hands into his pockets.

"I don't know," Jasper slid the letter across the table. "Open it up."

Avery hesitated. He had stolen a book from the school building when he was twelve. Jumped off the bridge into the river - really against the rules. And skipped out on work last year to fiddle with his new motorcycle, Jasper thought he was sick that day. Every single one of those transgressions led him to think about imprisonment or decapitation at the hands of Lafayette's most dangerous protocol officers.

He opened the envelope delicately. The folded paper inside was thick and glossy. He unfolded the letter, took a deep breath and read at his most deliberate pace:

Mr. Jackson,

You have been selected to participate in the Outer Domain Representative Assessment. Please arrive at the Briarcamp Outpost no later than 6 June at 8:00 PM. The assessment will commence promptly at 8:00 AM on 7 June. Any late arrivals are subject to a protocol infraction. Further instructions and toll road vouchers will arrive in a separate delivery.

Best,
Lt. Bryce Robertson-Quade

Avery methodically digesting each word. Reread it twice. He then sat down.

Chapter 3

Unusual Usual Visits

Bea's neck prickled as slipped down a lamp lit sidewalk on Lafayette's east side. Large well-kept lawns stretched out before reaching elderly estates. Her salt and pepper hair, windswept from the brisk midnight jaunt, sat atop her weathered caramel skin. She dressed intentionally plain. No buttons or zippers to catch reflection and her pockets were empty - the house key stowed under a spinach plant in the garden. She was ready to shift into the shadows if anyone appeared on the prominent street. There was a hint of a limp that she rolled through gracefully in her haste. She was getting too old for this.

She marched up the narrow driveway of a particularly massive estate, arched and spired along all sides. Then pushed open a jade colored side door. It had recently been repainted, a rarity in Lafayette, where paint was difficult to come by.

She peeked into the expansive kitchen sitting in glum emptiness, and shivered. Her nose caught the scent of lavender mixed with the woody aroma of bourbon. She knew where to find the housemaster. Up a wide curving staircase and down a heavily carpeted hallway, she glided toward his library. As always, his smoky presence drifted into her mind as she approached. Her most recent thoughts were sifted through. Her most significant and private thoughts of quite rebellion against The Chancellery, however, were locked away far from his reach. She had years of practice locking them away in a mental safe of sorts, undetectable and impenetrable even to him.

Kenyon Hubbard, Lafayette's Third Generation Fender, sat in one of two stretched out leather chairs in the office. A drooping body betrayed angular features with a gown folded across his chest. He swirled a glass of the amber liquid in a bony hand. Another half-filled glass sat on a round table between the chairs.

"Good evening," he said in a cold, sour voice.

"Hello," Bea responded.

"Most people try a little harder, Beatrice."

"I'm not most people," she said and curtly sat down, not touching the drink, and pushed him out of her thoughts with her own abilities.

"After fifty years..." he took a taste. "I should expect that by now."

In the prolonged silence, her senses started to calm as he drifted away from her mind. She had indeed known Hubbard for decades. As young children, their paths had crossed in peculiar circumstances - She the daughter of a pipe fitter, he the son of the Fender of Lafayette. Fate seemed to keep their lives intertwined throughout the years. For reasons she could not quite explain, Kenyon had kept her as a confidant and she had witnessed his victories and his struggles from a unique vantage point. And the association had also proven to be rather lucrative for her career.

"How are things?" she asked finally.

"Tiresome." Hubbard had fought off many challenges to keep control of Lafayette, he had grown weary as a result.

"We're getting old, Kenyon," Bea commented, looking away.

He pulled another swing. She looked over at the heavily curtained windows and to the bookshelf of glossy-covered novels from a bygone era. Each time she visited, she was tempted to crack open one of those books: a desperate office romance or a fancy lawyer traveling the world to find her way. Alas, she knew her limits in this place.

"You do look it," she said, concern finding its way into her voice. "Tired."

"Groa wants access to the Record Book. So does one of my lieutenants," he said ignoring her comment. "The pile of formal requests is growing," Groa was the Fender of Carrick City, and by all accounts the leader of the three.

Bea leafed through a glossy stack of official documents printed on both Lafayette and Carrick City letterhead. In a terse, official tone each requested access to the Record Book.

"Bryce is getting cocky, his requests are quite presumptive," she said without looking up. Hubbard sighed.

Lt. Bryce Robertson-Quade was Hubbard's most trusted and powerful lieutenant. His aspirations for city control were well known among certain circles.

But both in the room knew the answer to these requests. Hubbard's eyes flickered with frustration.

"What is their preoccupation with the Records?" she asked.

"That is not for you to question, citizen."

"Ahh, yes indeed. My apologies," Bea said sitting back down casually. "Please convey to them that the Record Book of Ables remains complete and up to date. As is my duty, no?"

Hubbard scowled, "Yes, it is. And that wife of yours... is she behaving herself?"

Bea cut a sharp glance at the Fender, which was answer enough.

Another silence stretched out. The kind that made her wonder why it was he summoned her to his estate several times each year. In the foggy distance he started to retrieve shared memories of their childhood. She allowed this intrusion, although the exercise had its own brand of sadness.

At some point, Hubbard stood. Bea cocked her head.

"Outer Domain assessments start soon," he said proudly.

Bea remained expressionless. The *representative assessment exams* were a cruel sideshow that gave outsiders false hope of power and control in the wild parts of The Chancellery outside the city walls. She hated these exams, poor people.

Hubbard sneered as he picked up her thoughts on the matter, "Desperation is good entertainment," he said.

She shook her head, resting two fingers on her temple.

For another half hour they rambled through tense and diverting conversation. He inquired about her cabin on the island, another item for which their association helped her attain. She deflected. Then a comment was made about the time and Bea was allowed to leave. A chill had gripped the air during her visit and she clutched her thin sweater as she tried to rid the clouds of his presence from her mind.

Chapter 4

Keep Your Eyes Open

Sun slanted across the porch as Avery stood in the open doorway of the cottage. He jammed his fingers into the top creases of his jean pockets.

His gaze slowly arced across the bowed branches of the forest that surrounded his home, to the rusted barn door and then to his squat motorcycle waiting in the gravel clearing. The first floorboard creaked slightly under the pressure of his left foot, as it had his whole life.

Jasper crouched near the knobby rear tire of the motorcycle, inspecting the transmission while Avery stood nervously on the porch. Over the previous two days they had feverishly prepared for the compulsory trip north to Briarcamp where the assessment exams would be held. His mother had insisted on covering the repairs with some of their hard-earned savings, which made him uncomfortable. Nevertheless, they replaced leaking gaskets and the snarly first-gear, tightened the rear suspension and attempted to fix a misbehaving fuel gauge. His mother reupholstered the seat and now red stitching neatly ran along the seams.

No one in Woodway knew he was leaving. He'd be back soon enough and it felt like not that many people would miss him. If he had really tried, he could have gotten a message to his best friend Beck in Garfield. But Beck left two years ago and not come back to visit Woodway. Embarrassing himself in front of the Lafayette soldiers and then returning home wasn't something he wanted people knowing about.

Dishes clinked in the kitchen.

"What can I help with?" Avery asked, turning back into the house. The kitchen was an assortment of different colors and varying sized everything that they had collected over the years. A clutch of purple hyacinth, his mother's favorite, sat in a mason jar on the table.

"Do you want your eggs scrambled or over easy?" His mother asked quickly.

"I'll take care of it" Avery said.

"No, no – the least I can do is make you breakfast."

He grinned, but did not respond. Before she could react, he walked over to the counter and grabbed a carton of brown speckled eggs. They kept a small coop on the side of the house; eggs were saved for special occasions.

She had raised Avery in this house. The creaky front porch was where they spent summer nights naming fireflies as they glowed on and off. The small garden on the east side of the barn was where they grew carrots and potatoes. But the kitchen was always where his mother burned the eggs.

"The suspension still squeaks," Avery said in a voice that couldn't fully conceal his nerves.

"Maybe that'll keep you from going too fast," she said.

"You know mom," Avery said as he cracked the first egg into a cast iron skillet. "I think that bike's in better condition now than when it was new maybe a million years ago. I'll be fine." Though he wasn't entirely convinced he would be fine.

"It's not you that I'm worried about," his mother conceded.

Browned pieces of bread popped up from the toaster and the skillet sizzled.

"And I expect at least an email once you get to Briarcamp," she continued. "If they allow that sort of thing."

"Yes, mother," Avery responded.

A tense silence hovered as he tended the stove and she moved throughout the kitchen. Jasper soon shuffled in and poured coffee into squat mugs.

His mother stared at the floor. The muscles in her neck were pulled tight, fingers pushed against the edge of the table.

"What's wrong mom?" Avery asked as he finished the eggs.

Her eyes jumped back to the room and she cut a stare at her son.

"I'm fine. Just thinking about when we got this table." The top was a mix of blue paint and worn wood grain. "You were just a baby. Your uncle made it for me," she said, the strain remaining in her face. "He carried it all the way over here one day. Right up the front stairs by himself. Then we sat here while I adored the color. And you, mister, proceeded to climb onto his lap and spill his iced tea!" she added, pointing a finger squarely into his son's chest.

Avery's face broke into a broad smile. Jasper chuckled as Avery spooned eggs onto three plates. Jasper claimed he could manage just fine without him for a few days. But Avery planned to return as soon as the assessment was complete. There was no way that Lafayette would select him to become the next Woodway Representative. Not a chance.

"Remember to mind your Protocol when you're in Briarcamp. And do your best on those exams," his mother said. "And be polite."

"And be polite," Avery mouthed back.

It would be good to get away for a few days, Avery thought to himself. Though his boot shook under the table. He took a big gulp of black coffee before shifting to center himself on the plate.

"Mom, I'm a grown man," Avery said over the lip of his mug.

"Well, thank you for that grown-man son."

He caught her burning stare.

Jasper cleared his throat and leaned in. Avery knew his uncle could hear the frustration teeming in his head. It was unfair sometimes.

"Go over your route for me one more time," Jasper said

Avery nodded, "I'm taking the L10 out of town until it hits 7A. The map at the school says there's a tollbooth there." A second drone had arrived yesterday and unceremoniously dropped a package containing vouchers and confirmation documents on the front stairs. "Then it's a straight shot. 7A for two-hundred fifty miles to Briarcamp."

"Hubbard and Ashburn watch that road pretty close. You should be fine," Jasper said with no hesitation. Ashburn was the Fender in Garfield, some five hundred miles away. He and Hubbard squabbled over Outer Domain territory in these parts.

"Even if the Fenders keep a close watch, there are lots of people out there on the road that answer to no one. Do you understand?" His mother added.

"Mom, I can handle myself. You've raised me well. I get to see some of the world, ya know," Avery said.

She looked at him in silence. Avery could see the thoughts churning behind her controlled exterior.

"I know. But us moms tend to worry," she replied simply.

"You can probably blame it on Jasper," Avery said.

"There are many things I can blame on your uncle Jasper," she said, seemingly to allude to something beyond their breakfast discussion. She then picked up her fork and stabbed a block of eggs.

Breakfast finished in silence as Avery's departure time quickly approached. Jasper collected their plates and shooed Avery and his mother out of the kitchen. She double checked the contents of his riding bag, a full canteen, a tin of coffee, two acorn butter sandwiches wrapped in wax paper, his passport and paperwork, a role of faded cash, a tire pump, his hatchet, and climbing gear. A hatchet was useful for all manner of activities in the grove and served as protection if needed. It was a Keeper's prized possession. The climbing gear was packed out of habit.

In the warming sun, Avery knelt in front of the bike and checked the oil. The solid frame against his hand gave him a sense of fortitude. He looked at the powerful machine and hoped it would hold together through the journey. Before he knew it he would be back home and cleaning up that fallen house in the grove. It would be cool to get beyond the Woodway fence for once. Not so cool if he got attacked by bandits, though.

He rose, turned the key into the ignition, and swung on his helmet. With the engine humming behind him and the summer heat gripping his skin, he turned to his mother. A tear escaped and ran down her cheek. He checked the fuel tank for the twelfth time to calm the nerves climbing from the pit of his stomach.

He swallowed against a tense throat, "Time to hit the road."

"Be safe," his mother whispered as she tightened his pack.

They hugged for a long while. Jasper walked out of the house wearing a gentle smile.

"I'll be fine. I'll will," he whispered.

Jasper came down and grasped Avery's shoulder, "Keep your eyes open kid. Not all doors are meant to be opened. Stay on that route, it'll get you to Briarcamp just fine."

He paused, "Yep, L10 north to 7A. Easy. And I'll keep the bike under a hundred."

His mother slapped him on the back of the helmet. Avery smirked. He shifted over the warm frame.

His mother walked closer to the bike. Her arms were still crossed close to her chest, a hand pushed against her cheek. Just a few feet from the bike, she watched her son make adjustments and pull on riding gloves.

He looked down at the small cluster of gauges and then over to his family.

"Love you guys," Avery said. These were words that he didn't say out loud very often. But in the moment, they just sort of came out.

"I love you too," his mother responded. Jasper held a clenched fist across his heart. A gesture Avery had seen from his uncle only twice before.

With that, the rear tire spun up bits of gravel and a cloud of dust trailed behind.

He clipped into second gear as he reached the tree's edge, gripping the handlebars firmly. The bumpy driveway dropped into speckled shadows, down through a small ravine, and then back up to L10.

The speed was calming. It was raw, unapologetic action. The *what* and *if* of those hours spent watching the world go by from the Witness Tree transformed into the *here* and *now* simply by shifting gears and heading north.

Understand and execute, his uncle would always say. It was time for him to execute.

L10 was clear and straight. The canopy remained dense, shading the road from the most intense heat, but allowing occasional splashes of sunlight to scatter across the road.

* * * * * *

His mother and uncle watched Avery ride away. The rising dust cloud blurred his outline. Without the engine's rhythmic hum, silence enveloped them, seemingly conscious of their presence. She looked out toward the barn without focusing. Memories she had long since abandoned resurfaced. With her son entering the clutches of The Chancellery, she found it impossible to ignore Avery's earliest years and not to worry about what he might encounter. Jasper, always mild mannered, brought her a fresh cup of coffee and, sighing, sat on the top step.

"Keep your eyes open, Avery Jackson," she said to the silence.

Chapter 5

Through and Across

Avery rode out of Woodway with his mood buoyed on a nervous cloud. Three miles outside of town the road came to a T in front of three abandoned grain towers with crumbling dome tops. With only a short pause, he pushed off and headed east.

Avery paid little attention to the structures for they had always stood as the strange, hulking gateway to Woodway. What he did not know is that his approach had activated a series of sensors hidden in the tall weeds. Set within the hole-filled canopy of the tallest grain tower, a multi-function camera came to life. A zoom lens clipped into place and focused on Avery, taking three high-resolution photos. These images were packaged together and broadcast to a receiving station hundreds of miles away. The camera received a confirmation code and quickly powered off.

The time-addled road wrapped around the edge of the old farm property. Avery leaned into the curve and then pointed north with the engine firing hard. He rolled his shoulders back, and loosened the vice grip on the handlebar. He passed a dilapidated fence and was beyond the reaches of Woodway for the first time.

L10 ran north with gradual bends, but with little change in elevation. The sun was drifting toward its highest point and burned off the morning dew. He clipped off mile after mile through overgrown landscape that he had for so long looked out upon. The roadside was often obscured with thick a carpet of tall golden grasses tangled with vines.

Here and there, shopping centers sat mostly collapsed. Relics of fast food joints, oil change shops, banks, post offices, and 24-hour gyms stared blankly at the road through bare windows and tattered paneling. Faded stop signs hung on rusted posts at the occasional cross street. Avery slowed to scan left and right, but didn't stop. He was unsettled by his current surroundings. The forest of Woodway was quiet, yet still active with life. He was a forest child and understood that rhythm. But these places felt harsh and out of sync.

The afternoon wore on and the elevation started to rise. Deep blackened craters ten feet across marked the earth to the east, scars of a forgotten war. He released the throttle just a bit as he scanned cautiously. The engine sputtered and coughed up a hill.

Nothing was alive within twenty feet of each crater. Browning grass struggled to grow even in the spaces between. His mouth started to dry, the sun blaring at full volume. He pulled to the side of the road, let the engine idle, and pulled off his helmet to get some relief from the insane temperature.

He peeled the backpack off his shoulders and drank nearly half of his water bottle. In the chaotic landscape visible from the top of the hill, the blue green hue of Sentinel Groves looked like scattered pocket squares. His uncle Jasper had mentioned other groves and other Keepers. But this was his first time ever setting eyes on Sentinels outside his Skylark grove.

More clusters of blackened craters were scattered across the wide spreading barrens. What had even been bombed anyway? From the traveler's eye, they looked to be clustered in empty fields.

Accurate details of the planetary collapse were now mostly lore. Lost in the halls of newsrooms, cell phone memory cards, and in the later years, military equipment. Avery thought about the stories he'd heard from the older boys at school. More than two hundred years ago, one hundred and forty eight, but who's counting, the world went haywire. Storms a half year long bruised and battered some areas. Drought, disease, and continental sized earthquakes ripped apart others. Wars raged where no one really knew who was fighting whom.

Leveling, that's what scholars started to call the global catastrophe. It was hypothesized that, perhaps, the earth was just reacting to our hold on her. We humans had achieved once unimaginable feats. Shaped nature, cured diseases, and became arguably the planet's singular dominant force. Maybe she was just responding to our too much-ness, dramatically recalibrating to a new balance. So they called it: Leveling.

Regardless of the name, the human race had been essentially driven to its knees. Forced to edit how we existed.

Avery shook off the thoughts after a brief rest, situated himself back on the bike and headed off down the hill. The road was steep at first; he picked up speed by allowing gravity to pull him down and onto the flat terrain.

Another hour's ride and he approached the 7A interchange.

Intertwined ramps and thick metal spans curved in every direction. Just before the interchange stood a large gate and small cinder block structure.

His approach had unknowingly activated another set of sensors hidden under the first bridge. A small camera powered to life. It rapidly captured three photographs of his approach, packaged the images files, and transmitted them to the same storage facility. The monitoring system received a confirmation code and powered down.

A tall soldier exited the guard building. His grey and green uniform was several sizes too small, as if someone had sent him the wrong size. He tugged on the sleeves, and then held up a hand for Avery to stop.

"Where you headed?" he asked as Avery stopped.

"I'm, ahh, on my way to Briarcamp."

"Passport and paperwork."

Avery presented the neatly folded material.

The soldier remained stone faced, "Official business?"

"Yeah, I guess so. For the Representative Assessment," Avery said.

"Can you confirm that this is your K-Code and verification number and no one has tampered with these documents?" he said in monotone.

"Yessir."

"Please hold."

The soldier spun and pulled a rectangular device from his hip pocket. Electronic tones sounded as he scanned Avery's passport and travel voucher. He briskly returned the documents and pressed a button on the instrument screen. The gate arm swung up. Avery revved the engine and pulled on to the entrance ramp for 7A North with a wave to the lonely soldier. The pavement transitioned from rough asphalt to concrete. He made a mental checklist of all the items in his bag while gradually gaining speed up the entrance ramp and resisting the urge to stop and physically re-re-check all the items strapped to his back.

Sporadic traffic started to appear. Large cargo trucks mostly, vehicles Avery had seen before. It was comforting in an odd way. He felt less alone, less in the wilderness.

He was happy to have the first leg of the journey behind him. His nerves slowly waned with the each nondescript mile on the smooth toll road.

Open highway allowed him to make good time as the fierce sun waned away toward dusk. The open road eventually started to wind a bit more, but the temperature still held like a soggy blanket against his skin.

He was about to dip into the left lane and speed around a chugging cargo truck when sharp blue-white headlights caught his eye. He held his gaze an extra second and made out three distinct sets gaining quickly, the cargo truck groaning louder over his shoulder. He accelerated, dipping into a lower gear for extra power.

Headlights appeared suddenly, washing the entire road harshly. The vehicles materialized at incredible speed, gaining nearly two miles in the short time it had taken him to pass the truck.

He leaned hard. His front tire soon weaved along the faded white edge line. The cargo truck's deep jumble was replaced by the shouting of supercharged engines. He glanced over again and recognized the long, angular outlines of Fender escort vehicles. They pulled together in a tight V formation, no more than three feet apart.

Farther into the shoulder he pulled. His tires kicked up gravel against the bike's undercarriage. The roar of the three powerful vehicles screaming toward him now drowned everything out. This would be the lamest way to die, he thought, to be run off the road in the middle of nowhere.

If he grabbed the brakes on the rough surface, he was sure it would flip him end over end. Out of pure reflex, he looked over yet again. The three black-as-smoke cars flew past without any acknowledgement of his presence. At that point, he had released the throttle.

Just as he was able to inhale deeply, the cargo truck flew past blasting its air horn. Avery leaned away from the massive rear tires pelting him with a second round of gravel. Well, shit. When he looked up, six red taillights were barely visible. Frustrated and with no other option, he pushed back into the open road. He now could not ignore the soreness in his mind and body. The grey evening sky was starting to fade further toward darkness and he pushed on - keeping his eyes on the round glow of his headlight.

Five miles on, maybe ten, clean and bright road signs for the Briarcamp Outpost started to appear at regular intervals. The white diamond and green medallion was located in the corner of each sign.

Towering light poles illuminated a wide exit ramp. The lane was lined with walls and forked in two directions. A large *Outpost* sign pointed to the right, with a smaller *Lodging* sign pointing to the left. Avery pulled left. The civilian town of Briarcamp was tucked away just south of the sprawling military facility. He entered a block of tidy brick houses, and slowed as he saw a group of people milling near the entrance of a small pub not far from an intersection. Just below the stop sign, which was notably unfaded, was small block H with another arrow pointing left. Easy enough. After a second look at the gathered strangers, he turned. Warmth spilled from a house with a large sign hanging from the porch that read *Interchange Hostel*.

Engraved in narrow letters on the front door were two words: Safe Passage. He parked out front. Inside he found a pleasant grey haired man sitting at a worn wooden desk.

"Hello young man," he said with a wide toothy grin.

Avery released the tension from tired shoulders, knowing he had completed the day's travel. The man asked for Avery's name.

"Jackson," Avery said. "Avery Jackson."

"Ahhh, yes. The last of the Assessment candidates. Very good."

The attendant then collected a surprisingly low amount for payment, which Avery paid from the roll of cash in his pack. From there they shuffled up the stairs, where the attendant showed Avery his room on the third floor. It had a rough wooden floor, a narrow bed along the wall, and a single nondescript chair. Avery dropped his bike helmet onto the seat and old man showed him the bathroom at the end of the hall. He explained the intricacies of the faucet and handed Avery the room key on a large ring. He patted Avery on the shoulder before heading toward the stairs.

"Excuse me, sir. Can I ask you a question?" Avery asked as the old man exited the tiled bathroom.

"What's that my boy?"

"I saw a pub down the street. What I mean is, if I was an outsider looking to get a drink or something...would I run into any trouble?" Avery asked with a crooked expression.

"Kid, everyone's an outsider in this town," the old man chuckled and descended the stairs.

Well, that was that.

Avery tested the faucet and ran cold water on his face before returning to the room. Weary from a long, scorching day he slid down to the wooden floor and stared up at the ceiling. He was still alive. Perhaps a bit more confused than twenty-four hours ago, but alive.

After resting his eyes for a few moments, he made toward the slender staircase and quietly out the front door with the large key ring in his pocket. In the distance, the tall lights of the interchange radiated into the night sky. He turned toward the pub with his hands pushed in his pockets.

Several blocks down the road, he came upon a narrow, dark lot situated. Tall, coarse grass protruded onto the sidewalk. Avery continued his quick pace when a familiar outline caught his attention.

Three black outlines seemed to hover close to the ground. As his eyes adjusted, the outline of the angular headlights solidified. They were spaced exactly, matte paint fading almost entirely into the night. The escort vehicles. What the hell? Why weren't they on the military side?

He paused. The vehicles sat in complete darkness.

Pulling his hands out of his pockets, Avery shook his head and continued to the pub.

The dull, shabby bar permeated a dank smell of hops. No one seemed to notice his arrival. Along the left wall, a slender bar extended toward the back of the room. To his right was a tangle of people facing inward toward small round tables. He scanned the room until he spotted an empty stool at the dimly lit bar. Perfect. He slid on to the empty seat without looking at the neighboring patrons.

Though the old man at the hostel had said that everyone was an outsider here, he definitely didn't feel that way. From a distance, everyone seemed to know each other. But under the veil of dimness, Avery could feel at ease in his anonymity.

He shifted his weight from side to side on the tall wooden stool. A slender man with gaunt features and slicked back blond hair was seated next to him. A short glass of clear liquor sat just in front of his crossed arms. He acknowledged Avery with a node and smirk. To Avery's left, a pair of coiffed women were engrossed in conversation. They faced away from him, yet his nostrils were assaulted by their perfume.

As he turned his head back, a bald headed bartender walked up.

"What can I get for ya?" he asked. Avery had drunk a total of seven beers in his entire life. Zero of which he knew the name.

"Whatever's on tap," Avery responded.

"He'll take a stout," said his neighbor.

Avery shrugged a tentative *sure, why not.*

"You got it."

"Thanks," Avery rasped.

"What brings you to this fine establishment?"

"A thing," Avery leaned to his left and looked over. He wasn't about to tell this strange dude what he had going on.

"You looking to win?" the hawkish man asked.

"Win what?" Avery asked.

"The assessment." The stranger was now staring directly at Avery, making him uneasy. How did this guy know Avery was part of the Assessment?

"Just trying to get home in one piece." Avery conceded as the bartender slid a glass of dark beer across the bar top.

"You travelin' by yourself?" The man asked.

Avery paused. He didn't know much, but this wasn't where this conversation should be going.

"Why." He asked flatly.

"Most people ain't as stupid as you. They travel in groups," he pointed around the bar.

"Yea."

Avery pulled a sip of his stout. The strong taste migrated through his nostrils. He slowly looked around the bar with more scrutiny. With the exception of the overly manicured girls next to him, folks were clustered in groups. He started to notice that no two clusters seemed to go together.

At the front of the bar was a deep booth separated from the rest of the tables. There were three tall, square jawed men sitting at the back of a crescent shaped booth. A shadow from the doorway concealed the detail in their faces, but Avery noticed that they all were dressed alike.

The man leaned in, "You see, even the Lafayette soldiers travel together."

Avery's head swung around to face the bar, and then back briefly toward the booth near the door. His unease with this weirdo was temporarily overwhelmed by curiosity.

"Those three? " Avery whispered.

"Aye, they come through every so often," He said. "Just keeping to themselves. Total squares. If I were to say, they're keepin' an eye out for trouble this side of Briarcamp."

"Huh." Avery couldn't think of much else to say.

"Let me ask you something," the stranger's gaze flicked over to the soldiers then back to Avery. "You need anything for tomorrow? They'll try to push your buttons. You know, a little somethin' extra to keep you up and fresh."

The stranger casually presented a bag containing three different colored pills.

Maybe coming to the pub wasn't such a good idea.

"I got uppers, downers, enhancers. All from good sources."

Was this happening? Was he actually getting presented with an actual drug deal? Nope. Not tonight. Eject.

The physical act of standing up took a few minutes. He sat rigidly, looking straight ahead, unsure how to end the thing. Then he just stood up, pushed a few dollars under his half empty beer.

"I'm all set," he didn't want to insult the guy, so he added: "Thanks though."

The stranger seemed unfazed. He palmed the bag and asked, "You gonna finish that?" pointing at the beer.

"All yours."

"Good luck."

"Yeah." Avery headed for the door.

He hadn't noticed the two women now staggering in front of the dark booth while the three soldiers smoothly stepped out and onto their feet.

Casually, he pulled open the heavy metal door and gestured toward the soldiers. Without a word, they walked around the drunk women and outside. Avery chuckled to himself and slid out behind them. The soldiers were already a block into the darkness in the opposite direction of Avery's hostel. He paused and watched until one of them looked back and he snapped around.

The door crashed open behind him and heals clicked on the pavement.

"You guys are ass holes!" One of the women yelled

There was some muffled commotion. Then a spray of pink sparks light up the night sky. Avery turned; they were coming from one of the girl's fingertips. She wore a murderous expression, letting the sparks spit overhead. The display illuminated the soldiers who looked very uninterested a distance away.

"We don't like stupid idiots in uniforms anyway!" The girl screamed.

Her friend slapped at her hands, "Stop it. Damnit, Kristin. Stop that." The sparks fizzled. "You know what they do to Ables?" the friend pleaded.

Avery wanted away from this entire situation. He made for the hostel, staring down at the toes of his boots. His shoulders and hips throbbed and his mind was overclocked. He crossed the street at a gentle angle, dug a hand into his front pocket and pulled out the large key ring. The rest of the house lay dark. He checked behind him one last time. The street was empty. Maybe the women had gone back into the bar. Maybe they had been arrested. He took the porch stairs two at a time, opened the door, and locked it behind him.

He headed up the stairs to his rented room. He pulled off his boots, and then padded back down to the bathroom to brush his teeth. Minutes later he had three alarms set: 7:30, 7:32, 7:35, and was soon asleep face down on top of the covers.

Chapter 6

Under Their Nose

Darkness had befallen Lafayette and crickets drowned out all other noise. Mitchell hustled along an empty road flanked by weed choked trees and ancient, rusty construction equipment. His pace was hasty, almost reckless. Cracked pavement crunched underfoot. A thick beard covered his face and he carried a rucksack.

The city wall loomed at the end of the block. Set deep into the rough brick face were two arched doors. Each was more than four inches thick and coat of grease repelled any rust from forming. He swung the small pack from his shoulder into the weeds along the edge of the wall. At the base of the door, a metal grate covered a shallow drain.

He drove scarred fingers into the openings and heaved the grate out of place. The opening was no more than a foot wide. He checked around, waited a bit, checked again, then quickly ran his hands along the doorframe, and coated his chest with the oily substance. Grabbing the bag, he sucked his ribcage tight to his chest and dropped into the drain opening. Decomposing leaves and musty bits fell onto his face as he dropped into clutching darkness. He shuffled under the doorframe using his heels and fingertips.

A rat squeaked near his ear. Or maybe near his feet. He writhed helplessly. Rough fur brushed against his leg. Feverishly, he pushed sideways. Tiny claws scurried past his torso. The suffocating space pushed at him. He shifted and seethed until moonlight peaked through the cracks of the far side drain opening. Only his left arm was free. He pushed up on the grate. It budged a few inches but slammed back down. Again, he pushed up - it shifted off center. Shoulder first, he squeezed up and out, air rushing back into his lungs.

Not far from the wall, a cargo truck sat behind an abandoned gas station. Under the hinge of pump five, as planned, he recovered the key. For several miles, the truck rumbled southward in the cloak of darkness. W Series drones patrolled these parts. This was when he felt most vulnerable, his eyes constantly checking the mirrors and the sky overhead.

When Highway 7A came into view - its wide lanes spotted with the occasional light tower, he flipped on the headlights and climbed a ravine onto the open road.

He clamped down, forcing himself to stay attuned to the road. Miles and hours of murky, empty road were filled by the groaning engine below his feet.

Exit 37 soon eased into view. He turned the hulking vehicle off the highway. A line of trucks was parked along a row of unmarked buildings. He pulled into an empty stall. By the time he climbed out of the cab, a mousy man with blonde slicked back hair stood by the rear bumper.

"You're late," he drooled.

"No. I'm not."

"Whatever."

Mitchell pushed the sack into the man's chest.

"I can only assume the full payment is here."

"Plus two percent," he said, anxiously running a hand over his beard while the man stuffed the stack of bills into a jacket pocket even though it was far too warm for it. Three bags of white oval shaped pills were placed in the bag that previously held cash.

"Next trip is my last trip," Mitchell said with the bag now back in his hand. "That's the agreement."

"You know, you've done so well. We should consider a more long term arrangement," The little blonde man jeered.

He seethed under an expressionless shell.

"I'll be here in five weeks, midnight. My. Last. Delivery." His eyes cut across the trucks.

"Yeah, yeah. You were more fun when you were high," The dealer slinked away.

Back in the truck cab, Mitchell slammed the steering wheel with his hands. Spit flew from his mouth. The bag full of pills mocked him from the adjacent seat as he headed back to Lafayette.

Chapter 7

Among Your Peers

Avery bolted upright. He searched for his watch, which he discovered had fallen behind the bed. He squeezed an arm between the bedframe and the wall. As he pried himself free, the first of his alarms started to chirp - 7:30. His heart rate settled as he sat up. In a jittery haze, he dressed and checked the Assessment directions for the fiftieth time: 8:00 AM, Building D.

Breakfast was a sandwich from his pack. In reality, he was not all that hungry. The hostel was quiet enough to hear every creak and crack. Once outside, he made for the Outpost.

Briarcamp stood dreary in the morning grey. Walking down the middle of the street, he passed a row of houses with paint peeling and curtains drawn in every window. Traffic hummed from the highway in the distance.

The vacant lot that had hidden the escort vehicles the night before was now empty. Rectangular depressions in the weeds were all that remained.

A guard station marked the entrance to the military side of Briarcamp. Green warning signs hung from a tall barbed wire fence. MILITARY PERSONNEL ONLY. ENTRY PROHIBITED WITHOUT PROTOCOL REVIEW. Beyond the rusting chain link was a row of hangars, dome-topped on one end, barracks-like on the other. The gateman checked his papers and scanned his passport.

"Third building on the left. Through the front door and turn right," said the soldier. "And don't look around, citizen."

Avery took his papers with a nod. He strained his peripheral vision as he walked. Sparse structures with narrow windows, a line of timeworn tanker trucks, and a squadron of

41

marching uniforms were all he could see. He had expected a grand fortress with impressive weaponry, guarded by thousands of highly trained soldiers and what not. The Outpost was actually rather underwhelming.

Taped to the mustard green door of Building D was a sign in block letters: ASSESSMENT EXAMS. He could taste the sandwich on his tongue as he pushed inside. Offices with brass name placards ran down the hallway. The low ceiling gave way to a vast, corrugated hanger with a concrete floor polished to a reflective sheen. The air was chemical. Parked on one half was a tarp-covered aircraft looking like an oversized ghost. And spaced across the open half were three square tables, each with two chairs. Seventeen minutes early, Avery was the first to arrive. A soldier approached.

"Where are you from?" the soldier asked.

"Woodway."

"Jackson?"

"That's me."

Avery really had to pee.

"What's your Linkerage score?" the soldier asked.

"My what?"

The soldier looked blankly at him, "Where's your phone kid?"

"I don't have one," he responded. The only person he knew who had a phone was Becky back at home. The thing didn't even work, but she proudly carried it around and took bad pictures.

"Truth and truth?" the soldier asked while he marked something on his clipboard.

"Totally." Avery said flatly. Note to self: Ask Becky about Linkerage.

The soldier informed Avery that there would be two examinees, from each of the three villages in Outer Domain Area 21B. He did not know what that meant, other than there would be only one other Woodway examinee. Who could it be? He was then directed to the table closest to the hangar doors. His armpits were now noticeably sweaty.

Next to arrive was a young girl, no older than twelve. Her eyes were wide and arms crossed tight across her chest.

"Where are you from?" the soldier asked, lacking any manner with the child.

"Chesterfield," she squeaked, looking like she might burst into tears at any moment. Chesterfield was a meager encampment far to the west of Woodway. All Avery knew was that they mined an old landfill.

"Sit there." the soldier pointed to the middle table.

Avery tried to smile without smiling when she looked at him. Then a short man, with a white mustache and rolling limp, scurried into the hall. He waved and whispered to the skinny girl before the soldier intercepted and directed him to the last open table. Avery didn't know how to sit in order to look relaxed, confident, dangerous, and indifferent all at same time.

Next to arrive were two men with toad-shaped bodies. Squat and muscle bound, their skin tanned and clothes tattered. One was older and smugger. He held both arms out from his body and smiled when they entered. A step behind him was a younger man, maybe Avery's age, and with a big nose and long torso. The soldier rushed over, they made small talk. The older gentleman slapped the uniformed man on the shoulder and his laugh echoed in the hangar. He was seated with the mustached man, while the younger boy was placed across from Avery. When he sat down, he glared over at Avery with an arm thrown around the chair back.

"Hi." Avery said.

"Sup," the kid responded. "What's your name?"

"Avery."

"I'm Brian. You from around here?" he asked.

"Here? No. Woodway."

"Where's that?" Brian asked, his eyes narrowed.

"South a ways." Avery did not want to give up too much information, Brian looked pretty dumb. The way he sat there like he didn't give a shit about anything also made Avery mad.

"How about you?" Avery asked eventually.

"Settlers Walk." Brian checked behind him. A blocky tattoo scrolled up his neck.

Avery had only overheard stries of Settlers Walk. It was a town built inside an old shopping mall, a fortress of sorts from the first Area War or something. Its walls were built from rubble and crushed cars. The 'New Settlers', as they called themselves, had a penchant for attacking other villages for no particular reason.

It was then that Quincy Pratt, reigning Woodway Representative glided into the hanger. With his nose pushed toward the ceiling, he paused on Avery for a half second before spotting the soldier. He wore a faux uniform buttoned tight across his neck and straining against his belly. He protested at his seating assignment with the young girl. But the Lafayette soldier ignored the retort and pointed sternly to the open chair.

"What a spack," Brain said under his breath.

Avery's face burned, he should have known Quincy would be here. At precisely 8:00 o'clock, a more senior looking official entered the hanger. He conferred with the attending soldier, checked files, confirmed the identity of each candidate, and finally addressed the group in a distant tone.

"Welcome to the first exam of the Outer Domain Representative Skills Assessment," he said as the other soldier placed a flat electronic device with a small projecting lens in the center onto each table. "You have been selected either because you displayed notable skills or someone has referred you." He turned on his heel, "Each table will be presented with a survival simulation. Your job - as a *team* - is to allocate the resources provided to maximize the survival of your community. You will have thirty minutes. At the end of those thirty minutes your strategy will be assessed. Scores will be provided at the end of the day."

Avery looked down at the projector device and over at the goon who was now his partner. Why did they have to work together? Group work was the worst.

"You may begin."

Avery snatched the projector and pressed buttons until a small blue tinged screen appeared between them. A long list scrolled down, each item accompanied by a thumbnail image.

"What does it say!" Brian barked.

Avery's mind stuttered, overloaded, them stuttered again. The letters were a jumbled mess. His heart was going to explode. Breathe, just breathe and read the words.

"Tell me what it says," Brian stammered.

Avery paused, then spun around the projector to his teammate.

"What are you stupid or something?" asked Brian.

"Just read it out," Avery quipped, feeling stupid.

Brian started listing their assignment manifest.

"We have twelve people, all adults. Andddd... a hundred units each of water, grain, scrap metal, sun screen, and fuel. We gotta survive for two years in a northern climate. Anddd, that's it."

They argued at first. Brian wanted to hoard everything, become the group leader and allocate materials based on loyalty. No one would be loyal if they all died, Avery stated. Then more stuff for us, Brian countered. Woodway survived because they shared and rationed resources, Avery kept telling Brian. But he was stuck on building power. Power begets more power. This went on for fifteen minutes.

Frustrated and terrified they would run out of time, Avery asked for two minutes to rough out a plan. He wanted use half the wheat and water to plant in year one and collect seed at harvest. Hopefully they could find a reliable water source by year two. Use enough scrap metal - say thirty units - to make shelters, use the rest to barter for more food. Same with fuel, save half for winter, sell the rest. They didn't have any vehicles, no need for extra fuel. Brian didn't understand the concept of cold winters; he was now focused on building a battle tank.

"We're not building tanks here, we're building a community," Avery exclaimed.

"Five minutes!" The soldier called out.

Avery reviewed his plan more slowly and Brian gradually came around, but insisted on hoarding all of the fuel in case tank building materials became available. So they compromised. Avery didn't know how to use the device; so he walked through the details a third time as Brian input them on a small touch screen.

Time was called.

They were instructed to proceed to the drill yard for Exam Two. They all rose and exited the hanger.

Quincy tugged on the back of Avery's shirt in the hallway.

"What are you doing here, Jackson?" he hissed.

"They picked me. What was I supposed to do, not show up?" Avery whispered without looking back.

"You are wholly unqualified to be considered for this position."

"Shut the hell up and leave me alone." He pushed Quincy away.

The sun had awakened fully during their first exam and the rumbling notes of the military outpost hummed in the background. A large rectangular area had been roped off on the open pavement. Inside, oil drums were placed at random to create an obstacle course. Soldiers stood at each corner of the course. The assessment participants clustered around a soldier leaning against a folding table. Brian and Avery stuck together for some reason, both unsure if they still needed to be teammates.

"Alright, this is your second exam," the soldier called. "It is a timed obstacle course. Nine flags will appear on the top of some of those drums." He clicked a button and arrow shaped flags popped up on top of the many nine drums. "The flags are your course. Run through the slalom and across the finish line as fast as you can. Don't touch anything. Don't bump anything. Just run. "

They all seemed to wait for more instructions - glancing eye contact with each other hesitantly. The soldier looked annoyed.

"That's it?" Brian asked.

"Yes. That's it. You, step up to the line." The soldier clicked the button again and the flags dropped down. Brian shuffled up to a white line with sweat beading on his temples.

"Clock starts when the flags appear."

A different set of flags popped up to create a winding course. Brian chugged into action, his short legs spinning without gaining much speed. He lumbered around the first three flags before knocking over two barrels, attempting to hurdle the next three, and spinning inefficiently around the last flag. He looked like an idiot, but returned to the group with his chest out and wearing a wide grin.

Soldiers reset the fallen barrels. The older New Settler was next - rumbling through the course in an awkward waddle. They high fived after he completed the course.

Next, the pair from Chesterfield. The mustached man showed surprising quickness but lacked a youthful spring in his step.

The young girl ran next. With her hair now pulled back in a tight braid, she swam through the barrels. She bent gracefully around each flag and finished in a blur. Definitely in the lead...But he could run faster than her. Right?

Already sweat soaked, Quincy demanded to be next. Which left Avery to stewing. Woodway's current representative rolled along, knocking over several barrels in the process. When he finished, the corner observers again reset the fallen obstacles.

Avery jogged up to the line, his head spun from the broiling heat. *Understand and Execute.* The flags dropped. A long pause. It felt like 30 minutes of pause. Then nine new flags jumped up and he launched forward. Leaning hard and trying to maintain his speed, he twisted through the course, pivoting confidently at each barrel like he was running through the grove. When he crossed the finish line, his mind was clear, heart pounding. He felt good. But the soldier scowled at a tablet when he turned. Maybe not so good.

"Go again."

Avery jogged over, "Run again?" he asked.

"Timer messed up. No one's that fast. Run again."

Before he could think straight, he was lined up and new flags appeared. He flew down the course with a better understanding of how his boots felt on pavement, how to propel himself around the barrels with his arms swinging high. The second run felt even better.

He finished and cautiously returned to the group of uncomfortable contestants. Two soldiers consulted the timing device.

"It's right," Avery heard. "14.70 - that's his time."

He felt every pair of eyes burn into his chest.

"Guess that's it. Good running kid," the soldier said without taking his eyes of the tablet computer.

And that was that.

Quincy gawked with his hands on his waist. Avery kept his distance.

"Body assessments are next."

What did that mean? It sounded intrusive.

Without a word, they were walked to a large glass building with a sign that read: AREA COMMAND. Passing through a featureless doorway, conditioned air blasted Avery's sweltering skin. The entire interior was shades of beige with blaring white light. It had a clinical aroma and felt like a place where people came to get punished.

They were guided to gigantic elevator, that could have accommodated an elephant if necessary, and were taken up to the 6th floor. In a square waiting room were lines of cracked vinyl chairs. A reception desk sat behind glass at the end of the room.

"Wait your turn. Any talking *will* result in disqualification," the soldier returned to the elevator and left the group.

Avery sat alone, wanting to distance himself from any potential whispered protocol infractions.

The mustached man and young girl sat together and Quincy stood in the corner looking like he might burst out of his fake uniform. The toad guys from Settlers Walk sat with cocky grins.

Slowly, their names were called one by one. The dry air now chilled Avery to the point of shivering. He anticipated going last again, but was summoned shortly after Brian.

The medical facility was staffed with a small team of nurses dressed in blue and soldiers wearing weird caps over their boots. Inside a small room, Avery was directed to change into a stiff gown and nothing else. He asked where his clothes were going. That was his only pair of jeans. But no one responded as he was walked into a procedure room.

Inside the narrow room he sat on crinkly wax paper and waited some more. After counting to one hundred, thirty times, the nurses entered. This marked the start of every possible exam he could imagine. Blood sample, urine sample, hair sample - eyes scanned, heart scanned. breathing test, balance test, kick-a-heavy-bag test. A second blood sample. He was then instructed to sprint on a treadmill. After powering along at full tilt for eighteen minutes they stopped the machine. Was he doing good? He felt good.

Then he was moved to a darker room, strapped to a bed, and pushed into a tube that chirped and groaned in different tones for a while. And finally to the last station: sensory deprivation. In an egg shaped contraption he floated naked, face up, in some lukewarm, viscous substance. No light. No sound. In the absence of any sensation, time blurred and his mind fluttered from cloudy thought to cloudy thought. Woodway. His bike. The craters. Beer. Woodway. Becky's boobs. That time he broke a plate in the kitchen. Briarcamp. His toes. He eventually drifted toward a blue trail of smoke. There were pulses of soft light. It felt as though he was going farther into himself. Deep down. Until that sensation of flowing energy pushed up against something solid and the image left him.

When the chamber finally cracked open, he had to cover his eyes from thebrightness. Back in the small room he found his clothes folded and neatly placed on a chair. His limbs felt like gelatin and his mind felt like a cotton ball. His watch read 5:57 PM.

"Individualized exams are next," the nurse said. She pressed a gloved hand to his bare torso. Was this part of the exam? When she left, he dressed. A soldier then took him back to the colossal elevator and outside again. The heat hit him and he winced. He kept going back to the blue smoke feeling. It was strangely instinctual – like a new experience that felt total normal. But he needed to focus on this last exam.

Around the back of the imposing structure stood a small woodlot that felt out of place.

Avery then saw familiar branching and dark blue-green leaves. A young Sentinel Oak pushed against the other vegetation.

"These trees keep coming back. Stupid weeds," the soldier said as if reading from a script. He opened a crate set against the building and pulled out an axe.

Out of habit, Avery advanced to inspect the tree - the trunk, straight and true, foliage a good color. Though he saw no other partner trees. That's not how it worked. Based on the diameter of the trunk, it was more than five years matured. There should be companion trees within fifteen paces. But there were none.

The axe was pushed into Avery's hands. The composite haft tapered to a glinting blade.

"Cut it down," the soldier commanded.

Avery's stomach sunk. The soldier stepped back.

"This is your exam," he called out.

Avery's vision spun, but he forced his legs forward to the trunk. The axe rotated in his hand, the weight pressing against his palms. He aligned the blade against the trunk no thicker than his arm. *Don't do anything stupid*, he heard his uncle's voice in his head. *They'll try to push your buttons*, he remembered from the man at the bar. Maybe he should have bought one of those pills.

"Citizen..." the soldier said in a low voice.

Avery shifted his legs and swallowed. He moved around the other side, slowly pushed underbrush from the trunk before repositioning in the low stance. In five strikes he could easily drop the tree: High and low along the far side, one - two. A chip off the back, three - four, and a final blow to drop it away from the building - five. That simple, *Understand and Execute*, do it and he would pass the exam. He'd maybe even be named the Woodway Representative for it. That would show Quincy. Take away his direct line to Lafayette. That would be sweet.

He threw the first cut, but it was off center and had none of the power of his typical strike. The blade mostly bounced off the trunk, chipping the bark and not slicing into the meat of the tree. He repositioned and checked his stance. Then it hit him.

This wasn't what Keepers did. This wasn't him.

He stepped back and dropped the ax with a thud.

"No," he looked at his toes. "I won't do it."

The soldier remained still and expressionless as if he was waiting for Avery to change his mind. He felt like he was out of his own body, watching the scene from two overhead.

"I won't cut down the tree," he said, sweat pumped from his temples.

The soldier tapped quickly on the tablet, held it at arm's length and snapped several photos of Avery standing there with the axe at his feet. He then motioned, "Follow me."

What did this mean? Disobeying a Lafayette soldier was a serious protocol infraction. Was he in deep shit?

With no further detail, Avery was escorted through the Outpost. During the walk he scanned for familiar faces. But the base was still. His papers were crumpled in his back pocket, though they seemed useless at this point. When they arrived at the exit, the gatemen nodded and he was free to go. That was it? No debrief? Or complementary snack?

He shuffled down the dark main street. Yellow light peaked from several half hidden houses. He searched for signs of the others, wanting someone else to tell him they'd had the same experience, a pat on the back, or something. His skin felt taut and brittle, his mind depleted.

The hostel was again dark behind the porch lights. A small blue car was now parked next to his motorcycle - just another traveler passing through. He sat at the bottom of the stairs and tried to compute the happenings of the day.

His performance in the first two exams was good. At least he didn't hate the outcome. But the last exam was a complete dumpster fire. He tried not to think about the tree. What would Jasper think? Would he even make it home?

He was unable to move until darkness blanketed Briarcamp. Still warring with his inner turmoil, he shuffled back to his room and fell into a restless sleep.

Back at the Outpost, a secure line was being connected directly to the Tower in Lafayette to discuss an urgent matter.

Chapter 8

Upon Request of the City

The door crashed open. Avery flipped out of bed and tumbled to the floor at the feet of a crisply dressed officer.

"Get up," the master sergeant commanded.

Avery paused for a second, preparing himself for whatever punishment was about to be delivered for his protocol infraction the night before.

The soldier grabbed a fistful of his shirt and yanked Avery upright. Once he was face to face with the angular jawed officer, he wished he were back in Woodway.

"New orders, kid. Lafayette wants you in the city grove," he dropped Avery and read from a tablet. "The Shoulder, it's called. You are to leave immediately and report for work on 9 June. Here is all the necessary paperwork." He planted a folded paper on the young Keeper's chest.

Avery's mouth was bone dry.

"Is this for real?" Avery asked sheepishly.

The officer did not respond, turned and exited the room. His legs wobbled as he found himself alone and afraid to look at the document now in his hand.

"Can I call my mom?" he said to himself.

At the bottom of the stairs he heard a terse greeting and a door slam.

Don't freak out. Don't freak out. Don't freak out. He sat at the desk and opened the letter. A toll road pass, glossy hotel room voucher, and a simple printed card slipped out. The letter, which he worked through methodically, read:

Mr. Jackson,

Your skills assessment has been deemed to meet the needs of an open Associate Keeper position at The Shoulder, Lafayette's Sentinel grove. You have been provided the necessary clearance to gain entry into The City. Please arrive no later than 8 June to begin work on 9 June.

In Protocol.
Lt. Bryce Robertson- Quade

That guy again, he had sent Avery the first letter too. And it was clear: His protocol infraction not only had been tolerated, but had landed him a Keeper position in Lafayette's one and only grove. What? Sentinels inside the city walls?

On the card were his Assessment scores:

TOTAL_POSSIBLE // TOTAL EARNED
EXAM 1: 150 // 120
EXAM 2: 225 // 225
EXAM 3: 315 // 265*
EXAM 4: 110 // 6

The marks gave him a small sense of satisfaction, no information on that asterisk though. But he was quickly distracted. He considered the options: He could ignore the orders, slip out of Briarcamp and back to the seclusion and simplicity of Woodway, but that would not last. The Lafayette soldiers would most certainly find him. First the drones, followed by a team of soldiers, protocol prison after that - for not just him, but his entire family. His mother, his uncle. Maybe even the others he knew best in Woodway. Or he could run, disappear into the barren lands of the Outer Domain.

There really was no other option: He was going to Lafayette. The opportunity was big time.

Half-stunned, he packed what little he had and descended to the hushed first floor. The hostel attendant bobbed in a rocking chair on the front porch. A plate of various breakfast foods sat on a table next to him.

Avery toed open the door and nodded, his throat still paper dry.

"Good morning, Keeper," the old man said.

"Morning," Avery rasped. Had the officer told him?

Clueless on what to say, Avery just walked toward his bike. The blue car was still there. He could ride hard and maybe get to Lafayette before dark. Maybe 7A pointed straight to the city. But his preparation had not extended any farther than Briarcamp.

"Eat some breakfast before hitting the road," the old man said in a gentle tone.

This seemed better than the crushed sandwich he had left at the bottom of his pack. He returned to the porch and pushed two bran muffins and a hardboiled egg onto a saucer.

The old man continued to rock rhythmically while Avery ate.

"Lafayette is a beautiful place," he said knowingly.

"You've been?" Avery asked.

"Oh yes. I used to live there."

"Get out, really?"

"Indeed, a long long time ago."

"What's the best way to get there from here?" Avery asked, trying to take advantage of the opening.

"7A will get you to Lafayette, but not without some kinks."

Avery studied the man while chewing slowly.

"About a hundred miles north of here you'll run into the craters. Big ole' bomb craters from one of the Area Wars. Scars cut across the road. Hubbard can't seem to get them rebuilt on account of the bandits." His voice trailed off. "Or he just doesn't want them rebuilt."

"So that's as far as I can get?" Avery asked.

"No, no. You can pass...But." He paused and shifted forward in his rocking chair. "Remember to shoot low. Ride through the bottom of the craters. There's three of 'em. Bandits won't have time to react if you shoot low. Beyond that, take Wallace Avenue to the city gates. You can be there by evening."

Avery was leery of the man's urgency. Maybe this low route would lead him into a trap. Or maybe it was just honest advice from a man who had managed to survive a long time in this wild land. He collected his dishes and walked to the kitchen where he scrubbed them quickly and filled his water bottle. There were footsteps on the stairs, the screen door opened and creaked closed again.

Back outside, a jolly looking man was climbing into the blue car.

"See ya later Russell." He waved at the hostel attendant and smiled at Avery. The old man waved with a smile and the blue car pulled away.

Avery then checked over his bike. There wasn't enough fuel to get him to Lafayette. He would have to figure that out on the road. The old man stood now, leaning heavily on the porch rail. He held up a hand before Avery fired up the engine.

"If you find yourself in need out there, tell them you are friends of the Argus Bureau."

Avery started the engine with a roar.

"Thank you," he said over the rumble. "And thanks for breakfast, Russell."

The old man held a clenched fist across his heart in response; in the same gesture Avery had seen from his Uncle Jasper. He exuded strength beyond that of a bent over hostel attendant, but the quiet confidence of a brooding man.

Avery sped out of Briarcamp, passed under a massive bridge and leaned toward the circular entrance ramp for 7A North. Over the interchange flew a flock of strange black birds. They circled with heads pointing at unnatural angles and called out in four-tone screeches. These birds had been seen near Woodway once before. He had been young when it happened. But still vividly remembered his mother frantically pulling him inside the house and locking the door. Something about their presence sent a shiver down his spine.

He pushed his speed to get away from the birds. The road shoulder was scattered with debris and rusted scraps. Piles of trash. Scraps. Rusted components. The pavement was in good condition, though, with patches of bright new concrete.

Haze held over parts of overgrown fields and scattered stands of trees.

The morning miles were solitary. He was distracted by how much the old man seemed to know. That he was a Keeper. That he was headed to Lafayette. Feeling like there was someone watching him, he peaked over his shoulder often.

The terrain was flat and the road ran straight and true into the distance. He began passing clusters of cargo trucks chugging along and a scattering of small cars driving south. How the vehicles passed the craters, he was not sure.

Midday approached and Avery pulled off onto a clearing on the shoulder to cool off. An old cell phone tower stood in an empty field next to the road. He let the bike idle on the hot pavement, pulled off his helmet and drank from his canteen.

While he was stopped, a pair of laser scanners mounted to the top of the tower detected movement at the clearing. The scanners ran a rapid parallel pattern across Avery and his bike, allowing a computer to detect the outline of a person. This triggered a high-resolution camera half way down the rusted pole to focus. The camera tracked his face, snapping three images as he drank from his canteen. A third device estimated vital signs. When he returned to the open road, the three images and biometric data were packaged together, and transmitted to a storage facility.

Another hour of steady travel and the once sporadic traffic started to bottleneck at the first crater. All the cargo trucks had strangely disappeared. Dilapidated sport-utility vehicles, many with boxes strapped to the roofs, condensed in a single line, curiously leaving the left lane open. The drivers had dusty, sweat soaked faces. Heat rippled off their vehicles.

Several of them pulled out from the slow moving convoy to follow Avery in the left lane when he sped passed. The road opened onto a grisly crater, more than a quarter mile in diameter. It engulfed the entire landscape in front of him. Clear blue sky and jagged grey-brown met at the horizon. When the bomb had hit the center of the southbound lanes at an angle, the blast propelled dirt, concrete and metal into a massive pile where the northbound lanes once ran. A large drainpipe lay broken open, spitting brownish water out onto a bare slope.

He eased off the accelerator to scan for clear lines of travel. A rutted path veered to the left and disappeared into crater - the low route. It seemed to pick back up on the far side and snake up the opposite slope. Another path shot directly up a smooth arc to the crest of the debris pile. With only a hundred yards before the two diverged, Avery checked both sides of the highway, looking for movement. The high route looked clear and simple. However the words of the old man remained: Stay low and out of trouble. Maybe. He could hear tires behind him growing closer and accelerated to the high ground.

He looked back to see two of the SUV's following him. The slope steepened, he dropped down a gear to climb. The handlebars shook violently. Just as he released his breath - a puff of dust. Three thick braided wires snapped taught at chest level creating an impromptu barricade. Adrenaline rushed into his system.

He pushed back off from the handlebars, gripping the bike with all the strength in his legs. His torso snapped back hard, helmet smashing into the rear fender. Every muscle in his body tensed. He wasn't sure if his eyes were open or closed. Blood pounded in his eardrums as he barreled forward blindly. One, Two, Three. His body then snapped back into action. He flipped forward, catching the handlebars with his right hand, nearly throwing himself over the front of the bike. In his periphery, he saw blurry forms of strangely dressed men stepping from behind twisted pieces of metal and piles of concrete.

The bike slowed without his continued grip on the accelerator. He caught hold of the center of the handlebars, stabilizing himself and then pulled the throttle wide open. The engine yelled and the rear tire churned gravel. Behind him the first SUV smashed into the thick trip-wires in a ferocious clamor.

Don't look back, he told himself. He leaned through the turn and powered down the other side. He was at the edge of full panic.

Patches of pavement and debris marked the next quarter mile before the second crater cut across in the same pattern as the first. He sped through the maze until he again found two paths. Without slowing he veered downhill, twisting around tight switchbacks. All he wanted was speed. The terrain made that impossible.

Ground water lay in a thin layer at the bottom of the second crater, weirdly reflecting the pure blue sky. In the rippling reflection, he saw movement along the rim of the crater. Slow moving forms looking down from hiding spots. He drove through the pool, hoping it would stay shallow.

It was thick with oil and sediment, but only six inches deep. On the far side, he climbed up the switchbacks and out onto the roadbed.

Not far from the edge of the last crater, a ragged group of five bandits stumbled toward him. Shit. Two of the men wore rifles slung over their shoulders. Both swung up their weapons.

Avery veered toward the tree line. The first shot hit a pile of metal ten feet behind him. Avery ducked low against the bike. He was going to die. A second shot kicked up dust as it hit a concrete pile just over his head. Glancing toward the tree line, he saw an overgrown gate. He again opened the throttle. A third round hit his riding pack as he careened toward the gate at full speed.

The front tire crashed into a heavy frame. Rusted hinges protested loudly, but the gate swung open. He expected to abandon the bike and head out on foot. But to his surprise, he landed on clear pavement and screeched to a halt. Shrouded by a dense canopy and thick vines, a narrow road ran off in both directions with a freshly painted yellow line running down the center.

Another shot ricocheted off the gatepost. Yells in a coarse mixture of English and a language he could not understand sounded from outside. He pushed off to the north, blazing across the smooth pavement. Through the trees he saw the last crater fade into the distance. The tunnel road seemed to be depressed several feet. He drove into the afternoon, running parallel to 7A at full tilt. The tunnel dipped and curved away from the highway in some places. His panic dulled into a general terror.

Miles along, he approached a square green sign hanging from a slow branch that blinked: STOP. He came to a tenuous pause, the chance of an ambush seemed high. A metallic panel was bolted to a thick tree branch.

"Soldier 378564, report status," a harsh voice ordered.

Avery's stomach tightened. He looked around, peered through the dense vegetation, and saw no one.

"Soldier 378564, report status," the voice repeated.

Avery killed the engine and leaned toward the box.

"Soldier 378564, reporting. All clear, ready to proceed to next...checkpoint," Avery said in a voice much deeper than his own.

"Reports of attacks at Craters 1 and 2. You must have just missed them. Three escort units checked on a broken access gate, found no signs of intrusion and are proceeding northbound."

"Roger that."

"378564 - please hold."

Several seconds ticked by with the open line humming. He frantically checked the tunnel.

"378564 - ahhh, seems to be record malfunction. Records indicate that you cleared this checkpoint two hours ago. Please hold your position, escort team will be passing your locations in approximately 8 minutes, they will be able to clear you for further northbound travel. Control, out."

He needed to get off the tunnel road, now. He fired up the engine and took off. There was no way his worn out bike could outrun the high-powered escort vehicles. If the bandits were bad, those patrol soldiers were a fate far worse. He held close to the tree line, looking for another gate; it only seemed to be getting thicker.

For miles he scanned both sides before he saw a narrow crescent of clear sunlight. At the apex of a curve he found a gate covering a narrow bridge out to the highway. The ground sloped steeply at the bridge and the gate was padlocked closed with a chick chain. Just as he stopped, the familiar whine of supercharged engines appeared in the distance.

He pulled the hatchet from his bag. Aligned the blade with the chain, then chopped with every ounce of strength. Three strikes and the chain let go. With the hatchet placed back in his pack, he idled his bike onto the bridge, a stray nail scraped against the sidewall the rear tire. Air now hissed from a small hole. There was no time. He surged onto the highway and no more than two minutes passed on the open road and he heard the trio of vehicles scream by.

The next twenty miles were spent stopping to pump air into the leaky tire. He was covered in dust and his t-shirt stuck to the inside of his riding jacket. His back ached. The old man at the hostel had been right about the craters. Who was he?

He was also running low on fuel. Soon a small sign for Exit 37A appeared. In a mile, he rumbled off of the highway and onto a wide packed gravel lot. A large cinder block building sat sullen and shabby. *North Route Hotel & Inn* was painted on a faded wall. Perpendicular to the hotel was a row of buildings with no signs and a line of trucks in various forms parked outside.

Avery parked his bike around the entrance of the hotel. He coughed and rubbed his eyes as he stepped off. Maybe they would know where to find gas and a tire patch.

A woman appeared from somewhere. Wild hair rumpled on the top of her head, her eyes and mouth were sunken into her face far too much for someone her age. The bones in her arms protruded under almost transparent skin.

"Got any spare change?" she asked in a sandpaper voice.

Avery reached into his pocket and flipped her several loose coins.

"Got anymore?" she asked.

"Not right now," he said, walking quickly to the motel entrance.

"Yeah, yeah." She shuffled away. Avery noticed a revolver tucked into her sagging waistband.

The motel lobby was paneled in dark wood. There was a small counter facing toward the door and several overstuffed chairs arranged neatly on a patterned rug. Behind the counter stood a tall man with long hair pulled back into a ponytail, and cigarette tucked behind his ear. He twirled a pencil in his right hand.

"Hi," Avery said cautiously.

"Hello."

"I've got a bike out there. I'm riding toward...err, riding north. Any idea where I can get a few gallons around here?"

There was a long calculating pause.

"Sorry man, no fuel 'round here."

"Tire patch?" Avery asked.

"No dice."

Avery heard loud voices coming from the buildings down the street and saw the women loitering outside the window. Not good. He felt a million miles from home, beat up and stranded.

"Sorry, ahhh. I forgot to mention this, but...but I'm ahhh, I'm friends of the Argus Bureau," Avery said looking at the man directly. Let's see if this works.

The man scanned Avery's face with a different type of intensity.

"Where are you coming from? Where did you start your trip?" the man asked tersely.

"Woodway. ITwo days south of here."

"How did you get here again?"

"My bike," Avery said, stepping toward the counter.

"Right on. Yep, ok - Let me see what I can do."

Avery had at first doubted the man at the hostel, but the experience at the craters now gave him every reason to trust the gentleman's suggestions. The attendant moved urgently now.

"Follow me."

They exited the motel lobby.

"Right around those trucks there," he said, pointing to the far side of the clearing. The begging woman turned away and muttered mindlessly.

The motel attendant then marched in that direction. Avery pulled the bike around slowly. The rear tire rumbled, almost completely empty.

Beyond the line of buildings an ancient fuel station lay in disrepair. Several pumps sat on their sides, rusted completely through. The roof tipped to one side perilously. A garage was in better condition. The fading afternoon sun threw shadows across the open door frame. Avery turned wide and watched the tall man disappear into the darkness. A bare fluorescent bulb blinked on and he motioned for Avery to pull inside.

With remarkable speed and little effort at conversation other than to inquire about tire pressure and request the occasional extra hand, the attendant had the motorcycle's tire patched and fuel tank filled in less than half an hour. Avery tried to pay the man what money he had, but it was refused.

When he reluctantly pocketed the wad of cash and climbed onto the repaired bike, the attendant simply stuck out a fist. Avery pushed out his gloved left hand. Their knuckles connected and a rush of energy flooded his body with the same blue tinged sensation he had felt during the body exam back in Briarcamp. His eyes and heart awakened. The path ahead was in perfect focus for what seemed like miles beyond the exit with the edges of his vision blurring.

His hand returned to the handlebar, and the blue sensation vanished. The rude shock to his senses sent the bike tipping over and he crashed into the gravel. Frantically he clambered to his feet and heaved the bike up right. Befuddled, he looked over at the attendant who grinned but seemed to be emanating orange smoke from his shoulders and arms. Having spent the last two hours in constant life-threatening situations, Avery jumped back on the bike and accelerated away from the garage. He raced onto the highway. What the hell was going on today?

Avery sped through the afternoon. He kept a smooth line along the lane marker on the pavement. His mind was back at Exit 37A. Over and over, he re-played that half-second of energy, power, and focus. Replayed, reset, replayed, reset. He passed the first cargo truck on the road and remembered a comment from his uncle. Years ago they were walking out of the grove after clearing undergrowth from around a struggling tree. The memory came back to Avery with clarity, as if the slow cadence of his uncle's voice was inside his helmet.

"You'll learn one day. You'll learn to see," he had said. Was this what it felt like to be an Able? No way. That was impossible. But the road and the heat started muddying his focus.

Traffic on 7A increased as he drew closer to Lafayette. Once again the cargo trucks inexplicably thinned but this time they were replaced by brightly painted cars and the occasional battered SUV. He was determined to get to the Lafayette Ambassador Bridge before dark, but held back from weaving through traffic to avoid drawing undue attention.

Signs started to appear for the city. Avery merged in behind a familiar shiny blue car at the exit for Wallace Avenue. The same blue car and happy looking man that had stayed at the Briarcamp hostel. A massive overpass arched over the highway and curved to the west. Half way across the bridge, another sign read in white letters: *Walter Ave to Lafayette - 5 Miles to Checkpoint.*

Walter Avenue was a meandering boulevard. Trees soldiered along each side, evenly spaced in a strip of neatly mowed grass. Beyond that, dense vegetation took over. The wide median was similarly maintained. He was accustomed to the tattered places of the Outer Domain, the formality of it all intrigued him.

A mile down the boulevard a massive pillar rose into view. The hulking base tapered upward to a height of almost thirty feet, capped with a strange metal booth with angular iron bars protruding at random angles. Avery and the blue car traveled together now, encountering similar structures every mile. Each topped with a unique cap.

After passing the fourth pillar, the grade dropped and forest thinned. Avery slowed a bit, allowing the distance between him and the blue car to increase. The river appeared, a blackish green line of water shimmered through the trees. The avenue then straightened and a line of thick metal gates reached across the road. Behind the gates, a bridge soared high over the choppy river below. Pillars flanked the bridge. Unlike those on the road, they were topped with startling statues of crouched crow-like birds, like those he had seen flying over Briarcamp, with wings held high over their screaming faces. Their metal talons clawed at the pedestals.

Three groups of soldiers stood in the middle of the road. They wore the standard dark grey and green uniforms. The blue car was pulled off to the right, the driver, the round faced man with wild tufts of blonde hair, was being questioned by three soldiers.

Avery drove up to the second group and pulled off his helmet.

"Passport and registration," the soldier said.

A second soldier stood several paces away, as the third circled behind the motorcycle. He pulled a rectangular device from a hip pocket and scanned Avery's licenses place.

"Passport. And Registration. Please."

Avery reached into his breast pocket, both his passport and vehicle registration were damp with sweat. He handed them to the guard along with the letter of order.

"Idle your vehicle and stand by," the soldier sneered.

The other two met near the back of the bike. The device that scanned his license plate was held out to scan his passport and registration. Avery heard two beeps from the reader.

The soldier then returned and pointed to the bridge.

"Scan your passport at the inward gates at the far end of the bridge. You are required to pass full protocol inspection prior to leaving Zone 1. Is this understood?"

"Yep." Avery swung on his helmet and revved the engine. He had no idea what that meant, but he was anxious to get moving again.

The uniformed man pushed open the large gate and motioned. Avery passed through and accelerated onto the bridge. The concrete walls were high, cables and pillars towered overhead. No traffic flowed out of Lafayette.

When the bridge crested, a muscular skyline came into view. Lafayette was an old, bad city. Towers rose up like clenched fists in the haze. Directly in front of the bridge stood the tallest buildings. In the middle, stood a slender orange brick tower. Intricate detailing ran up the seams. Its more impressive details were turned toward the city for which looked out upon. This was The Tower.

Other dull nondescript buildings fanned out from this central cluster. Vacant rectangles of land scattered throughout the landscape, like pieces that had been ripped from a model set.

Over the northern bridge wall, Avery glimpsed a slender crescent shaped island. It was covered in thick forest and speckled with rooftops. From what Avery knew, these were the estates of Lafayette's elite and influential.

A set of gates ran across the road on the far side of the bridge with electronic scanners positioned at each drive lane. Avery's hands shook as he pushed his passport against the reader. Here goes nothing. The gate opened slowly. He dropped into first gear and rode across the threshold. He had arrived in Lafayette.

Section 2

A Further Range.

Chapter 9

Old, Bad City

The gate swung closed with a deep clang. Avery was in the city. In the shade of the tall, grimy gate structure, he sat for several moments as the vibration rang in his bones. He was glued in place, clinging to the last semblance of what he knew as normal life. Then the next gate panel opened and the blue car drove through and stopped next to him. Avery was too distracted and overwhelmed to pay proper attention.

Across an empty field and behind a hulking concrete wall, a gritty train station with a half reconstructed tower of stone and glass stood next to line of open-air platforms. On the far end, separated from the rest, a massive, white locomotive stood with steam curling from its roof. The spear shaped nose swept back to a line of dark glass panels near the top of the cabin. Its width was more than quadruple that of a normal train. Metal wheels and coiled suspension as tall as a house stood at each corner and in the middle. Behind the locomotive stretched a long line of low-slung cars.

Beyond the train station, the city sprouted through a tangled grey web of pavement and thick forest.

"That's the Blade Train," the driver of the blue car called over.

Avery pulled off his helmet, "I've never seen it in person. Pretty sweet," he said.

"Sure is!" the man said with casual ease.

After a beat, he added, "You were in Briarcamp this morning."

"I was..." Avery said struggling to conceal his hesitation.

The man, round faced and chubby, gave a thumbs up.

"Means you need to clear Protocol Inspection then," the driver of the blue car called over.

How had this guy cleared the craters? What was his angle?

"Where do I do that?" Avery asked.

"At Hubbard's Tower," he said, then waving his hands in feigned terror. "The Towwweeerr."

"Ok," Avery responded. In the face of all things new, Avery did not want to admit he was helpless.

"You have no idea where that is."

"No," Avery was forced to concede.

"Follow me," The driver pulled away from the gates in a dust cloud.

Avery spun on his helmet, then gripped and released the brakes nervously. He could follow this guy. Or he could drive the other direction and not get stabbed in an alley. The blue car slowed, and the man threw out another thumbs. What the hell, Avery thought, he could always ride away if this went sideways.

Avery gunned it down the access drive and they proceeded to take a straight shot toward downtown. Lafayette differed from Woodway in almost every way possible. The road was, for some reason, wider than the highway and dotted with hulking structures of industry and the occasional rubble heap. Avery followed cautiously with the city center condensing into tighter streets and taller buildings. Traffic on both the street and sidewalk swelled. Unlike the Outer Domain, the cars in Lafayette were shiny and well maintained. The residents were clean, plainly dressed, and seemingly distracted. Pairs of soldiers patrolled the streets.

The two travelers pulled into a snarled traffic circle under a tall wedge of a building. Traffic tightened as roads converged from multiple directions. Avery felt claustrophobic. In the outside lane, he revved his engine in the melee.

The scale of the city struck Avery. Ancient buildings reached up and up, staring at each other from across the sea of pavement, half bathed in bright sunlight. It was as if each tower was not only so much bigger than him, but almost noble. They held their secrets in windowsills, patterned stone facades, and oxidized copper.

He cruised up a central boulevard, now tight to the blue car's bumper. The slender brick Hubbard Tower appeared, shadow clad, standing long and leering. Diamond patterns of tile and slender glass weaved through the brickwork along each facet of The Tower. The top floors narrowed and reached to their pinnacle with a multi-pointed star of brick and stone. Near the third story, a crumbling raised concrete railway ran behind the building.

The temperature dropped as they pulled into a tall, stained garage connected to the tower. Uniformed officers appeared, scanned their passports a third time and requested keys. Reluctant to relinquish his bike, Avery inquired sheepishly.

"For inspection."

The single key was pulled from his hand.

His travel companion waited by the wall of the garage.

"I'm Henry." He introduced himself with a firm handshake as they ascended into dusty stairwell.

"Avery," Avery said. "And thanks for the help back there."

"You bet. I remember that 'oh shit' moment when I first came into the Lafayette. No one tells you where to actually do this Protocol Inspection thing."

Henry's bustling nature put Avery at ease. It wasn't the cagey demeanor of others he had encountered on the road. He was a head shorter than Avery, barrel chested and moved with unapologetic confidence – like none of this Protocol stuff fazed him in the least.

The stairs opened onto an barrel vaulted lobby of stone. Matching stone soldiers stood in the entrance - one holding a key, the other holding a sword. The space bustled with activity. An entire wall was lined with tall counters behind which various uninterested city officials attended to the various functions.

Henry led them to a line simply marked: INSPECTION. A wiry kid, with his nose against his phone, pushed between Avery and Henry. This ended their brief interaction, but it would not be the last time the two would cross paths.

The queue snaked back and forth before a row of four counters was armored with the same stone of the surrounding hall. The rude kid in front of Avery hadn't even looked up. He recognized the device as similar to the one Becky carried around in Woodway.

At the first counter, Avery saw another stern guard dressed in the crisp dark grey coveralls. A white diamond was stitched into the breast pocket, and a single narrow stripe of green ran up the collar. He was from Lafayette.

At the second, was a slender man with his feet propped on the counter, his fingers pressed into long unkempt hair. He wore a bright orange shirt with several of the top buttons undone and an unamused look on his face. Clearly a representative from Garfield.

A massive, forlorn man with a scruffy beard and shoulders nearly touching both partitions manned the third counter. His oversized proportions gave him a superhero look. His uniform marked him as an officer from Carrick City.

The line crept forward as others were processed through the line of inspectors. Avery scanned the buzz of civilians and soldiers. After some anxious line standing, a herculean figure appeared up the far stairwell. Uniforms and citizens alike heeded his approach. He was broad with light hair and two silver lines running up the collar of his uniform.

He was a Lancer, like the spear throwing soldier. He seemed to be keeping an eye on the Inspection line. And looked like a fricking Viking.

Avery was called to the first counter. Henry gave him another jolly thumbs up.

He handed his passport to the clerk who slapped it down onto the warn counter top, and flipped to the first page. From behind the partition the Lafayette representative pulled out the standard rectangular device, scanned the passport. On the second page of his passport, there was the line of three colored glyphs spaced along the top of the page: Green, Yellow, and Black. Avery kept a nervous eye on the lurking Lancer.

"First time Lafayette?" The attendant asked.

Avery nodded.

"Stay away from the Thicket Blocks."

The attendant pulled a narrow metallic marker from his pocket, drew a straight line through green rectangle, and pushed Avery's passport across the counter.

"Thicket Blocks?" he asked, in a hushed tone.

"Abandoned city blocks, nothing good happens there," the attendant said and pointed to the next counter.

Avery sidestepped. The wiry attendant was chewing gum with his mouth open. Avery presented his passport.

"Sup," the dude said between chews.

"Living the dream," Avery responded.

"Uhhhh huh."

Barely looking down, the attendant scribbled on the yellow rectangle and threw it back. What a dickhead, Avery thought.

"You're the best," he said turning toward the third counter.

"Yeah yeah, keep it movin'."

Under much different circumstances, they too would meet again.

The bear man looked like a zoo animal whose years in a cage had drained him. The passport looking like a post-it note in his hand. On a large tablet set on the counter, the Carrick City attendant tapped several times with his giant fingers.

"What is the purpose of your trip to Lafayette?" he asked.

"I ahh, I'm starting a job on Monday, following my - errrr – orders," he said, pulling out the paper of order. The attendant read.

"Your intended length of stay in the city?" His gaze seemed to look straight through him after looking up from the letter.

"Ummmmm."

"Please answer the question."

"Several years, let's say - seven." Avery shrugged.

"Criminal past?" the attendant asked.

Avery thought about crashing through the gate near the second crater on Highway 7A.

"Nope," he responded.

The attendant swiped a circular puck smoothly across the black rectangle. An arrow appeared at forty-five degree angles with a small puff of smoke. He then produced a beat up smartphone.

"This is for you," he said, pushing the phone across the stone counter.

"Oh I don't need a phone. Thanks."

At that moment, a pack of soldiers swarmed Henry. Grabbing him roughly by the shoulders, they pulled him away in loud protest.

"Hey! Hey! What's this all about?" Henry yelled, straining against their hold.

"Check my papers!"

The massive Lancer approached and addressed Henry.

The giant attendant tapped the phone against the stone, ignoring the commotion. Avery was concentrated on the scuffle and grabbed it. He barely heard him say, "You are expected to maintain a certain LAFAYETTE LINKERAGE score. If you fail to do this, you will be subject to punishment."

Avery pushed through the line as a team of soldiers shackled Henry with thick cuffs.

Avery seized up. He timidly slipped away from the counter, assimilating into the crowd. The soldiers were rough with Henry, twisting him toward the floor and sneering about Protocol Infractions. Avery wanted to push forward, help Henry, provide an alibi, do something. But the newly approved passport weighed a thousand pounds in his pocket. His feet did not move forward, but backward to the stairwell.

"I didn't do anything..." was the last Avery heard. Then there was a sharp slap and crack.

Avery ran down the dark stair and to the stall where he had left the bike. It now sat empty, other than a seated inspector.

"Hi, ummm, I left my bike here. A 90x..."

He checked the rest of the garage and did not see Henry's blue car either. His insides were in turmoil. The soldiers would come for him next, he was sure of it. He needed his bike, pronto.

"Your vehicle has been permanently confiscated," the inspection agent said.

"What!" Avery exclaimed.

The agent flipped open a tablet cover and read,

"The motorcycle is out of compliance with engine emissions standards for Lafayette. And has also shown a power to weight ratio above set standards. Such compliance violations are strictly prohibited by Protocol Section 12.4B - 3."

In stunned silence Avery was shown the door. In the din of evening rush, he wondered downtown with no clear focus other than to put distance between himself and the Tower. Fast walking residents jostled against him as he wandered aimlessly. There was an unexplainable strangeness to the city that Avery couldn't quite place. People seemed detached. Focused on their phones and in a hurry to get somewhere other than where they were. He tried to keep up with the pace, but it felt foreign.

Second to his hatchet, that bike had been his prized possession. What kind of place was this? They could just arrest Henry? Just take his bike? Emission Standards? What had Henry done? What had he gotten himself into?

When it was properly dark, he pushed both hands into his jacket pocket. The stupid phone and...the hotel voucher. Yes, yes, yes.

After asking several strangers who just ignored him, a soldier pointed him in the direction of the hotel.

Three blocks later, he ambled into cool, conditioned lobby air. A green suited woman smiled at him from behind a simple desk. This was his first time staying at a hotel.

He checked into his room without issue and took the elevator to the fifth floor. The room was a small yet a comfortable affair. The window was open with a slight breeze baffling long white curtains. He dropped his bag on the carpet and peeled off his riding jacket. Out of the pocket fell a small folded piece of paper with scrolling penmanship. It read:

A useful little list of things to know about Lafayette.
1) Somehow there is always traffic downtown. Rarely anywhere else in the city, but always downtown.
2) Find a place to live with people you can trust.
3) Stay away from the perimeter fences and walls. Surveillance drones patrol all the borders.
4) On Saturdays, no cars are allowed on the roads.
5) All of Hubbard's soldiers wear a white diamond on their chest. A green stripe on their collar means they are high ranking, two stripes means they are a Lancer. Take heed of that.
6) When in doubt, follow Protocol.
7) Try not to ask too many questions.
8) Hubbard and Ashburn do not get along. Hubbard and Stanton are firm pals.
9) Know the soil your plants grow in.
10) Stand Strong.

It must have been from the old man at the hostel. He returned it to his jacket pocket. Out of his window he could see the blank side of a tan building and toward the front of the hotel was a triangular shaped plaza filled with people. In the far distance he could see a gradual bend of the river. Long, arrow straight avenues radiated from the tall core of downtown and cut through the city fabric at wide angles.

After watching the city pass by and recovering a moderate level of sanity, Avery plopped down on the bed and pulled off his boots. He laid back and looked up at the tan ceiling texture. His mind and his body had been clenched for three straight days. He noticed the muscles in his face were pulled tight. He tried to breath and relax. With some discomfort, he wiggled his jaw and sighed.

Anonymous footsteps in the hallway reminded him that he had a bathroom, with a shower. He stood in the shower for nearly a half an hour, enjoying the endless supply of warm water.

Feeling refreshed, he dug out his only clean pair of underwear and a fresh shirt. They were crinkled and smelled slightly of canvas and motor oil. Once dressed, he felt like a new man.

He then filled a small glass with tap water, pulled the last sandwich from his bag, and sat down at the narrow desk where a tablet computer was mounted to the surface. He tried to focus on the tasks ahead of him. Step one was: a finding place to live.

On the back of his room key card, he found a sixteen-digit passcode that allowed him access to the wireless connection. When he opened the browser, a message appeared on the screen: *Please be advised. Internet activity is regularly monitored for fraudulent, and insolent activity.*

"Noted," Avery said to himself. The message was replaced with a search window.

He browsed for rooms and apartments for rent. The connection was fast and consistent, a far cry from the sporadic access to which he was accustomed. After a sandwich worth of searching, he ran across three different forums that posted available lodging. He knew very little about the layout of the Lafayette neighborhoods. With an aerial map, he added a pin with the general information for each property.

One particular post required any new roommate to own a sword and be able to conjure spirits. Another, which was located only two blocks from the hotel, was only accessible by fire escape. Many locations were asking for an exorbitant monthly rent or did not provide contact information.

After two hours, he powered down the tablet in frustration. When he turned back into the room, the jagged bullet hole in his riding bag caught his eye.

He emptied the contents of his bag onto the bed. A pencil thick hole pierced through the coffee tin, grounds trickled from the exit wound. He gently placed the tin on the desk and wrapped it in the plastic bag from the bathroom.

By the time he finished reorganizing the sparse contents of his bag, which now contained his only worldly possessions, the city had started to quite under a gray sky. His eyes were heavy with exhaustion. Tomorrow he would continue the housing search.

He laid looking up into the darkness for a long while. The only light entering the room was from the window. As his eyes adjusted, he started to see the ceiling texture. He forced his eyes closed. The back of his eyelids danced to phantom swirls and images of The Tower lobby. His thoughts jumped to Henry and to his mother. Slabs of guilt weighed on his entire body.

He stepped back out of bed and turned on the desk lamp. A small circle glowed in the corner of the room, making the other walls stretch. He again entered the access password and again read the warning about insolence. To his mother he sent a quick email.

In the subject line he wrote: Change of plans - Lafayette!

> Hi mom, I'm writing from my hotel room in Lafayette! Crazy, right? The exams went well, I guess. Well enough for them to order me to be a Keeper in Lafayette...The last 24-hours have been a whirlwind. But, I'm safe. The city is tall and loud. But, I'm safe. I'll call Jasper when I can.
> love, A

He hit send.

Now awake, he adjusted his position and looked through the housing forums with groggy eyes. The first two were not any less ridiculous than his previous search. Another house offered a room if you brought your own missile launcher.

But he then opened the third forum and saw a new post that caught his attention on Forest Avenue:

Quirky household seeking new roommate to fill current vacancy. Our house is located in a friendly neighborhood just a few miles north of downtown. We're entirely and enthusiastically Protocol compliant. Looking for a trustworthy, independent, and engaging individual. Small room, on second floor, is available for immediate occupancy. Rent is negotiable, let's just talk about it. Must love dogs.

Avery scanned through several images of a small home with and a large porch filled an eclectic group of smiling faces. It felt like a good fit.

His fingers tapping quickly against the keyboard icons, he drafted a short message about himself. After reviewing the images again, he hit send and crawled back into bed. This time, falling to sleep after a while.

He did not see the tablet glow with a new message.

Hi Avery,
You sound like an excellent fit for our house. If you're interested, feel free to stop by anytime tomorrow to take a look around. Hope to see you soon.
Best,
Beatrice

The room posting was deleted shortly after.

Chapter 10

Outer Domain Surveillance

Standing some miles from downtown Lafayette, a tower stood proud and alone. With a wide base more than two blocks across, it stretched high above the featureless structures in its shadow. The unseen basement sunk deep into bedrock and a dedicated elevator system scurried between subterranean levels.

This was Hubbard's Protocol Center. Five separate divisions monitored various parts of Hubbard's empire.

The featureless hallways were lined with pods of protocol technicians. Frosted glass doors blocked the view into each cluster. Desks were wrapped with wide monitors and positioned just out of view from neighboring workstations. The air hummed from a harsh ventilation system banks spinning servers.

Each division operated autonomously and lay scattered across the various levels. No two groups worked on the same project, monitored the same people, or analyzed the same data.

A management center was located on the first basement floor. Technicians clocked-in for their shifts at a large circular counter, received a set of tasks on a portable drive, and shuffled to a randomly assigned desk.

Each Fender controlled a loose sphere of influence around their city - the Outer Domain they called it. The borders of the three fiefdoms were blurry and often a source of squabble between Fenders. But Hubbard controlled much of the land north of Lafayette before it faded out into wilderness. Scattered amongst the tattered northern towns were surviving industries that helped keep the city running. A metal fabrication complex, a dairy operation, farm fields, and a few random storage facilities. To the south, Hubbard's Outer Domain included an ancient nuclear power plant and extended further south along major corridors, including 7A. A cold, windy river, and a nondescript village called Woodway marked the farthest southern boundary.

A nameless officer plopped into a stiff backed chair and wheeled up to a bank of monitors. He verified his identification with a long passcode and voice sample, then plugged in his day's work. Shortly after, a folder popped up on the screen. There was a long list of date-stamped packets: images, 3D scans, and location information. Keystrokes from the surrounding desks tapped along with the murmur of dry air blowing down.

He started sifting through data, which came from various monitoring devices along the southern edge of the domain. Despite claims by field officers about the precision of the sensors, birds, squirrels, or even gusts of wind often activated them. Those images were promptly deleted with a sharp pinky strike.

Halfway through his shift, a specially marked set of data packets appeared from his queue. The green tab noted that the contents had been flagged by upper level command for detailed review. The location information showed the far edge of Lafayette Outer Domain. The first images showed a motorcyclist with square shoulders riding north out of town. The technician pulled a bit closer to his desk and zoomed in. The high-resolution photo showed wrinkles on the riding jacket in precise detail, yet he could not make out the rider's face.

A license plate number was captured in the next three photos. He drew a window around the plate. The computer quickly detected the values and confirmed the registration. Additional packets of images then showed the rider approaching Briarcamp. A final packet showed the rider speeding out of Exit 37A but strangely nothing in between. He plotted the points and confirmed there were two more checkpoints missing in the route. After creating a small text file that contained the license information, a description of the vehicle, and a REASONABLE JUSTIFICATION FOR CONCERN, the packet of images were moved into the queue for further consideration.

Upon completing this task, a window appeared directing the technician to contact the lieutenant's office immediately. He was confident that it was simply a system malfunction and was hesitant to make a direct call to the officer on duty. For an extra minute, he hovered over the files and finally decided to dial the provided extension. After briefly describing the surveillance data, the technician was instructed to hold the files in his open queue and await a visit from the lieutenant. A very rare occurrence.

A few minutes later a towering, serpentine officer bustled into the room. Lt. Bryce-Robertson Quade, known within the Protocol center as Hubbard's most ruthless enforcer, loomed over the monitoring station, bringing a cold rush into the technician's mind.

"Show me the images," the lieutenant commanded, standing close.

The technician slowly scrolled through the progression, noting the locations as he went.

"Sir, the last confirmed location of this vehicle was at the Hubbard Tower, Vehicle Bay 6,at 18:35 yesterday."

Lt. Quade sighed in response.

"Give me control."

The technician rolled out of the way and Lt. Quade leaned over the keyboard. He rapidly entered a string of commands that brought up a restricted access directory. After entering a password, a myriad of files on this specific traveler appeared which were closed in a flash after he dragged and dropped the new images into the directory.

He deleted the originals from the queue and stepped away from the station.

"Return to your normal duties," Lt. Quade ordered. He straightened the shoulders on his uniform and tugged crisply on both sleeves. The technician nervously rolled back to his station and returned his review duties. Lt. Quade then disappeared down the hallway, heels clipping on the polished floor. He dialed an unregistered number on his phone as he entered the elevator.

A woman's voice answered.

"He's here," Lt. Quade said and then ended the call.

Chapter 11

Must Love Dogs

Avery made an appointment to visit the house on Forest Avenue at 9:30AM. He was brushing his teeth, when a knock came at the hotel room door. Surprised, he swiftly washed out his mouth and pulled open the door. A floral scented woman with a bulging chest and long legs bustled into the room with a squeak.

"Avery Jackson, so good to meet you!" she exclaimed pulling him in for a tight-armed hug. Her breasts felt strangely firm against him.

When she pulled away, he tried not looking bumfuzzled.

"Hi. Should I? Am I?" He was the smoothest talker of all talkers.

"I'm Crystal. I'm one of your Pre Loads and I noticed your Lafayette Linkerage score was *shockingly* low and had just checked into the hotel. Sooooo, I thought I would stop by and say Hiiii."

"Oh. There it is." Crystal grabbed the chipped and scratched phone sitting on the hotel desk and tapped it against her own, much shinier phone. She then scrolled through his phone quickly.

"And you're a Keeepeerrr. How mysterious and impressive." She handed it back to Avery. "I've heard, from a very reputable source, that the acorns out of our grove are the very best."

"Thanks," he said, brandishing the phone and trying to meet her eyes without getting distracted. "What exactly are we talking about here?"

"Lafayette Linkerage. Linkerage for short. It's the city's social network. Everyone's required to maintain an account. Plus, it's awesome, the best way to meet people and keep that score up. And I have an exceptional score, *obviously*. Champagne Class 5. Which is, of course, why they pre loaded you with me," Crystal explained as she wiggled back toward the door.

"Avery, you're in excellent hands. Just remember to check-in often and start getting those links. We'll get you up to speed. 'mmk?" With that, she was gone. Her sharp scent lingered.

Avery threw the phone on the bed. That was weird.

When he was done getting ready, he found several notifications of link requests. A younger accountant guy with an impressive haircut, two young ladies with proportions similar to Crystal, and a bearded man with tattoos running up both arms. Accept all. His Linkerage score grew 7 ¾ points. Well, that part was fun. After that, he dressed, organized his belongings on the desk and headed out into the city.

Down from the hotel he found the streetcar line that headed north out of downtown. The spartan platform brimmed with people inattentively waiting for the next train.

A narrow automated ticket booth was the only electrified element in sight. He sidestepped closer, not wanting to look clueless. Several buttons sat below a cracked screen and a narrow slot blinked for cash. From his pocket he pulled crumpled bills. The machine pulled in his first bill and promptly spat it out. The second bill: buzz, buzz, spit. The third try: buzz, buzz, spit.

A distant clang and metallic screech of an approaching train. Avery nervously flattened the bill against his leg. The two people who had gotten in line behind him were starting to get annoyed. Crap.

Seemingly from the heavens, a short girl with a mess of auburn hair and dressed in hospital scrubs, stepped over. A calming hand rested on his elbow.

"Gotta select your ticket first. What kind do you need?" she asked, looking at Avery with a curious smile. Her face was round and kind.

"Out and back. Is that a thing? I need to go to Woodbridge and then, ya know, get back here," he blurted, sheepishly.

"A double." She tapped the screen and the half eaten bill zipped into the machine. A small ticket printed and popped out.

Avery thanked her with relief in his voice.

"You bet." Her smile made it hard to look away and Avery found it hard to look away. "Five stops up - don't forget to scan it." She added.

And then the train, faded panels and half the windows missing, rolled around the corner. A rush of people exited the twin cars before those on the platform shuffled on, scanning tickets as they went. Avery boarded and grabbed hold of a greasy overhead bar. The train was stuffy and smelled like armpit.

The redhead was a half car back, chatting with an older gentleman. They glanced at each other. Avery managed an awkward half smile before turning away to conceal this round of embarrassment. The train lurched forward and settled into a halting rhythm. It stopped once more just beyond the crumbling elevated track, taking on a few more passengers. Then marched out of downtown. The wide Avenue, Woodward, was lined with brick and stone structures of two or three stories. Some small cars and trucks with the green Lafayette colors chugged along next to the train. Avery was overly aware of everything around him and watched the redhead in the window reflection.

Several minutes outside of the squeeze of downtown, a familiar pattern of blue green leaves peaked over the rooftops. Sentinels. He ducked low and in the process kneed a man in the thigh. Apologizing and making too much noise, Avery leaned against the overhead bar, affording him another glimpse of Lafayette's grove, The Shoulder, before it disappeared behind the city.

The next stop was the fifth from where he started. With a half turn he waved to the redhead, who didn't notice. Though her seated neighbor nodded with a confused brow. The train stopped and he jumped out, ticket still clutched.

"What an idiot," he muttered under his breath. From the platform, he marched along a wide sidewalk. Woodward Avenue was another warped and potholed road that seemed to stretch a million feet across.

Several blocks along, he saw a small sign for Forest Avenue and turned right. Each house held close to the narrow, shaded street. Squat front yards were filled with gardens, patches of scraggly grass, and tall trees along the sidewalk. He passed several folks who looked up and smiled. On the third block he slowed and hunted for address 1435.

As he read the numbers on mailboxes and front doors, he found himself growing exceedingly nervous. He didn't even know these people. Why was he nervous? Nevertheless his insides pressed against his rib cage.

1435 Forest Avenue was framed by two large Sycamore trees that shaded the entire yard. A narrow driveway ran along the right side. A cobalt blue door with a small, square, stained glass window sat at the back of a deep front porch. The second floor had a small bay window tucked under the steep gable.

Meeting new people was something he'd done terrifyingly little of in his life. Woodway was small. He was maybe like eight years old the last time he'd met a new person? Scenarios where this would be an unmitigated catastrophe ran through his head.

As he turned to walk up the driveway, a breeze rustled the leaves overhead. A cattle dog sat on the front porch, with its brown and grey head resting between outstretched paws. When he came closer, the dog rose. It looked at Avery as someone looked at an old friend. Head tilted, warm and calm, ears pointing straight forward. As he walked up the steps, its head pressed into his palm and circled around him, holding close to his leg. He pulled back the squeaky doorknocker several times and waited - the dog by his side.

Several slides and clicks came from inside and the door swung open. A stocky man with shoulder muscles the size of an ox and tan skin appeared. He threw his arms into the air.

"Avery! Que Pasa? How are you?" he grasped Avery's right hand and slapped him on the shoulder.

"That's me," Avery said.

"I'm Paolo."

"Good to meet you man."

The dog sat down on its haunches next to Avery.

"Aw man, you just made a new friend. Mia doesn't like anybody," Paolo said.

Avery took a quick breath, trying to hold his chest in tight. Did he come to the wrong house? But Paolo knew his name.

"I'm sorry. Someone named Beatrice responded to my email...Does she live here?" he asked.

"Aw yeah! Lemme get her. Step on in." Paolo disappeared into the house, leaving the door open onto a foyer and a narrow staircase.

Mia walked inside and looked back at him. He took several tentative steps.

From around the corner a short woman with caramel skin and silver hair appeared, pulling a pair of reading glasses from the bridge of her nose. She wore a blue button down shirt with the sleeves rolled up to her forearms and khaki shorts.

"And you must be Mr. Jackson. I'm Beatrice." She reached out and shook Avery's hand firmly. "Ever so nice to meet you."

"Hi Beatrice. Thanks for getting back to me so fast," Avery said with a nervous twinge. "And good to meet you too."

"I got good feelings from your message." She waved one hand in the air and pushed the front door closed with the other.

"And no one but my very dead mother actually calls me Beatrice. It's Bea. Come in."

Avery followed her out of the foyer into a high ceilinged kitchen centered on a large island. He stood back, hooking his thumbs into the pockets of his jeans.

Bea walked in and leaned against the counter. Paolo followed. She looked at him quizzically, studying his face.

He smiled at them both. Who was this quick talking Latino man that looked like he could be a prizefighter? Was Bea his mom? No - they looked nothing alike. There was no way to avoid running through scenarios of who lived in this house.

Bea broke the silence with a calm voice. Her words stitching together in neat sentences.

"Avery, I'm sorry. I forget that we've never met. Please, have a seat and take a drink. I'll give you the low-down."

She pulled two stools from under the counter.

"Sit."

Avery sat and Mia stayed close.

"How long have you been in Lafayette?" she asked.

Paolo walked out of the kitchen, slapping Avery on the shoulder. The blow could easily have knocked him into the basement.

"I got here yesterday. I'm staying at The Book downtown," he stuck his thumb toward the city center, he thought.

Bea pointed in the opposite direction with a chuckle.

"You said you're from Woodway. That's pretty far south. What brings you to the City of Lafayette?" Bea asked.

"It's for a job. I got conscripted to work at The Shoulder. It's the Sentinel Grove here in the city, I guess. Start Monday morning." Avery smiled urgently.

"Then you're a Keeper."

"Yep."

"Young, outside kid, comes to the big city following Fender's orders. And now he needs a place to stay," Bea said.

"Hubbard didn't really leave me any choice. Your posting was the first that sounded halfway sane. What is with people in the city and weapons? If you're in need of someone trained in swordsmanship, I don't think I'm your guy," Avery said matter-of-factly.

"Mmmmm, there are plenty of crazies in this town. I can't say we're 100% sane here. But some people think that Hubbard and his men are out to control their lives and break in and steal their women and children..." Bea shook her head.

"Oh! That reminds me, I'm supposed to work on my Linker-do or something score," Avery pulled out his phone.

"None of that shit in this house," Bea scoffed. "Put it away."

"Ok." Avery pushed the phone back in his pocket. The screen read with no less than sixteen new link requests.

Bea rubbed the skin on her neck. "You are working for them now, I guess. So keep straight. But you'll learn that keeping to yourself has some value inside these walls." She said.

There were a hundred questions that he wanted to ask her, but she seemed to be holding back a bit.

"Got it," He responded. "So, is Paolo your son?" more aware of the absurdity of that question once asked he asked it.

Bea leaned away, feigning indignation.

"Heavens no," she said. "Paolo works for me."

Again, Avery sensed that that she was holding back further comment.

"Ok, so I get it. He's on the payroll to...." Avery stopped. Foot in mouth.

Bea burst into laughter.

There was an undeniable comfort between them.

"Kiddo, I haven't been around a penis in decades. And I've known Paolo for years and years. He works for me, in the most legitimate way. Runs several of my labor crews and has been living with us for four or five years now."

"What is this place?" he blurted.

Bea just grinned. She crossed her arms and started to explain the situation on Forest Ave, letting the open atmosphere continue to flow:

She was married to Florence. Together, they had lived in this house for almost thirty years. For a long time, they tried to have children of their own - desperately wanting to fill the empty rooms with a family. With no success, they started opening their home to people in need of a place to stay.

"Like yourself." Bea touched Avery on the shoulder.

She did not in fact run a male escort service, but a construction company that repaired roads, fences, water pipes, and the like throughout the Lafayette. Florence was a gardener who grew vegetables and fruit trees on several plots scattered around the city. Bea promised to make introductions, but explained that she was, at the moment, currently transplanting beets in the backyard.

There were four rooms. Paolo had one. Mitchell stayed in a room upstairs. Bea described him as the quiet one and that he knew the inner workings of this city better than anyone.

Bronwyn lived in the basement room and she was a gardener like Flow. Her mother had been killed in a car accident on the west side, and she had moved into the house after Flow found her walking down the middle of empty street one night.

"And the last room is currently empty," she said.

Behind him, Mia whined quietly.

"Oh, and then there's Mia. She's the best damn mutt anyone could ask for. Part cattle dog, part something else. Wolf maybe. She keeps us all out of trouble...And seems to like you. That's something," Bea said with a wink.

He looked over his shoulder; Mia was watching them with the same intent expression as when he arrived.

"Yeah, Paolo said that too. I guess I'm doing something to trick her," Avery said, still looking over at the dog.

"Ahhh haa, not much gets passed her. If you were no good, we would all know it," Bea said. "Come on, lemme show you around the place."

She walked him around the main level, which was floored in worn hardwood. Adjacent to the kitchen was an area with a long table and high-backed chairs. Around the corner was a compact common room with a burgundy sofa facing a large fireplace and several overstuffed chairs. Bea stopped occasionally to show Avery various items on the walls, and review their backstory. Off the foyer was a set of glass paneled and curtained doors that opened into Bea's office. A desk centered in the room was covered in neat stacks of papers and the back wall was constructed as one floor to ceiling bookshelf. Tucked under the stairs was a cramped bathroom.

On the second level, a narrow hallway ran through the middle of the house. Located at the front was Bea and Flow's room, with the bay window poking out. Across the hall was Paolo's room. They passed by a large bathroom, with shining white tile on the floor and walls. At the back were two small rooms. The first was heaped with loose scraps of papers, maps, and scales.

Across the hall was a mostly empty room of similar size. There were large windows on the back and sidewall. The roof sloped down and clipped off the corner of the ceiling. A mattress was tucked under the windows. Greyish carpet covered the floor and it smelled stale - like it hadn't been used for some time.

Bea leaned against the doorframe as Avery walked around, looking at the corners of the room.

"A few months back we tried having a soldier trainee stay in here. It ended in a lot issues. You know, us lesbians are a troublesome bunch."

"That's what I hear," Avery joked.

"So, what do you think?" she asked.

He looked in the shallow closet.

"I like it. I think this could work. Do I need to get approval from the Mrs?" he asked.

"Let's head out back. I'm sure she'll love you." Avery stuck his head in the bathroom on his way down the hallway and got a whiff of fresh pine needles.

Back in the kitchen, she pulled open the screen and they stepped onto a patio. The back yard was deep and filled with various garden things. The narrow driveway ended in front of a small garage. A faded red pick up truck was parked with the tailgate down. Avery could see Paolo and a bearded man unloading palettes from the back. Adjacent to the garage a narrow swatch of grass curved up to a large garden plot. Neat parallel lines of lush greens, tomatoes, and herbs covered the earth.

Bea, shoeless, tiptoed along the grass line until she encountered a woman kneeling near a disturbed patch of beets.

"My dear, can you take a second to meet Avery? He's the one looking at our spare room. He's a Keeper," Bea said, tilting her head to the side.

Florence looked up matter-of-factly. She was a plump woman, wearing bright green rain boots, turquoise t-shirt and a floppy wide brimmed hat.

"Well shit, you should have told me he was here," she said scowling. She stood up and pulled off her gloves one at a time. Avery stepped over a pile of tubers and extended his hand.

"Hi, I'm Avery."

She grabbed his hand and gave it a good shake.

"Avery, it's a pleasure. I'm Florence, call me Flow."

She pushed the brim of her hat away from her face, dropped her hands onto her hips and looked at Avery.

"Any plans on becoming a Lafayette soldier?" she asked.

"Not in the least."

She looked at him for several more seconds.

"Well, if you're a Keeper, you're a keeper," she said, looking back down at the garden.

"You like beets?" she asked.

"No, not really," Avery responded quickly.

"Yeah, neither do I. I don't know why the fuck I always grow 'em."

Bea leaned in and kissed Flow on the cheek.

"Come over and meet Mitchell." She motioned toward the truck.

Paolo looked over and smiled.

Avery gave a half nod.

Bea peeked around the truck, "Mitchell, come out here for a second, would you?"

A bearded man with scraggly hair drenched in sweat walked around the far side of the truck. His shirt was dirty and frayed and he looked down at his shoes as they scuffled against the pavement.

"This is Avery. He's interested in the empty room we have upstairs."

"Hey," Mitchell said, glancing up at him. Avery noticed that his hands were calloused and scarred. The marks also ran up his forearms.

Paolo stood the back of the truck, "M, he's legit."

Mitchell wrapped his fingers on the hood, "Yeah." Then walked back into the garage. Bea frowned and crossed her arms.

"It takes a little while for him to warm up," she said.

Bea and Avery walked back into the house. He grabbed his bag from the kitchen counter and Bea went over the terms of the rent. The first month was free, and he was welcome to move in at any time.

To Avery, the place already felt like home. There was a warmth he couldn't quite explain. His phone buzzed again, he decided to ignore it for the time being.

As they walked to the front door she asked about his dinner plans - which he had none. So she told him go back to the hotel, get his stuff and be back to the house by 5:00.

Avery smiled inside and out as he walked back down Forest Avenue. Mia had returned to her post, sitting next to Bea. He turned and waved. The morning clouds had drifted away, leaving a scrubbed blue sky. This city was transforming into something real. Bustling with noise, stories, and contradictions.

He had made his way down Woodward Avenue and was about to walk up to the streetcar platform when a Lafayette patrol truck passed him and slammed on the brakes. He paused, two soldiers jumped out and approached him.

"Don't move citizen," they commanded. Avery held up his hand. He swore to himself, wondering what he had done.

"Registration and phone." The two soldiers were now up in face.

"In my pocket," Avery said, struggling to speak.

"What was that?"

"In my back pocket," Avery repeated.

A hand roughly dug out the passport and new phone from his back pocket. Avery's jaw clenched. His bag was now pulled off his back. People at the platform watched coldly. There was a familiar beep. He knew he had passed Protocol Inspection like twelve hours ago and had scanned his ticket on the train.

Then the shooting pain of a boot in the back of his left leg sent him crumpling to the sidewalk. There was commotion. He was stunned, unsure if he was allowed to move. The boot returned, pushing him over. The soldier leaned down and presented Avery with the screen of his new phone.

"Lafayette Linkerage is meant for the safety, security, and social well-being of its citizens. A score this low is a serious Protocol Infraction." His score was 12 and 5/8ths and 22 link requests were listed below. He couldn't speak – his face pulsed with fire.

"Good thing you have a special visa," one soldier scoffed, while the other rooted through his bag and found his hatchet.

They dropped the phone and passport on Avery's chest.

"Get that score up, citizen." They marched back to the truck, his hatchet now in their possession and took off with a hiss.

Avery turned away from the watchers, rose off the pavement and dusted himself off. With the back of his hand he quickly wiped away tears. The streetcar clanged down the avenue and stopped at the platform. No one came over, they all entered the awaiting car. Though three more link requests arrived on his phone. His stomach had spun in knots. More uncontrolled tears got pushed away. What had just happened? He knew everyone in Woodway by name.

Walk it off, just walk it off, he told himself.

For an hour or so, he trudged through anonymous blocks trying to reconcile the morning's events and accepting every anonymous social connection listed on his stupid phone.

After awhile, he returned to the platform and took the next train back downtown. Once again they passed under the crumbling concrete bridge that seemed to mark the entrance to the city center. He caught a glimpse of the mean looking top floors of the Tower.

Finally back in the hotel room he dropped his bag. He was dripping with sweat. Through the tall window, a current of air circulated around the room. The bed had been made and in the bathroom he found his towel neatly folded.

He gulped down several cool glasses of water and stood under a lukewarm shower for some time.

After finishing in the shower and getting dressed, his watch read 1:53. He returned to the lobby, checked out of the room, and in unnatural fashion, introduced himself to strangers with variations of: *Hi, I'm Avery and I'm new here. Can I link with you?*

Most people obliged by tapping phones with him, though they seemed a little off-put by the interaction. At least he'd talked face to face with people before adding them as a link. When he was sick of doing this, he found a bank of tablets mounted in the back of the lobby and checked his email. No less than twenty messages from his mother, all frantic. He tapped a response, keeping it brief and leaving out the more challenging bits.

```
Hi mom,
        I'm safe. I found a place to live today.
I'll be near enough to the Shoulder, not far
from Woodward Avenue. I haven't quite figured
this place out yet. But I start work tomorrow. I
miss you all. Will be in touch.
        love, a.
```

Before he could close the window, a new message appeared. His mother must have been camped out by their half-functioning computer.

```
        A - Please, please be safe. (I know you
know this.)
        love from mom.
```

* * * * * *

Bea returned to the backyard, running her toes through the soft grass. Crouched in the garden a few feet away, Flow rested on both knees.

"Whadya think?" she asked, looking over at her wife.

"I think he's going to work out swimmingly." she said.

A beet got pushed into the soft ground.

"Yeah. Me too."

"Are you just saying that?" Bea asked.

"Truth and truth, my love," Flow said. "He's a good kid. Glad you found him."

"Yeah," Bea said in a long breath.

"And is he?" she asked.

"Yes."

"You're sure of it."

"Absolutely."

"Well, if nothing else - this 'ill be entertaining."

Chapter 12

Among Friends

The fifth streetcar stop appeared and Avery exited the packed train. His Linkerage score was now in the green, one hundred and ninety four points. But he had never felt so alone. Every time he thought about the soldier walking away with his hatchet, he wanted to punch someone. When he passed the opposite platform and made his way along the bumpy, ugly Woodward Avenue, he tried to control his brooding anger. Plus he didn't want his new housemates thinking he was a grouch.

Paolo again greeted him at the front of the house. The kitchen hummed with activity and was filled with the smell of fresh herbs and cooking vegetables. Hidden behind the center island, Mia let out a single bark and then padded over, tail wagging.

Flow manned a large pot at the stove, and Bea chopped carrots at the center island. She looked up and smiled, then turned and snapped Flow on the butt with a dishtowel.

"Hey!" Flow turned around and saw him. "He decided to return! Welcome, welcome." She turned back to the pot as it threatened to boil over. "Dinner in half an hour. Go get settled upstairs."

Bea grinned a crinkled smile at Avery.

"Come on, I'll show you up to the room," Paolo said.

The two walked toward the stairs. Mia clinked behind until the edge of the kitchen and then sat down, keeping an eye on them and ears pointed back toward the cooking. Avery dropped his stuff in the open room and let out a sigh.

"Hey man, you're part of house now," Paolo said. "Bea and Flow are the real deal. Pulled me off the street and put me straight."

Avery nodded with a tense smile.

There was a pause. They both inspected the floor.

"Avery, for real - good to have you. I'll leave you be. If you're late for dinner, I'm eating your rolls. Don't say I didn't warn you." He threw up a peace sign and ducked out of the room.

The lump in Avery's throat settled and he took a deep breath. A new home, that meant something. The carpet was soft on the bottom of his feet after he pulled of his boots and socks. A set of fresh linens sat on one of the narrow closet shelves. After making the bed, he unpacked the sparse contents of his bag. His hatchet cover sat empty at the bottom.

A small picture of he and his mother got pinned to the wall next to the door. When he left Woodway, he thought they would be seeing each other again soon.

He was smelling his already-worn shirt when a soft knock came at the doorway. Leaning against the doorframe was the housemate he had yet to meet. He was greeted by her goofy face grinning underneath a mop of hair that fell long over her shoulders.

"Hi," she said in a warm voice. "I'm Bronwyn." She was wearing a patterned dress and pair of rubber soled boots.

"Avery, guess I'm your new housemate." Avery stepped over to shake her hand.

"Aw," she protested, stepping closer. "I'm a hugger. Come on in." And they hugged.

"Welcome to the casa, Avery. Paolo hasn't scared you away yet did he?"

"Not at all, it's great here." He meant it too. No one seemed to have a filter - it was refreshing.

"I hear you're from Woodway." Bronwyn sat down on the floor and leaned against the wall. She was calm, curious.

"Yep, you been?" Avery asked half joking.

"Never in my life."

"It's a small town. Too quiet," He said. "I lived there with my mom and uncle down the road 'til they called me up here."

"S' that her?" Bronwyn pointed to the photo.

"Yeah," Avery nodded, keeping his hands busy folding his last pair of clean underwear.

Bronwyn laughed with an open smile and Avery looked over curiously.

"Being around when someone's folding their underwear. That's a thing right? Like, you don't just see *everyone* folding their underwear. I'm claiming this as a bonding moment."

Hiding the boxer briefs behind his back, Avery had a good laugh.

"Bonding moment staked and claimed," he said and then pushed them into the closet.

They chatted about oak trees and gardening and beer. He described the grove that his uncle kept and she talked about the garden that she tended on the west side of the city. However, the past seemed like a difficult subject in this house.

Avert glanced down at his watch, "Flow said dinner in a half an hour. That was two minutes ago."

Bronwyn pushed herself up to her feet, "We should get downstairs before Paolo steals all our food."

"Seriously, though. With haste." she headed down stairs.

At the bottom of the stairs, voices mingled, and plates clinked. Mia was still sitting near the edge of the kitchen. She stood up and turned toward the table when she saw him.

Bronwyn was pouring wine. She looked over at him and pointed at an empty glass.

"Please," Avery said quietly.

With light steps, he rounded the corner to a table full of housemates. Sitting at the head of the table was Bea, with Flow to her right. Bronwyn and Mitchell sat on the far side next to her. Paolo was stationed on the other end of the table and saw Avery who was casually watching the scene with one hand pushed into his jean pockets.

"The man of the hour!" he called.

There was a chorus of hey's, hey there's, and well wishes.

Even Mitchell had a slight smile on his face.

Avery smiled true, though he was feeling overwhelmed. A hand pressed against his back softly and a large glass of red wine appeared in front of him. "Welcome kiddo, now let's eat." Bronwyn said as she tip toed around him and sat down. The last seat was for him.

It was then that he noticed a script letter carved into the top wood panel of each chair. Their first initial. On the back of his, a square-ish "A" was stenciled onto the wood grain. This was a splendid place.

"Avery, sit your ass down," Paolo said.

Avery sat, pulling his "A" chair closer to the table. Bea raised her glass and everyone quieted.

"Well. Isn't this just a lovely scene? We haven't had a chance to sit together in quite some time. And it just happens that we are welcoming a new member to the house today. A worthy occasion for a feast, I'd say. I want to give Avery the warmest welcome. He's new to the city, but I can already tell he's good people. Let us be good people, together. Cheers."

"Cheers!"

Glasses raised and clinked. Avery's heart warmed.

"NOW LET'S EAT!"

Next to him, Paolo bowed his head and prayed silently.

The table burst with delicious seasonal color. A basket of dark wheat rolls were passed around first. In the middle of the table was a massive dish of steaming, curly pasta. There was salad, and quartered apples, and generous amounts of alcohol for the special occasion.

Avery answered questions about Woodway, his childhood, and his journey to Lafayette, but he mostly kept quiet and listened.

Bronwyn talked a lot about her three gardens. How the soil on the west side was better than the craggy stuff they had around Forest Ave. Avery asked questions about nutrient levels and drainage. Flow nodded and smiled as they bantered back and forth about the best way to adjust the soil pH.

Paolo interrupted, "Booorrrrrinng."

Bronwyn came right back, "Well, *please*, entertain us with stories about replacing pipes. Hmmm?"

"Those pipes take your shit away," Paolo quipped.

Bea looked over at Avery and changed the subject, "You start work tomorrow? At The Shoulder?" she asked.

"Yep. Bright and early. I was planning to leave some extra time, just in case I get lost. I haven't quite figured out that streetcar yet."

"I can give you a ride if you want," Mitchell spoke up for the first time. "I mean, we need to leave about the same time, probably. Anyway, just an offer."

"No, yeah, that would great. Thanks man." Avery was taken off guard. Avery also noticed that only water sat next to Mitchell's plate.

"Can you swipe us some of those high prized acorns?" Paolo asked.

Avery wasn't sure what he meant by that. The Skylark's harvest was plenty for everyone back at home.

Flow waved Paolo off with a nasty glare and they continued with dinner.

After a hearty first plate, Avery took a second helping of pasta and let the conversation regain its natural cadence. Bea mentioned something about a water main that had burst on the east side of town last week. It had taken her crews almost three days to get the leak under control. She looked over to Paolo.

He made a face at Bronwyn who slyly gave him the finger in return.

"Those pipes are so old," Paolo said with mouth full of pasta. "You patch one side and the other side bursts. Lots of times, it's the earth itself that's holding everything together."

For some reason, Avery's mind jumped to his arrival to the city along the wide, winding boulevard. And the strange towers that stood at each mile along the way.

He asked about the weird metal houses. Everyone looked around, no one spoke. Bea shifted her chair forward.

"Avery, those are nests," she said.

"Nests?"

"Yes," she said, then paused. "Hubbard has a flock of Jarons - big black birds that travel in packs. People think they're part animal, part machine. Anyway, they nest in those towers."

"But they looked empty to me," Avery said before fully digesting what she had just said. Large black birds that travel in packs, part animal, part machine. Jarons were certainly what he had seen flying over the 7A interchange on his way into Lafayette.

"They are. For now," Bea continued. "They all seemed to disappear a few years back. No one really knows where they went. From my perspective, good riddance. They terrorized this city."

Avery held a stern expression.

"Stay away from those birds. Full of the devil," Paolo said pointing to his eyes. "I've seen 'em just fall from the sky. They burst into flames when they hit the ground."

"You're full 'a shit," Mitchell responded.

"No, I'm serious! Hubbard's got some sort of spell or something on them. I saw it with my own eyes," Paolo exclaimed.

"Just give them some distance if you see them and you'll be fine," Mitchell said flatly.

"Hey, sorry for bringing up such a downer," He shrugged. "All new to me."

Bronwyn chimed in with her warm voice, "No worries Avery, we've all been there. I had one breathe fire on me once - I BARELY ESCAPED WITH MY LIFE!"

The entire table burst into laughter.

"Fine! You don't have to believe me," Paolo exclaimed.

Flow stood up from the table, "Who needs a refill?"

Most everyone raised glasses. Avery noticed Bea was drinking water too. Flow returned with two open bottles of wine, one red and one white. She filled her own narrow glass with white and passed both around the table. The bottle of red ended up with Avery. He poured a healthy amount. Avery then looked over to Mitchell and raised it up.

Mitchell shook his head and just raised his water glass.

"I'll take that Avery," Bronwyn circled around and took the half filled bottle of red back into the kitchen.

The group chatted until the sun dipped below the trees. Summer heat lingered, but it was comfortable in the house.

Flow eventually stated, "Let's get this cleaned up, shall we?" They all stood and gathered dishes. Bea walked over to Avery's chair, "It's your first night here, I officially absolve you of any cleaning duties. Come on, let's go out front and enjoy this weather."

Bea and Mitchell walked toward the front of the house. Avery stood up, but paused to stand behind his chair. He hadn't noticed, but Mia had been lying behind him the whole time.

Bronwyn hummed as she grabbed dished from the table and ushered them into the kitchen where Flow moved about.

"Where does this go?" he asked, carrying his own plate into the kitchen.

"Right here, darling," Flow said dropping it into a pile. "Now get."

He eyed a large pot near the stove, snuck over and slid it to the sink. Before anyone noticed he was scrubbing. Since he was tall enough to reach the sink, dishwashing had always been Avery's job back at home. With a grin, he worked on pasta stuck to the bottom.

Flow cleared her throat, "What part of: *Now get*, did you not understand young man?"

"Sorry, didn't compute," Avery said. "Dishwashing is a higher calling for me." He didn't budge from the sink.

Paolo walked back from the table with the last pile of dishes, "You're crazy, I like you already, but you're crazy." He deposited leftovers in the refrigerator, grabbed another beer, and made his exit.

Avery kept scrubbing with a grin. Flow and Bronwyn moved around him. Drying, organizing, and wiping counters. In short order, they had the kitchen and table gleaming.

Flow wrapped her arm around Avery's waist, "Hey, thanks for the help stinker. I hate to admit it, but you just earned some brownie points."

He smirked. Full wine glasses waited on the island when they finished and moved to join the others.

The group was scattered around. In the golden hour, orange rays ran across the street. Flow walked over and sat on the arm of the Adirondack chair with Bea. Mia minded her post near the stairs while Bronwyn found a seat in the grass near where Paolo and Mitchell threw an ancient football.

"A! Come show us your game!" Paolo yelled from the grass. Avery sat his glass down and headed down the stairs.

He jogged out onto the long grass. Paolo took two steps back and flung the football in a tight spiral. It was a tad high. Avery adjusted mid step and snatched it from the air.

"Alright," Paolo said.

Avery stepped back into the middle of the yard, making a rough triangle with his new housemates. His throw wobbled its way to Mitchell. He didn't mention that he had only thrown a football once in his life.

They continued to toss the ball lazily. Several times, they intentionally aimed at the ladies on the porch. Flow simply returned the ball with laser aim. Bronwyn joined in, but decided to stick to lounging in the grass when her dramatic punt attempt ended with the ball bouncing down the street.

Light slowly faded from the sky, but the group continued to sip on drinks and sort of do nothing together. It was as if each of their engraved letters came together to form a sentence on that warm summer evening.

Chapter 13

Associate Keeper Jackson

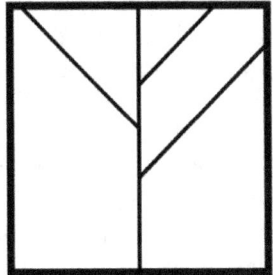

The Shoulder

The hallway was dim with first morning light. All the other doors were closed. Avery had checked his climbing gear twice over before deciding to head downstairs. This was the moment he realized that he actually lived here. This would be the place that he would see every morning and every evening. And very much not Woodway.

At the bottom of the stairs, a single light was on in the kitchen. Bea sat at the island, with her reading glasses and a wide cup of coffee. He heard a familiar clink and Mia's head popped up from the floor.

"Good morning Avery," she said not looking up.

"Morning Bea," He cleared his throat, "Morning," he repeated.

"I hope I didn't wake anyone upstairs," Avery said.

"Heavens no. A freight train couldn't wake that boy," she looked over her glasses.

He rubbed the back of his neck.

"Coffee's on the pot. Help yourself."

"Excellent. Thanks." He poured a full mug and leaned against the counter.

"Mitchell will be up precisely seven minutes before you have to leave," she said.

"Got it," Avery nodded. The coffee was deliciously strong.

"Sleep well?"

"Yeah, slept great. Are you always up this early?" Avery asked.

"I'm up with the chickens most days. I like the peace and quiet. Most of my guys are gonna be doing fence and bridge work for awhile."

"Fence?" Avery asked.

"Mmhmm. The south end of the city, where you came in, is bounded by the river. To the north is the old sunken highway. It's filled with garbage and burned out cars now. Most of the bridges are gone, so that's easy to patrol. But to the west...there's a fence. A big fence. It's a brick wall in some places. It's triple thick chain link and barbed wire in others. I've been telling Hubbard to just build the damn wall along the entire west side for *years*."

"You've met Hubbard?" Avery asked quickly.

"Yeah, I haven't seen him in a long time," She lied. "He keeps to himself now. I have to deal with his damn lieutenants these days. A filthy bunch of Lancers. Anyway, the chain link is easy to cut through. And people do it often."

"What for?" Avery asked.

"Any reason you can think of. Mostly to get the hell out of this place. But there's a healthy black market for just about everything in Lafayette. Electronics, food, women, drugs. Easiest place to get things through is that fence." She shuffled to another printed schedule. "Paolo's actually fixing one of the northern bridges this week."

"I like him," Avery said. " I mean, I like everyone so far. But, ah..." His voice trailed off and he shifted a bit, unsure how to end that sentence.

Bea smiled, but her eyes stayed stern.

Avery was fully awake now, his senses sharpened by the jet fuel coffee.

He asked, "Am I off about Paolo?"

Bea peered over her glasses, "He's the most loyal, trustworthy person I have ever met." Her lips pursed. "Just don't get on his bad side."

Avery was done asking too many questions, so he let the issue go and made himself some breakfast. Later he would find out from Bronwyn that Paolo had grown up in a rough area north of Lafayette. The story was that he snapped when another kid insulted his mom. Paolo broke both the kid's arms, punctured a lung, and cracked his skull in three places. He was still swinging when five other kids managed to pull him off. The kid's uncle had been the gang leader in town. A price had been placed on Paolo's head. His father, a scraper that Bea knew, smuggled him into Lafayette. And that was that.

As Avery finished his breakfast, Bronwyn appeared from the basement with sleep still in her eyes. She grunted and reached for a coffee mug. Avery washed the plate he used for breakfast and headed back upstairs.

The fixtures in the bathroom creaked, but the place was spotless. He ran cold water on his face and brushed his teeth. He pulled on a pair of jeans, and a faded green t-shirt with a sagging pocket on the front. In his bag, he packed all of his climbing gear, but no hatchet.

Mitchell soon appeared, waved zombie-like into Avery's room and disappeared into the bathroom. The early morning calm wore off, replaced with a feeling like a stuffed animal was pushing on his insides.

The shower was running when Avery again passed by the bathroom. He walked downstairs and Bea was gone. Mia sat by the back door, so Avery walked over. His finger ran across the 'A' stenciled onto the chair back.

A moment later Mitchell came sweeping into the room. Both his shoes were untied and his shirt was missing a few buttons. He grabbed an apple from a bowl on the counter.

"Let's do this," he said heading toward the side door.

Avery sprung up and followed Mitchell out the door. The large pick-up truck was parked next to the garage and Avery trended toward the passenger side.

"This way, chief." Mitchell motioned with an apple filled hand.

The garage door crawled open. There sat an ancient Jeep, mostly rust with some olive-drab paint remaining, next to a tiny fire engine red roadster.

Mitchell jumped into the Jeep. Avery yanked open the passenger door, tossed his bag in the back seat and climbed inside. It smelled of gasoline and old upholstery. The engine cranked and spat to life.

Avery looked over at Mitchell as they turned out of the driveway, "The entrance to The Shoulder is just past...."

"Yeah man, I know where we're goin'," Mitchell quipped.

Avery nodded stiffly.

Traffic was almost nonexistent on the Woodward Avenue and sky was clear.

For several long minutes he listened to the engine strain against third gear. The silence didn't seem to bother Mitchell who was driving with one hand on the steering wheel and the other holding the apple.

"What do you do?" Avery finally asked.

He remembered what Bea had said about him knowing the city.

Mitchell glanced over and then back to the road. He tilted his head, which made Avery assume he was about to say something. He sensed that Mitchell was at odds with something.

"I'm a cartographer," Mitchell said eventually, quickly glancing over again. "Ya know - Like maps."

"Yeah. Totally. That's cool," Avery said squinting.

"What kind of maps?" he asked.

"Lots of different kinds."

"Ok."

"Do you really care, or are you just trying to be polite?" Mitchell asked.

"Naw man, I'm really interested. I climbed trees for a living. How much dorkier can you get? Do you sorta work for Lafayette like Bea and Paolo?"

"No. Well, yes and no. It's complicated," he said, keeping his eyes on the road. "I work for myself. But Hubbard's guys come to me when they have a problem."

"Got it."

"I plotted the trees in that grove a yours a few years back," Mitchell added.

"Oh yeah? How'd that go?" Avery asked.

"Boring."

Mitchell looked over his shoulder and then pulled into the center turn lane.

"Anyway, a lot of information got lost way back, when the wars and shit happened. Roads, utilities, building outlines. Anyway, I make maps. It's boring."

"That's pretty awesome, actually," Avery said, keeping his eyes away from the glare as they turned.

"Yeah, ok."

"Did you use location services on your trip north?" Mitchell asked.

"Just got my phone at Protocol Check. Don't even know how it works," Avery said.

"Give it here." Mitchell motioned with one hand.

Avery handed over the stupid, scratched up phone without hesitation. Mitchell swiped and tapped as he drove and soon had a map on the screen of their location on Woodward.

"This a real thing?" Avery asked in astonishment.

Mitchell nodded, "Somehow they've managed to keep a few of the satellites in orbit. Not super accurate anymore though."

They turned and hummed along a narrow road with small houses on one side and a large vacant lot on the other. Avery noticed Sentinel branches peaking over the rooftops.

"I'll swing by around 5:00 tonight. Cool?"

Avery was now too distracted to respond. They circled around in front of a massive gate with brick columns on each side. One panel was swung open just a few feet. Inset on the gate was the Shoulder's branch symbol. Beyond the fence stood a neat file of Sentinel Oaks in wispy fog. Off to the side, he saw a low-slung station building, dark framed windows and covered with a slate roof.

The Jeep squeaked to a stop.

"Yeah, 5:00 works great." Avery pushed open the door and stepped out, still ogling at the gate. He eventually came to his senses and snapped toward Mitchell.

"Hey man, thanks for the ride," he said.

"No problem. First day, don't screw up." And Mitchell was gone.

Avery had one foot inside the gate when he realized his bag was in the backseat of the Jeep. His stomach dropped to the earth. He whipped around and sprinted toward the road, looking in both directions. Before he even had a chance, he would be headed home. Laughed out the door.

He kicked the loose pavement, with his heart beating in his ears. He headed toward the embarrassment of being completely ill prepared for the job of a lifetime.

The Jeep then careened back down the road. Mitchell cut a tight circle around Avery, slowing just enough to toss the bag over the top cage and scowl. Dust pelted him in the shins and the bag hit him square in the chest. His blood pressure dropped as Mitchell once again sped away.

A stillness hung in the air. He felt disconnected from his body stepping through the gate and into the grove. A wide gravel drive drew straight between the middle rows of stately Sentinel Oaks. The ground was covered with a thick carpet of clumped grass. The Keeper station looked at him ominously.

He knocked on a door covered in peeling green paint.

A tall, slender man with a greying beard opened the door and called out in a smoky voice, "Heyo! There he is. Come on in Avery."

He shook Avery's hand with powerful, long fingers.

"Hi," Avery said, stepping inside. It smelled like aging acorns and cigarettes.

"Name's Wallace," the man said.

"Wallace, it's a pleasure. Glad to be here."

Avery noticed right away that Wallace wore an outfit similar to his. Worn boots, tattered jeans, and a faded t-shirt. Keepers think alike.

"Step over to the office. Jim's in there," Wallace said.

They walked through the door into a square office with three desks each on opposite sides of the room. Bookshelves covered all the open wall space. Leaning back in a desk chair was a shorter man with a circular face, wire-rimmed glasses, and a balding head. His eyes were a piercing blue.

Avery wanted to show his confidence, so he walked over and introduced himself firmly.

"It's my pleasure. My name's Jim," the short man said. "Welcome to the Shoulder...the most exceptional grove in the city."

"Only damn grove in the city," Wallace said, sliding into another chair. "Most of our harvest goes straight to Hubbard and his inner circle. Not much in the way of Sentinel acorns for the rest of the city."

Avery's palms were sweating after feigning the confidence in the introductions.

"Take a seat Mr. Jackson." Jim pointed at the third chair.

He leaned forward and pushed down into the old desk chair.

Wallace swiveled around to wide a computer screen, and an ancient printer clanged to life near the back of the office. Avery's new desk was barely visible under piles of paper, random tools, and several glass jars of acorns.

Jim rolled toward the center of the office, "Wallace's collating all the paperwork necessary to complete Hubbard's Employee Assessment," he said.

"It's a lot of fun," Wallace chided. "We kill a whole tree printing these damn things."

It took a lot of effort to keep his eyes from wandering across the bookshelves bursting with records, binders, and file folders.

Wallace rolled over a bit closer.

"You're the first new employee in almost ten years. Probably the first outsider to work here, I'd say. We gotta follow the rules."

Avery felt obligated to continue.

"Well I'm very humbled by the opportunity. The orders came as a complete surprise. I, ah, yeah - such an opportunity for an OD guy like me," Avery said.

Jim leaned back and rested his hands on the back of his shiny head.

"Glad you get it," he said. Jim was looking at Avery with a driving gaze. He wore an anxious grin, but his eyes scanned quickly across Avery's face.

"What happened to the last guy?" Avery asked.

There was another long pause.

Wallace's chair creaked behind him. He shuffled over to the printer.

"You said that I'm the first new guy in ten years. What happened to the old guy?" He asked again with some hesitation.

"Truth and truth, we don't know for sure." Jim held his hands in the same position on the back of his head. "His name was Stephan. Everyone called him Phan. An excellent Keeper. His knowledge about these trees was second to none. One day - he just vanished. About six months ago, on a Monday morning, he didn't come to work. Tuesday morning, didn't come to work. It wasn't like him, we started to get worried. He lived alone on the west side. Near Wallace, actually. So we made a visit. House was empty, nothing was out of place. It was just empty." Jim exhaled long and slow.

"And that was that?" Avery asked.

"Mr. Jackson, you'll learn to not ask a lot of questions around here. If something like this happens, you keep your head down and stay on course. That's what we did. A few months passed and we scraped by with just the two of us. Then a Lafayette officer arrived here one day and said they had identified a qualified replacement."

Avery felt like he had just been hit in the stomach. He cleared his throat.

"Guys I'm really sorry. I didn't know."

"Aw can it. Things happen. If you're good enough for Hubbard, you're exactly what this place needs," Wallace said from his desk.

The words sounded honest to Avery, but they seemed soaked in sadness and anger. Wallace handed him a stack of papers easily an inch thick, still warm from the printer.

"They need all of this?" Avery asked. His voice sounding cracked and pitchy. That stack would take him forever. It was like asking him to read the entire Internet by tomorrow.

"Get ready to answer questions about everything in your life...ever. And we'll need those by tomorrow. Technically we're breaking Protocol by having 'unsanctioned personnel' working on the grounds," he said.

"Understood." Avery weighed the pile of papers in his palm and lamented the simplicity of his life back in Woodway. It felt like that life was getting slowly scrubbed away by a dull eraser.

Jim got up and walked out of the office. Avery looked at the words on the top page, not able to focus on a full sentence. He flipped through the thick stack and saw page after page of questions. The last page had a thick rectangle with the words *Blood Sample* printed at the top.

Jim returned, holding his Keeper's gear in hand - a full harness and a tool belt.

"C'mon, we're wasting daylight. Let me show you around."

He fastened the tool belt around his waist and pushed the harness into a small bag on his desk. Avery stood up, tightened his own bag and placed the stack of papers on the empty chair. Perfect, he'd get to jump right in.

"You coming, Wallace?" he asked.

"I've got a bunch of work to do here today, paperwork out the ass," came the retort.

"Later then I guess."

Jim exited the room and Avery followed close behind.

The shade thickened as they moved into the heart of the grove. The air was still and warm. At Skylark in Woodway, the trunks were about two and half feet in diameter, crowns reached a fairly uniform height of forty feet. Here, each massive tree stood to nearly twice that height, and precisely spaced trunks almost four feet in diameter.

Jim slowed a bit. "So there are four hundred trees in the grove. Mostly your standard *Quercus senitinetalis*. There is a poor performer or two on the west end. Henry, Lafayette's first generation Fender commissioned the grove. They say this spot was originally a ghetto that was turned into a huge housing development with a park in the center, Henry had it burned to the ground and, somehow, they coaxed the trees to grow here. Who knows how they pulled it off, but we're looking at a stock that's about a hundred and fifty years old. Everyone seems happy and healthy, we try to keep it that way." He stepped off the path and looked up, Avery followed his gaze. Just below the first branch, which was almost a foot in diameter, was a slender aluminum device with a blinking green light.

"Each tree also has a second generation monitoring stake, series 44w. They're pinned into the north side of every tree," Jim said, pointing over to the neighboring tree where an identical green light blinked.

"To make sure they don't run away?" Avery looked down and over at Jim.

"The spike gathers analytics," Jim stated. "More specifically, growth rate on a quarterly basis, nutrient and moisture levels, critical pathogens, and hormone levels during harvest season. All that data is feed into our server back at the station. We have records going back almost thirty years."

Avery was used to keeping records in his head, and the occasional note at the end of the day. His uncle, he was fairly certain, knew each of his trees like a family member.

"Cool," he said.

"Wallace is the data expert, not me," Jim said, hard faced.

They stepped back onto the drive and headed north. Jim continued describing things. The main drive ran directly north through the entire grove. A secondary service path traversed at an angle from east to west. Underneath was a live gas line. The terrain rolled a bit but only gaining a few feet in total elevation from south to north.

On the eastern edge was a storage barn. Jim warned him that it was rarely used and to stay away. Curious, but OK, Avery thought.

In the southeast quadrant was a small spring-fed pond at the feet of the Shoulder's largest tree. Susan B. Anthony, they called her. She kept an eye on the rest of the grove, standing an extra twenty feet taller than every other tree.

A wrought iron fence ran along the entire perimeter. The main gate was to the south end. A mostly unused second gate was situated along the west side in alignment with the underground gas line.

Together they continued north. Jim explained how the soil had been imported from outside of the city and mixed together with topsoil from an old park.

Bright sunlight started to sprinkle the path where the northernmost row of trees stood in step. The precise line of trunks opened onto a narrow overgrown grass field and then the fence. Beyond the fence were blocks of small houses with some lots vacant like missing teeth.

"We haven't been able to schedule time for mowing up here on the northern field - roughly two acres of tall fescue." Jim looked out at the field with squinted eyes. "But we like things looking very tidy. Sounds like a perfect job for our new Keeper." Jim looked at Avery as he wiped sweat off his forehead.

With the trees marching off toward the east, Avery felt as if he was leading the charge with an army that wasn't his own. This place was rigid. He was accustomed a grove with a few ragged edges.

"Listen, I'm going to leave you be for the morning," Jim said. "Explore the place, get a feel for her. She's not a huge grove, but she is exceptional. Be back to the station by noon. I'll have the mower blades sharpened and you can start on this north lawn. Capeesh?"

Avery was anxious to get out of tour mode and explore, "Yep. Got it."

"Welcome to the Shoulder," Jim said and walked away at his hurried pace.

Avery stood for while at the end of the drive. Eventually, he started off along the tree line, with the monitoring spikes blinking at him. Before reaching the eastern border fence, he turned back into the grove. Even under the dense shade, the morning heat had taken hold. His arms and legs started to sweat. Regardless, Avery's mood was buoyant.

He noticed how the large branches tended to swoop downward before reaching back up and fanning out into a dense system of shoots. And the trunks were ribbed with thick flutes pushing out from the earth and fading into a rough column at about eye level. The bark was dark grey with deep cracks and crevasses like the wrinkles on an old man's temples.

After zigzagging between the colossal trunks, he came across the small service path and followed it east, remembering the barn. The narrow path curved slightly, but never broke the rigid grid of the trees. Soon the outline of a barn came into view.

The two-story structure looked as though a stiff wind could blow it over. Eaves sagged and the door was locked shut with large padlocked chains, the windows were missing shudders and covered in dust and soot. He pressed his nose against the glass but could see nothing. For the neatness of The Shoulder, the dilapidated barn was out of place.

Just beyond the clearing, he found a single Sentinel that had branches curling away with yellowing leaves.

He looked to the Sentinels beyond. They stood tall and healthy. The monitoring spike oscillated from green to yellow. A sick feeling turned over in his chest. Was this the runt Jim mentioned earlier? Jasper would have removed a tree like this long ago. No Keeper takes pride in cutting down a Sentinel, but it was also their responsibility to maintain the overall health of the grove.

On the south side of each trunk, he checked the identification number. 327 - He would ask about it when he returned to the station.

A loud thud broke Avery's concentration and he jumped, scanning the area for its source. Another thud. It seemed to be coming from the barn. He circled the structure with silent steps. Nothing. He waited several moments, watching and listening. Nothing.

Before long, he convinced himself that his mind was playing tricks and headed back down the service path. The next mission was to find Susan B. Anthony. He angled back to the main drive and then to the southeast quadrant.

Starting to feel more comfortable, his pace increased. With confident movements he watched for patterns on the ground and unique branching overhead. Landmarks that would, in time, become second nature.

Vegetation with extra splashes of color soon started brushing against his knees.

A giant among giants, Susan was the only thing in the grove that broke from the grid. She stood at the edge of the shallow oblong pond. Thick, gnarled roots grabbed at the bank.

A small flock of birds chirped and sang as they jumped from branch to branch over the edge of the water. The glassy surface reflected textures of the forest canopy. Avery pushed through the undergrowth to the water's edge. Kneeling down, he ran his fingers through the cool water.

He then looked up at Susan B. Anthony, rising to his feet almost out of reflex. She didn't look like a dame, but more of a statue of an athlete who was frozen in a victorious pose. Legs planted on the ground, strong arms extended victoriously toward the sky.

Pushing through tangled undergrowth with his knees, he reached the base. At that moment he remembered the climbing gear that had been strapped to his back all morning. Excitedly, he fastened the straps and connections of the harness around his hips, slung the rope over the first branch more than thirty feet overhead and deftly ascended.

Stepping into the crock of the first branch, he took a deep breath. The rush of getting high above the ground was always the same. Down below, the pond shimmered. Driven by excitement he moved quickly, shifting from limb to limb. Shafts of sunlight peeked through the canopy and he finally looked out. His feet were well above the tops of the other Oaks, their domed clumps pressed together in neat geometry. Beyond that, the city unfolded into a panorama. The silence was different here. There was always the distant hum of tires on asphalt – city silence.

He watched and listened for a while. It was like one of Mitchell's citywide maps laid out before him.

And in time, a surprising feeling of freedom settled over him. Like a rope that had been coiled around his heart for a very long time finally loosened and fell away. He was a part of something bigger than himself in Lafayette, full of so many things that were yet to be discovered.

Realizing it was quickly approaching noon, Avery scaled back down to the first branch and reattached his rigging to the long rope. He repelled down with powerful strides. Pushing boot against bark followed by a split second of free-fall until he was back on the ground. Just as quickly as he had prepped for the climb, he had his gear stowed.

Two minutes before noon, he walked up to the station. Wallace was still sitting at his computer. Jim's desk was empty.

"He lives!" Wallace said, not looking up.

"Alive and well." Avery lifted the pile of papers off of his chair and pushed them into his bag. "This place is something else."

"Ain't it?."

Avery pushed his bag under the desk.

"Hey, lemme ask you something. What's going on with 327?" Avery asked.

Wallace glared back with a perplexed look on his face.

"327," Jim said, sweeping into the room in a huff. He tossed a paper bag onto Wallace's desk and swung another onto Avery's lap. "Happy lunch break...That damn tree has been the bane of my existence for three years. It is sick as a dog and we've tried every remedy possible."

"Why not just cut it down?" Avery asked. "Whatever's making it sick could spread to half the grove if we're not careful."

"That won't happen. I will not let it," Jim said with his back still turned.

Wallace cleared his throat cautiously.

Avery kept his mouth shut.

"Thanks for lunch," Wallace said. "Place just down the street that makes the best damn grilled cheese. Triple layer, three types of cheese. Heaven in a sandwich."

Avery opened the bag to find a large sandwich wrapped in wax paper. He spent the next half hour asking Wallace about the monitoring software.

Wallace had created the system himself, patching several different programs together. The Shoulder had an encrypted wireless network that connected to the all four hundred monitoring spikes and the perimeter fence, as well as the larger Lafayette Protocol system. He pulled up a dashboard that showed a three dimensional diagram of the entire grove and a list of different data layers running down the side.

Avery actually had some suggestions on how to analyze the distribution of moisture content and nutrient levels. Showing some surprise, Wallace took detailed notes as he spoke. See world, I have brains, Avery thought to himself.

"You can play with the computer game later," Jim interrupted. "Let's get that mowing started."

Outside stood a rudimentary push mower. He was well accustomed to hand tools, but this was unimpressive even by Woodway Standards.

"There she is. I sharpened the blades. It should cut like a knife through warm butter."

"And you'll probably need this." Jim tossed him a squeeze tube of green liquid. "Us Keepers are shade loving creatures. That sun will burn you to a crisp." Jim walked back into the office without another word.

In the tube was a runny green substance, but it rubbed into the skin easily. Sunscreen. Avery applied a layer to his neck, face, ears, and arms. He now smelled like stale seaweed.

The spinning blades squeaked and creaked, but it pushed forward easier than anticipated. A thin line of shining metal ran along each blade.

When Avery returned to the northern lawn, the midday heat was beating down with no breeze as relief.

Avery started mowing parallel to the tree line. The push mower whooshed through the long grass, but the going was slow. At the end of each row, he had to stop and pull dense clumps of chopped grass from the cage.

By mid-afternoon he was more than halfway through the lawn and desperately bored. He worked at a slow jog now, and estimated the increased pace would take a minute off each pass. His hands started to ache.

On a particularly fast row, the mower crashed into a fist-sized rock. The narrow handled jabbed into his stomach, flipping him over onto the ground. *Crap.*

Covered in grass clippings, he collected himself. Upon inspection, the rock had mangled two of the blades. He tried pushing the mower. The bent metal just complained. Really Crap.

Trying to improvise, he picked up the oblong stone and hammered against the blades. They held fast in the new bent up position. Not good. This was going to take some work and the day was starting to wane. He carried the mower over into an area he had already completed. Bolts held the frame together at each end, and with some luck and urgent twisting, he got it disassembled. The damaged blades had to be pried from their housing and again he used the stone to flatten the kinks. Surprisingly the metal behaved and he soon had five somewhat uniform blades back in the housing. But during the process two bolts had gone missing.

Now bathed in sweat he searched frantically. It was almost five o'clock. No more than half the field was mowed. Then Jim arrived.

"Care to explain what the hell is going on here?" Jim asked as he approached.

"Whaddya mean?" Avery asked, trying to buy time to find the missing bolts.

Jim said no more and grabbed the mower, which promptly fell into three pieces.

"I hit a rock," Avery said, reassembling things. "And tried to fix the blades."

"Don't they teach you how to look where you're going out there in the Outer Domain?" Jim screamed.

The scolding went on for another twenty minutes, focusing mostly on a Keeper's dedication to quality and Hubbard's elevated expectations. The only interruption was Avery telling Jim that his ride would be there soon.

Jim sent him off and Avery exited the Shoulder feeling like an idiot.

"Hey," Avery said, climbing in the Jeep.

"Hey," Mitchell said, pulling back onto the road.

"Is Jim still a big sack of shit?" Mitchell asked.

That produced a half smile from Avery.

"I'm sorry, I should say: A short, balding sack of shit."

"He's ahhh, interesting," Avery responded.

They turned onto the main avenue with scattered evening traffic. Avery didn't want to talk about his first day and Mitchell didn't seem interested in asking further questions.

"Thanks for turning around this morning. You saved my ass. I owe you one," Avery said.

"Watch whatchu say, I might take you up on that," Mitchell warned.

A siren broke out behind them.

Avery cursed and contorted in his seat.

"Keep your pants on," Mitchell said. A very familiar patrol truck blasted past with sirens blaring and green lights flashing.

After that, they rode home in silence. Mitchel backed the Jeep into the garage at breakneck speed and jumped out before the engine stopped turning. He ripped the keys out of the ignition and placed them on the left front tire. Avery just sat with his index finger pressed between his lips and watched him walk into the house. Losing his hatchet had felt like losing a limb, screwing up at the Shoulder was adding salt to the wound.

After some stewing in the garage, he walked toward the house on tired legs. From around the front came boisterous laughter - such a contrast to what he was feeling - so he headed in that direction. On the front porch Bea and Flow sat in their matching chairs.

"Avery!" Bea said in a kind voice. "You're alive."

"People keep saying that." He grinned under drooping eyes, trying to conceal the emotions that were telling him to pack up and leave the city tonight.

Flow leaned forward in her chair, "How was that first day of yours?"

"Good," he shrugged. "Interesting."

"Mmhmmm," Bea said, turning her face and looking at him curiously.

He felt like he needed to divulge a little, "The Shoulder is a lot different than what I am used to. Guess it'll just take some...ya know, time or something."

Bea and Flow kept quiet. With heavy steps scuffing against the wooden stairs, he walked up to his room, and sunk onto the edge of the bed. The light was dim and pensive, so he sat with his thoughts for a while longer.

Creaking floorboards and voices in the kitchen eventually jostled him back to the present. He kicked off his boots and turned on the small desk lamp. From his bag he pulled out the stack of papers.

Chapter 14

Sanctioned Personnel

The first several pages covered detailed personal information, and the simple forms didn't scramble in his mind as much as longer stretches of text. Yes he could remember his mother's maiden name. No, he didn't know his father's date of birth. He continued on, writing his visa number in the box at the bottom of each page, and reading quite fluidly.

Then a page with an embossed green strip along the edge marked the second section: Trends and Characteristics. This is where the fun started.

37.) Have you ever attended meetings in regards to the overthrow of government(s)? If yes, please provide details below.
No.

38.) Have you ever broken Protocol in an effort to find errors or omissions in monitoring code? If yes, please provide details below.
No.

39.) Have you transported materials illegally across Chancellery borders?
No. (He didn't even know there were Chancellery borders...)

40.) Have you ever assisted an individual in transporting materials illegally across Chancellery borders?
No.

These questions continued for several more pages until Avery turned to another cover page: Attitudes and Behaviors. His room was dark now and he realized that he was starving. He'd venture downstairs after this section.

103.) Are you sexually active?
Yes. (Well, actually no. But Yes made him feel better.)

104.) How many sexual partners have you had?
Two (That seemed like a reasonable number. Anything was better than the true number. Maybe he still had a chance with Becky. And now he was in a big city with lots of girls.)

105.) Are any of these partners of the same sex?
No. (Why did that matter?)

106.) Please provide names, addresses, and contact information for all aforementioned partners.
Avery fabricated wonderfully fake identities for both.

At the end of the Attitudes and Behaviors sections he dropped his pen and rubbed his eyes. His stomach growled. From the hallway, he heard footsteps on the stairs. Bronwyn appeared in the doorway holding a plate with two thick sandwiches in one hand and beer in the other.

"Hey," Avery said, leaning back in the chair.

"Mitchell said you had a bad-first-day face. I dare say that's deserving of food and beer." She held up both hands before sliding the plate and bottle onto the desk. "Ahhhh, Protocol papers."

"Yeah! I hope my insolence level is within accepted minimum," Avery said.

"You mean to tell me that attending meetings where prostitutes discuss the overthrow of The Third Chancellery Government of Lafayette is against Protocol?" Bronwyn asked with her palms pressed against her hips. "Eat up and drink up. I'm in the middle of kicking Paolo and Flow's ass in Scrabble."

"Thanks for the grub," Avery said as Bronwyn skipped down the hallway.

The night wore on and he overheard yells of Scrabble induced frustration, but he had to stay concentrated. If this paperwork helped him get off whatever blacklist he was on with Hubbard's soldiers in regard to Linkerage, it was worth it.

The seventh and final section was titled: Professional Experience. It covered specific details about Grove Keeping for which he knew nearly all the answers. He wrote out detailed paragraphs about proper limb maintenance, monitoring spring growth and how they each related to fall harvest yield. Jasper had taught him well. When he got to the last page, checked for spelling errors backwards and forwards, he remembered the square asking for a blood sample. It was the only question on the page. Was this for real?

From his toolkit, he pulled out a sharp pick and quickly poked the tip of his left middle finger. He pressed it against the paper and then held his finger against his palm to stop the bleeding. He glanced down at his watch. It was well past midnight. The house had gone quiet and crickets chirped in the backyard. He drank the last of his beer, sent a quick message to his mother - he was alive and well. Then walked to the bathroom with his toothbrush and a towel.

A quick shower and clean teeth washed away the lunacy of his first day. After setting his alarm, he folded himself into bed.

In the coming days and weeks Mia would take to sleeping at the base of his bed. Avery would wake with the first slivers of morning and they would climb downstairs for a cup of coffee with Bea.

He would then stand in the backyard and throw a tattered tennis ball down the driveway, Mia bounding joyously after it.

Mitchell would schlep out the back door with shoelaces astray and shirt crooked, always on time but never a minute early.

Work at the Shoulder were filled with grunt work. He properly fixed the mower and was instructed keep the northern lawn in pristine condition. He repainted fence pickets, cleared fallen branches, and washed the station windows on several occasions. His 'new guy' status was not about to wear off anytime soon, so he begrudgingly did as told.

In every free second he quietly increased his domain awareness. Patterns and peculiarities were jotted in his notebook. #283 had root knobs close to the surface. #87 bent over the barrier fence a little too much. #145's bark was darker than all the others. And during his lunch breaks, he pestered Wallace about the computer database and was soon able to manipulate the data himself.

In the afternoons he found time to strap on his climbing gear and pull himself to the highest branches of one of the four hundred Sentinels, four hundred views of the city.

The southwest quadrant had views of the river fading into the haze just before opening into a shallow lake. He saw the top of the wall that stood between Lafayette and whatever was beyond. To Avery, it just looked like forest, with only the occasional rooftop jutting through the green. Just inside the wall sat two large estates with square flags of different colors flying from their rooftops. These were the Ambassadors' houses, Wallace told him.

Hulking in the northern quadrant of the city, a dirty smelting complex of featureless structures and tall stacks belching putrid smoke. When the wind shifted, the acrid smell wafted through The Shoulder.

Even when he was swaying high above the grove floor, he felt like a little brother next to the dominant skyline. The Tower snuck watchful views between soot-covered buildings.

On one of his climbs, Jim walked beneath him, not noticing the pack resting in the crook of the trunk and rope hanging loose from the primary branch. As he paced underneath the tree, Avery heard his voice rise and fall.

Avery slid down to a lower branch. Who was Jim talking to?

"He cleared protocol...!"
"wha' should I 'av don...?
"Fine!"

After shoving a phone in his pocket, Jim stormed off.

Avery held the panic tight in his chest. It was in these moments when he encountered the ugly mysteries of the city and felt trapped.

Chapter 15

A Slice of What it is

Avery headed out from the Forest Avenue house in search of Fashni's Pizza. Mitchell had described it as the best in the world. They had actually made plans to go after work on a Friday. Avery was excited: an opportunity to get on Mitchell's good side, which until this point, seemed an impossibility. Friday after work came, and Mitchell was nowhere to be found. Avery had waited around the house until it started to get dark. No one else was home. Frustrated and hungry, Avery went to find this damn pizza place. Mia seemed interested in joining, but he slammed the front door before she could come along.

Flow had given him turn-by-turn directions the night before, that he promptly forgot. So now he wandered north.

A ways up and away from the house, he crossed some invisible threshold. The happy neighborhood harshly transitioned into something more derelict and ragged. Thicket blocks, maybe, or areas headed in that direction. The shells of houses reminded him of the fringes of Woodway. Shadow clad people gave him sidelong glances and moved away into overgrown corners with their heads down. Streetlights were dark.

His danger sense stayed quiet until three hard-boiled guys with shaved heads ambled toward him from the other side of the street. The leader was lanky with a scraggly mustache and wearing a dirty white t-shirt. Just behind were two younger looking cronies. They could have been brothers. One of them had his hands held behind his back.

For nearly a block, they followed close. Talking loudly and banging against objects along the way. Avery showed no outward signs of concern, but his heart quickened along with his pace. The next block was darker than the last and he planned to turn at the upcoming corner.

The group then came level with him, walking with exaggerated limps and wearing stupid grins.

"Evening," the mustached man said. They were all taller than him. Just ignore them and get out of here, he told himself.

Avery glanced over and continued with arms pulled in tight. Just ignore them and get out of here.

"I said hello," the leader-type said.

"Hey," Avery quipped. Four more houses, then there was a functioning street light.

"Don't look like you're from around here," said one of the droopy sidekicks.

"Yeah, don't think we've seen you before," added the other.

"Just passing through."

His legs moved as fast as possible without breaking out into a run, which was his next option. An arm slung around his shoulder. The mustached man smelled of alcohol and stale sweat.

"What's your name, kid?"

His face was too close. An ugly scar ran along his neck. Avery shoved off the unwanted embrace and the man backpedaled.

"Yooo, we were just saying hello. Did you put hands on me? Hector, did he just put hands on me?" The running option was quickly fading. Avery had been in one fistfight in his entire life and it hadn't ended well.

"Yeah 'e just did."

Avery's fists clenched. If he struck first, maybe he could take down the bigger one. The other two would be easier to handle. The trio were poised to strike when a fat man with a crazy beard came out of nowhere and chest bumped the mustached leader to the ground.

There was a whirl of pushing and shoving in the dusk. The bearded man, who looked strangely familiar, nodded to Avery. The curious scene made him pause for a beat. Something was in the air. A happy feeling floated into Avery's head as the big man talked in curious phrases.

"You three, on a bubble bath battleship," he commanded.

"What?" one of them blurted.

Avery wanted to move. But his feet were frozen.

"K, so there's a moose stuck in the Christmas Castle, right?" the bearded man continued. Tattoos covered his pudgy arms from elbow to hand. He pointed for Avery to leave, but Avery felt like Jell-O.

"Celery fungus on a cracker. That's just simple trigonometry."

The three other men now wore dumbfounded expressions and their arms hung limp at their sides.

"You'll let the Iguana go, on account of furious guacamole farts."

The tattooed man pointed again without looking over. This time Avery stumbled around the corner thinking about cotton candy but still remembering that he was in danger. He took what he thought was a straight shot back toward Forest Avenue and ended up running into Woodward Avenue. Well, that worked too. The fast walking and commotion along Woodward cleared his head mostly. He pulled out his phone and checked his list on Lafayette Linkerage, but the big bearded man, who Avery was confident had been one of his first links, was no longer there. There was no doubt that he was an Able. Where had he come from? Had he been following Avery?

The last of the fuzziness faded from his mind when, as fate would have it, a flickering neon sign came into view: Fashni's Pizza.

A closet sized building sat in a gravel lot. Avery swung open the door to a thick aroma of dough and melting cheese. A pizza oven was squeezed behind the narrow counter, behind it stood a pimple-faced teenager.

"Sup man."

"Hey," Avery said out of breath from excitement.

"You are in luck. Last pizza for the night." The kid reached back and grabbed the rectangular box off of a flower-covered shelf.

Avery pumped his fist in the air. He paid with part of his first paycheck. With the warm box in hand, he decided to stick the to busy streets on his return trip.

Paolo and Bronwyn were sitting on the front steps when he returned. Mia trotted over to him and pressed against his thigh as he came up to the porch.

"Hey there girl," he said scratching her behind the ears.

"A, what up doe," Paolo said

"Hey guys." Avery walked up to the steps with a grin and the wide box half hidden behind his back.

"Mia sure has found her favorite," Bronwyn said.

"It's only because I brought pizza," Avery said, pulling the box out.

"Yessir!" Paolo exclaimed.

"Help yourself," he said. "I got the last one of the night over at this place called Fasni's. Fassshni's?"

"That's supposed to be good luck!" Bronwyn said, grabbing a slice. Mia sat next Avery with her nose pointed at the pizza.

"Good man," Paolo said through a big bite of pizza.

Avery grabbed a slice, feeling a funny pride in his chest. "Well, I've been mooching off of you guys since I got here. So, anyway, thanks for that. Enjoy." He wanted to talk about his run in and that curious interaction with the bearded guy. For some reason he was too embarrassed to say anything.

"Cheers!" Bronwyn said, raising her slice.

Paolo ate most of the pizza, but no one seemed to mind. They chatted for a while, enjoying the nice weather. Paolo told a few stories about his childhood outside the city. From the sounds of it, north of the city boundary was tough. Even if Paolo left out the parts about nearly killing someone, Avery started to appreciate his housemate's rougher edges. Bronwyn kept quiet mostly. Avery caught her holding long stares out at the street.

When they were finished with the pizza and night had arrived, Avery asked about Mitchell as they walked inside. "He disappears randomly, what's that all about?"

Paolo shrugged and looked down at the stairs.

"Sometimes he doesn't stay here," he said. "Five years sober. My ass."

Avery scratched his chest, "Oh, but, ahh."

Bronwyn ran a hand across her throat.

He dropped the subject and closed the door. Without turning on any lights he attempted to navigate the stairs without making too much sound. Phantom lights dashed in his vision as eyes adjusted to the dim hallway. He was about to turn into his room when Bronwyn called from the stairs.

"Could we talk for a second?" she asked.

Avery jumped then turned to see Bronwyn's outline at the top of the stairs.

"Of course." he whispered, anxiously wondering what this could be about.

He flicked on his desk lamp.

Used to the jovial and frizzy Bronwyn, Avery quickly noticed she was all bound up.

"Your picture fell off the wall," she said, picking up the photograph of Avery and his mother, which was wedged into the top of the baseboard.

"Oh jeez - I hadn't even noticed," he said.

"I won't tell your mother."

Avery propped the photo up on his desk and sat the chair backwards.

"What's goin on Bron?" he asked.

She perched on the edge of his bed next to Mia.

"Promise you won't be mad at me?"

"Promise," Avery said.

"I'm leaving Lafayette," she said.

"What?" he asked.

"I've gotta do something new. Gotta get beyond these walls for a bit. Well, could be for a while. Maybe," Bronwyn said.

"What...ah....where you gonna go?"

"There's a little farm between here and Carrick City, and south a ways. It's tucked in the foothills of some low, snarly mountains. I'm headed there. They are expecting me. Should get there in time to help with harvest and get settled."

"Wow," Avery said. "That's awesome."

He was stunned.

"Thanks."

"If you're leaving because I smell bad. You can tell me."

"You smell like a proper Keeper, Avery," Bronwyn said with a half smile. "Just, ahhh, just need to get away."

"Aren't we two arrows cruising in opposite directions," Avery observed.

"I know, right? Outer Domain boy brought to the city, and a city girl headed to the Outer Domain. You're not mad at me?" she asked.

"Course not," Avery said. "We're gonna miss you though." He thought about how in Lafayette, more seemed to change in a day than changed in an entire year back in Woodway.

"....yeah. Me too.."

It felt like that wasn't the full story, though Avery struggled with the words to use.

"You don't have to leave," he joked.

"But I do," she said.

"Still, you know what I mean."

"I'll just make you guys come and visit me," she said getting up from the bed and heading toward the door.

"When you leavin?" Avery asked.

"Next two days, I think. I just got clearance from the department head at Production and Inter-Chancellery Coordination."

"Damn, soon."

"Yep," she said, her spunk returning with a little backward kick in the air. "I'll still be here for Hubbard's Solstice Gala though. And guess who gets Bea's extra tickets this year?" She casually dropped a shiny green and white ticket on Avery's desk.

"We need to find you a proper suit." Bronwyn rapped on the desk and headed down the dark hallway.

Chapter 16

Proper Attire

Avery had never worn a tie before. He struggled with the whole *loop, hold and flip* thing in the bathroom mirror. The time of the gala was quickly approaching and Flow called up to ask how things were going.

"Not so good," he replied. After flubbing the knot for the seventy-third time, he yanked the silver-blue fabric from around his neck and threw it on the floor. He'd borrowed the entire outfit, grey suit, white dress shirt, and blue tie, from Mitchell's closet.

"That's not how you do it," Flow said, entering the bathroom and grabbing the tie. She wore her own suit - dark blue with a neatly arranged yellow bow tie under her chin.

"I can't get it," Avery said with his jaw clenched.

"Well, I can see that," Flow said while untangling his failed knot.

"Come on, lean down here for the ole gal." She looped it over his shoulders

Avery squatted down. He didn't like how much he was sweating.

After measuring off the long side and straightening his collar, Flow deftly pulled together a tight Half Windsor. Avery then pulled on the jacket. Ok, maybe he looked pretty good in this thing.

"Handsome devil." Flow tugged on his shirt cuffs. "Now get downstairs."

Bea and Flow received four tickets to the annual Summer Solstice Gala hosted by Kenyon Hubbard at the Lafayette Institute of Arts. By all accounts, it was a big deal. One, because the city's connected and influential all attended. Turns out that the two ladies were in that group. So much so, that they had been regular attendees for the last two decades and were also issued two extra tickets. Second, it was one of the rare occasions when Hubbard, Lafayette's reclusive Fender, was seen in public.

Avery checked his hair, his teeth, re-tied his shoes, and hopped down the stairs two at a time. Not only had he never worn a suit, he had never been to a fancy event, gala, celebration-type event either. Celebrations in Woodway were usually bonfire-and-corn-on-the-cob type of affairs.

In the front room, the ladies of the house paced impatiently. Flow in her tailored suit, Bea in a black pencil skirt and crisp white shirt with a big collar.

"Bronwyn, let's go!" Bea exclaimed down the basement stairs.

Avery pushed his hands into the creased pockets and made eyes with Mia who was wide eyed from all the commotion. Paolo had no interest in attending; he sat in the kitchen ignoring them.

A minute later Bronwyn marched up the basement stairs wearing a floral summer dress and her trademark rubber boots.

"You could at least wear some decent shoes," Bea scoffed. She was wearing simple black heels.

"What's wrong this these?" Bronwyn pushed back.

"Looking good," Avery said.

"Why thank you," Bronwyn replied with a curtsy. That ended the matter.

"Let's just go. We're going to miss the train." Bea marched into the kitchen, kissed Paolo on the cheek, and they were off.

The group, dressed in their finest, walked briskly to the streetcar platform and caught a northbound train. A short while later they arrived in a bumpy stop at the Lafayette Institute of Arts. Set away from the street, the museum was a wide stone structure with grand stairs leading to three arched entranceways, each awash in spotlights for the occasion.

Avery stepped out of the streetcar and paused to take in the spectacle. Elegant residents in black ties and ball gowns gracefully approached the entrance.

"Avery, come on," Bronwyn urged. Avery jogged to catch up, pulling a ticket from his breast pocket. They joined a line forming at the bottom of the stairs.

Bea scanned the crowd knowingly while they waited. Her eye caught on someone in the distance. She leaned in to whisper to Flow who glanced over her shoulder and then gave her wife a sharp look. Bea then turned back to Avery and Bronwyn.

"Please be on your best behavior," she said tersely.

After soldiers in grey and green dress uniforms scanned their tickets, they climbed the stairs. The main hall was vast beyond anything Avery had ever seen. Marble columns reached up to vaulted ceilings covered in ornate patterning. The air hummed with a sophisticated buzz. Couples milled about across the polished floor. Waiters carried white trays of hors d'oeuvres, and alcohol flowed freely from bartenders stationed at each corner of the hall.

This truly was the grandest happening Avery had ever experienced.

"Isn't it great?" Bronwyn asked, tugging on his arm.

Avery nodded, not sure how to describe his mixed feelings.

"How did you get these tickets again?" Avery asked Bea who had just finished greeting what seemed to be an old friend.

Her eyes glinted. "Hubbard owes me a thing or two." She brushed a hand across his cheek.

Bea then took Flows arm, "Have fun kids. Stay out of trouble."

And the ladies strolled into the crowd.

While Avery watched them walk away, Bronwyn leaned over, "Hey, I see some people. I'm going to say hello."

"Oh, you want me to join?" Avery asked.

Bronwyn was already half gone.

"I'll circle back. Grab a drink, they're free."

Oh, so it was going to be like that, he thought. His people just dressed him up, brought him to the ball, and left him like a fish out of water with no one to talk too. *Fine.*

He shifted toward the nearest bar. Not knowing a single thing about mixed drinks, he ordered exactly what the fat man in front of him had requested. Which turned out to be an Old Fashioned.

The drink burned on the way down, but at least he had something to hold on to. Avery migrated to a sidewall. The main hall stood tall in front of him with a darkened gallery to his left and an atrium with a tall leaded glass roof to his right.

The event felt indifferent to itself in some ways. It was the inverse to what was going on in vast stretches of a city of thicket blocks and folks living in desperation. Avery wanted to show his mother and uncle where he was standing.

In short order he emptied two more Old Fashioneds and started to notice that there were three types people in attendance: aristocratic types that paid no attention to his existence, tightly dressed women whose proportions were a little too perfect, and soldiers of various rank who moved in groups.

The drinks hit him suddenly, filling him with a fuzzy sensation. He wanted to walk around, but the wall had a powerful magnetic hold on him. Where were his housemates anyway? He decided to stay where he was with his empty glass in hand.

A short while later, a towering, impressively dimensioned lieutenant flanked by four serious looking soldiers approached him.

Avery thought he was in the way of something, so he shifted over a few steps.

"You look familiar," The lieutenant said coldly.

Avery thought he was talking to someone else, so he shifted a bit more and glanced over his shoulder. Definitely no one there.

"Citizen, I'm talking to you."

Avery looked up; the soldiers were in a tight formation around their commanding officer. He felt a slithering presence in the back of his mind.

"I'm Avery," he said, shifting the empty glass and pushing a hand out. The officer ignored the gesture.

Buoyed by the alcohol, Avery continued, "I'm new here. From the OD, Woodway – a small, little town in the middle of nowhere."

"I know where Woodway is." The officer said flatly. "I grew up in Kettering Heights. A few hours from there."

"Really?"

"Yeah. A boring hellhole. Glad I joined the service...You're the new Keeper," The officer said knowingly.

"I, uh, ah," Avery stuttered. "Yeah." He felt as though a salamander was crawling around inside his brain. He blinked hard and shook his head. Was it the booze or was it someone invading his mind? Avery noticed the double stripe on the officer's collar. A Lancer. The feeling in his brain then vanished.

"Lieutenant Bryce Robertson-Quade," the officer stated and they finally shook hands. Avery knew that name. How did he know that name?

"Pleasure," Avery said. Then it clicked, this guy had written him! That was it. He was terrifying in real life.

"Do you play Trumbull?" Lt. Quade asked.

"Of course," Avery said. Why did he say that? What was Trumbull? Major fail.

The officer motioned for Avery to join him. They walked into the brick walled atrium. Younger soldiers mingled with the shiny looking girls and sinister characters lounged on oversized leather sofas. The air smelled of alcohol and Avery felt unsubstantial against it all.

In the middle of the space was a square court maybe thirty feet on each side and split into quadrants. A player was positioned in each quadrant and they batted around a comically large plastic ball that was at least three feet in diameter. A crowd stood around the court, taunting the players as they lunged and hit the ridiculous ball. It looked like a big, drunken game of Four Square.

"We're up next," Lt. Quade said. Avery deposited the empty glass on a table and stood next to the soldiers, hands pushed in his pockets. The current game came to a close with a soldier winning on an acrobatic flip and hit.

The court cleared. Avery cautiously took position in one of the squares, Lt. Quade and one of his soldiers in two more quadrants. Then Bronwyn appeared and took possession of the fourth square as she swung her arms and turned her head in little circles.

"Hey!" Avery explained. Where'd she come from? Did she know these guys?

Bronwyn smiled and gave him the finger as she limbered up. Then the game commenced. Trumbull, as Avery had suspected, was indeed just an outrageous game of Four Square that involved a revolving goal of protecting the Trumbull square. The giant ball had pretty serious hang time which lead to dramatic jumps, swings, and power slams. Lt. Quade played a focused game with his subordinate letting him score easy points as needed. Bronwyn played scrappy and held onto second place throughout the match. Points were tallied on a large flip board manned by a wispy girl wearing almost no clothing. The crowd built up around the Trumbull court as they continued. One corner had taken a liking to Avery, cheering him on as "Little Suit."

Avery held his own. He worked through his Old Fashioned induced haze and several more instances where he felt someone invading his thoughts. They were quick pokes to his subconscious as he moved to strike the ball, like someone was searching for a particular memory in his head. But he was enjoying the attention and excitement and chose to ignore the sensation. He overtook Bronwyn for second place as they approached match point.

"Beginners luck!" Bronwyn taunted and hunkered down for the next series. Avery had gotten a feel for the game and was feeling pretty cocky. Lt. Quade watched them as the ball was recovered from across the atrium.

"Avery Jackson!" a voice squeaked. Crystal, the plastic looking Pre Load that had visited him in the hotel now wiggled next to the Trumbull court. She wore a shimmering purple dress and waved urgently at him. Avery gave Crystal a little wave. His cheering section hooted and hollered, calling him all sorts of names, but he was now flustered and that invaded feeling fluttered back into his mind.

Lt. Quade controlled the Trumbull Square and started match point. Avery positioned himself well for the first strike into his quadrant and caught Bronwyn off guard. She was forced to extend and drop an easy shot into the faceless soldiers square. Which then got teed up for Lt. Quade, who drove a shot toward Avery that should have been easy to counter. But his vision caught Crystal who was eying him like a cat ready to pounce. That split second threw him off. He over hit the ball and the game was over. A group of well wishers attempted to embrace the victorious lieutenant. But, he coldly rebuffed them.

Avery's cheering section dispersed just as quickly as it had formed. None of them even knew his real name. He felt deflated as Crystal clipped over with arms stretched out.

"Avery! Hi!" her stiff boobs pressed against him.

"Hi," Avery got out. She held on tight for a while. Over her shoulder he saw something curious. Lt. Quade had shed his contingent of subordinates and was making for a side entrance with Bronwyn at his side. They were engaged in animated conversation as he entered an access code into a keypad and briskly pulled open the door. They disappeared.

Crystal let go and was pulling her phone from somewhere. He could see directly down her dress.

"Walk with me," she said and led him back toward the main gallery. He stalled, watching that side door. Why was Bronwyn with that guy? What were they talking about? Crystal had a weird command over him and he followed her into the main hall as she scanned her phone. A band now played, bass chords and saxophone echoing throughout the space.

Without looking up and holding on to Avery's arm with one hand, she navigated them through the formal crowd. She smelled really good. Avery felt like a dog being pulled along by its leash.

"I see your Linkerage score is doing well!" Crystal said squeezing his arm. His profile showed on her screen. There was a terrible picture of him that looked like it came from a security camera in The Tower. Where had that come from?

"193.5, a good score for how long you've been here." Crystal scrolled down, then back up, switched screens, answered three text messages, then flipped back to Avery's profile. She scrolled, checked a few more things. "Metrics are good, keep it up."

He hadn't said anything yet.

Crystal phone was then deposited somewhere. Avery looked back toward the atrium. He scanned for Bronwyn, Bea, or Flow. Nothing.

"Dance with me," Crystal said. She twirled; Avery held out a tentative hand and caught her. She spun back in and they were close and rotating gradually. Avery wasn't exactly graceful, but he did his darnedest to keep pace.

Crystal talked fast.

She was living downtown with her bestie and a cat named Prince. They technically weren't allowed to have a cat. But, whatever. And she was dating a soldier, Josh. Maybe she'd said Scott. But there was this other thing going on too and that was complicated cuz he was older and more mysterious. You know?

Avery didn't know.

She talked about her dress for a while. He was pretty sure he saw nipple a few times. According to Crystal, there was another girl at the Solstice Party with the same one. But that girl looked fat, so Crystal wasn't worried.

At one point Avery caught a glimpse of Bea who smirked and winked. She seemed to be thoroughly enjoying herself, so that put Avery at ease somewhat.

After some dancing and Avery not saying anything, Crystal looked straight at him for the first time.

"Are you a virgin?" she asked.

Avery stopped dancing and had a minor heart attack.

"Noo," He scoffed. Liar. Totally the worst liar.

Crystal pursed into a judging smile.

"Why?" Avery asked.

Then, in a saving grace, a group of her friends sauntered by.

"Susan, fucking, Powers," she called. The passing girls turned and screamed in delight.

Crystal pulled way and was instantly holding tight to one of them, which Avery assumed was Susan, fucking, Powers. Crystal had officially closed the Avery Jackson tab and wandered off with her friends without so much as a goodbye.

Well, ok then. Avery weaved through the hall looking for Bea and Flow. His head spun. He felt a new wave of disdain for the whole Lafayette Linkerage B.S.

He walked to the bathroom, splashed cold water on his face, then wandered through the galleries situated off the main hall. The hushed calm was a welcome relief to the chaos of the last hour. Oil paintings of the founding of Lafayette hung in a sequence in the last gallery. Hectic brush strokes depicted victorious Fenders defending some nameless foes and building up glorious cities from the ashes - which wasn't quite accurate, Avery knew that at least. Lafayette and the other two Last Cities had been standing before the Fenders took power those many years ago. The Chancellery was more of a sorting of the chaos of a previous lifetime, then the building of a 'new order'. He enjoyed the art though and the solitude.

When Avery returned to the main hall, the music had stopped and people were starting to group together. There was a nervous buzz as folks clustered near a low stage. Soldiers in full combat gear now lined each side of the hall. Avery circled around and found a small break in the crowd where he could see Lt. Quade standing stiffly at the corner of the platform.

A thick metal door soon opened near the back of the hall and the crowd quieted. Avery pushed forward curiously trying to get a better view. From the shadows, Kenyon Hubbard swooped out and on to the stage. He was smaller than Avery anticipated and wore a dark cloak that hung over a boney frame, which made him appear to be floating. His gaze was toward the back wall, not to his people. Lt. Quade rushed to his side, leaning in and turning away from the crowd. He nodded formally and ceded the platform to Hubbard.

A tense silence hung over the hall as Hubbard held court on the stage with his hands crossed across his chest. Avery was more amused than anything else. Was this guy going to say anything? He looked half dead.

Hubbard cleared his throat and held up a hand. Total silence ensued.

"Thank you all for coming," he said. His voice was somehow amplified and boomed through the space, "The Solstice Gala is an important tradition. I'm glad to have you all here at the Institute to pay homage to the great achievements of this city and The Chancellery as a whole."

Hubbard had a cold power that Avery felt even from a distance. His command of the crowd far outsized his physical presence.

The speech continued. Hubbard spoke to the importance of Protocol and the rule of law in maintaining safety for the residents of Lafayette. Bandits and other forces were a constant threat. Avery wasn't sure what he meant by 'other forces'. But he technically worked for this guy, so he listened intently.

Hubbard then transitioned to the importance of Linkerage. That a connected citizenry was a strong citizenry. It was a service that those outside the fence did not enjoy. Avery struggled with that. Back at home he hadn't had phone or a Linkerage Score to maintain and he was perfectly happy. But the crowd ate it up. A drunken contingent near the back of the hall cheered. Folks were taking out their phones, checking scores, taking pictures of their Fender, finding new links. Avery pocketed his hands, not touching his phone.

Riding the wave of goodwill in the hall, Hubbard moved on to speak about Ables. That those with unique powers had a duty to serve their Chancellery. After all, the first generation of Fenders had started as a quiet band of powerful, forward thinking Ables. More cheering and applause. Hubbard had everyone in the palm of his hand.

Then someone in the crowd started jeering. A small man with a bald head and barrel chest pushed his way toward the stage as he flung insults at Hubbard. Avery could only hear snippets.

Ables owe nothing to you!!

Filthy coward!! He knew nothing of people's struggles!!

Hubbard looked startled for a flash before hardening his gaze. A shocked pause washed over the hall. Then chaos.

Soldiers ran the man as he continued yelling. Lt. Quade rushed to a protective position in front of Hubbard. The crowd scattered. There was a loud crash near the front door. Screaming, shuffling, another crash. People ran in every direction. Avery was frozen. Images of Henry being attacked at The Tower flashed in his mind. The soldiers had the small man pinned to the ground in a seated position. Lt. Quade jumped from the stage and brutally struck him across the face. Hubbard slinked back to the dark doorway at the back of the stage. That insidious feeling leaked back into Avery's head.

Lt. Quade struck again and again. The old man convulsed on the floor, blood coming from his mouth. Avery's mind burned, he couldn't move his feet, he couldn't look away. Then Bea appeared.

"Let's go," she hissed.

She grabbed his arm and yanked him toward. Her presence cleared Avery's mind. He could move and think clearly again. They pushed through the panicked crowd. Crystal was clutching to one of the soldiers as Bea and Avery approached the front door. The soldier struck her to the floor.

A tall, tuxedo-ed man stepped in front of Bea just as they were about to cross through the door.

"Is this the doing of the Argus Bureau?" he asked.

Bea tried to push past, ignoring the question. The man held his ground, grabbing Bea by the shirt.

Avery sprung into action.

He wedged himself in front of Bea and drove an elbow into the man's sternum. This cleared the doorway. Bea ran out. Flow and Bronwyn were at the bottom of the stairs. Avery surged with adrenaline and some extra power welling in his chest. He geared up to strike the man - he was tall, but he was old. Avery could drop him no problem. Don't fuck with us.

"Avery," Bea snapped. "Let's go."

Another crash from inside.

Avery backed away and the four of them crossed Woodward and into the darkness of the surrounding blocks. Flow led them along a winding, backtracking path. Bea took off her shoes and proceeded barefoot. They crossed through vacant lots and down streets that looked familiar from Avery's trip to the pizza joint. No one spoke. Tires squealed and sirens wailed from multiple directions.

Bronwyn looked stunned. She moved with the group, trudging along with her boots squeaking on the pavement, but her shoulders slumped. Bea checked her phone as they walked, messages popping up one after the other.

They made it back to Forest Avenue. Paolo and Mia were standing on the porch as they approached. Bea and Flow moved into the house briskly. Mia ran over to Avery, he knelt down and scratched her ears as she licked him on the chin. Paolo and Bronwyn conferenced quietly near the door.

When he went inside, Flow and Bea were in the office. He trudged upstairs after Bronwyn disappeared without saying anything. He pulled off the suit and tie, depositing them on the desk.

His phone chirped. Two new messages. The first was a series of Linkerage requests he'd received during the Trumbull match. The second was a short message from his mother.

Hi A, hope you're doing well.
be safe. love mom.

He couldn't deal with either right now.

Chapter 17

Blue Smoke

connectory /*kuh-nek-ter-ee*/ noun. particular bond between a human, specifically an Able, and their key.

Like rubbing skin against rough brick, the alarm ripped Avery awake. He rolled out of bed, squinting against harsh light. His phone showed a strobing green icon. He swiped but the icon did not disappear. There was commotion downstairs. He had just fallen asleep after trying to process the night's events. Mia roused from the foot of his bed and barked.

Flow appeared at the door, "Level Three Protocol," she said. "Get dressed, come downstairs, we're going to black." She vanished, leaving the door open.

Avery jumped to his feet, looked out the window. Just above the black tree line, an angular craft chugged across the sky. Twin green lights flickered on the rear panel. Soon it disappeared behind the trees, leaving behind only puffs of exhaust.

He pulled on a pair of jeans and shoes and ran downstairs with Mia.

"What's going on?" Avery asked as he entered the kitchen, rubbing the sleep from his eyes.

"Level Three baby!" Paolo called out

Bea was pulling a binder off the shelf. Everyone circled around the kitchen island. Bronwyn stood with arms crossed, still wearing her gala dress. Paolo paced with his hands on top of his head. Mitchell was not there.

Flow stepped in from the back yard, and slid the glass door closed with a solid thud. Avery pushed his hands in his pockets while Bea flipped to the front of the binder and ran her fingers down the edge of the page.

"The back is secured," Flow said as she pulled the blinds shut.

"Pen," Bea said. They all looked around at each other, pressing hands against empty pockets. Avery pulled a pen from his breast pocket and slid it across the counter.

"Ok. The Level Three warning just came through. Is everyone here?" Bea looked around the room. She checked names off of the list as she went. Mitchell wasn't there.

"You said the yard was clear?" Bea asked in a stern voice, "Where's Mitchell?"

Silence.

Bea looked at them over her glasses.

"He's not here, Bea," Paolo said quietly.

"God damnit," Bea lowered her head and sighed. "Alright, get out your phones."

They all pulled out their phones. The blinking symbol had turned into a blank green screen with a pinwheel spinning in the center.

"Put 'em here," Bea said. One by one they lined up the phones on the counter. An official message appeared on each.

```
THIS IS A LEVEL THREE PROTOCOL //
HOLD IN PLACE UNTIL FURTHER INSTRUCTIONS //
RESISTANCE WILL BE MET WITH APPLICABLE FORCE //
END
```

Avery looked like a ghost as Bea ran through a checklist of items from the binder.

"Hey Bea," Paolo said quickly.

She looked up. He pointed to Avery.

"Oh, sorry. Avery! I forget you're new sometimes. This is a Protocol Night. Hubbard does this from time to time. There's a few different levels. Usually it's just an electronic check-in of everyone at each residence - Level One. No big deal. But Level Three is a whole different ball game. They send out the full military force, helicopters, drones, armored patrol, the works. Anything that moves gets scanned. If you're out of the place, you get detained or shot on site." Bea paused, "Must be looking for something."

Flow walked into the kitchen and threw her phone on the counter, "Where's Mitchell?" she asked.

No one answered. Horror struck her face.

Bea and Flow exchanged knowing looks. Mitchell, wherever he was, was in big trouble.

Bea closed the protocol binder, "So, we've all checked in. Save for mister Quelhurt. Stay inside. Stay quiet and away from the damn windows. You know the drill. I'll handle Mitchell's missing check in."

Avery's phone then started ringing. The screen showed an incoming call from Mitchell.

Avery swiped frantically to answer, "Mitchell?" he called.

There was commotion on the other end, a finger fumbling over the microphone. Avery flipped to speaker phone.

"Avv Avvvvery?" a slurred voice came through.

His chest tightened. He leaned closer to the phone.

"Mitchell? Is that you?" he said in a slow, clear tone. They all condensed around the phone.

"Aaa" the sound was distorted.

"Mitchell, are you OK? Where are you?" he asked.

"Avery, I'mmm in trouble." Mitchell's voice was slurred and distant.

"Where are you? Mitchell! Hey! Where are you?" Avery asked urgently.

Bea snatched the phone, made two quick swipes. The voice call consolidated on the top of the screen and a map of the city appeared below.

"Don't tell anyone elsss." Mitchell's voice faded.

"Hey! Listen to me. Mitchell, don't worry about that. Where are you there?" Avery asked.

"...Yeah I'm here."

"Do you know where you are?" Avery asked.

"...No idea. I'm sorr'."

"Ok." Avery wiped sweat from his upper lip, "Ok."

"I need you to turn on your location service. Got it?" Avery said.

There were strange voices on the other end of the line. Laughing, shouting.

"Mitchell! Mitchell! Listen to me!" Avery commanded.

"Heyy...I'm here," Mitchell mumbled.

"Listen. Turn on your location service," He said forcefully. "You got do that right now. It's a blue button on the home screen. Just press that blue button."

More fumbling across the microphone, the voices in the background grew clearer. *Fuck.* They were losing him.

Then a large grey circle popped up on Avery's map. Covering most of the city, it soon narrowed down to the west side. Mia sat near the door whining. The circle blinked and narrowed against slightly.

"Mitchell, are you there?" Avery asked again.

The circle stopped blinking and hovered over a neighborhood-sized region. Willing for more accuracy, he scanned cross streets where the circle had settled.

Then he heard Mitchell's phone drop to the floor with a thud. The circle disappeared and the line went blank.

"Mitchell?! You there?!" he called.

Nothing.

At that instant, a door inside Avery found its key and unlocked. There had been times before when he had only peaked through the cracks. Now it swung wide open and released a phenomenal burst of energy, elegant and blue tinted. He sprung up, in a blur, and blasted out of the kitchen.

He burst out of the front door like lightning. He landed lightly in the grass for several paces, then exploded out of the yard and cut into the middle of the road.

His vision sharpened, focused on a path illuminated in a subtle glow. All of his senses were calm and synchronized. The city blurred past, first through the neighborhood, then into the thicket blocks and beyond. His heart pounded and his lungs seemed to function at twelve times their normal capacity. With each breath, he felt more energized like he was holding the reigns of sixty jet engines screaming at full power.

In a blur, he cleared the narrow streets and veered onto an open boulevard. He banked left, wanting to go west. But against the unchecked flow of energy, he failed. He dug in his heels, sending chunks of pavement flying in all directions. He leveled a road sign, tripped on the curb and barrel rolled into a vacant parking lot. Two drones zoomed passed him, lights flashing on their undercarriages.

As he collected himself, Mia galloped up beside him. Her eyes a piercing black, ears slung back on her head. This is what he felt in a flash at Exit 37, but now in full color. Even with Mia's normal speed, there was no way she could have kept pace, unless, Mia was his key. Too much, that was too much to comprehend.

Together they made for the empty westbound lanes. The power was overwhelming and difficult. Twice more he overcorrected, flattening a rusted gas pump and trampling the roof of a parked car. But he urgently powered on, willing himself closer to the circled area etched in his mind.

Their speed was huge, streaking across the open night. He was aware of Mia's senses in fits and starts. Getting closer to the zone, an armored patrol vehicle screeched into the road, blocking his path. The drones returned, pelting the ground with a stream of bullets.

He didn't have time to deal with Protocol issues. In a reckless kick he launched over the armored vehicle and threw a punch at the closest drone. He found himself vaulting way high and way fast. His swing missed epically. Scanners tracked him, adjusting the weaponry. He was too fast, landing safely on the other side of the patrol vehicle. Mia came screaming around the front bumper and they accelerated away.

They crossed overgrown lots and ramshackle houses when green spears sliced over his shoulder. Avery recognized the Lancer's weapon; he'd seen it in action from the Witness Tree in Woodway. He dove off the road as another spear slammed into the tailgate of an adjacent truck. The air was filling with approaching drones and urgent radio calls echoed through the block. A third and fourth spear sailed through the darkness of the overgrown block. The Lancer was hunting Avery. A squadron of drones five across and two deep descended on the area.

Avery worked to collect himself. Deep breath, Avery, Deep breath. Mia's calm focus was with him now, he felt himself drawing on her fearless instincts. His eyes adjusted to the tangled darkness. A green spear glowed in the hands of the Lancer as he stood at the curb. The drones crept forward, jostling the vegetation. This actually helped conceal Avery from the Lancer.

Step by careful step, Avery worked toward the edge of the block. He could outrun their attacks if he had a clear path and open road. Any slow down and he'd be dead. The Lancer unleashed a spear that sunk deep into a tree at the opposite corner from where Avery was positioned. He heard a radio call: *Subject located.*

It was go time. They bounded over a long tangle of vines, hit clear sidewalk in stride, and flew west at impossible speed. He took his engines to 100%, letting all energy flow to his legs. Mia kept an effortless pace right by his side as they left the commotion behind them. They were still pointed in the direction of Mitchell. At full speed he was still able to read the street signs.

He scanned the broken cityscape within the zone, fiercely pushed forward. Whatever had distracted the patrols, it looked like he'd shaken the drones and soldiers. He overran several intersections, skimming across dew-drenched grass and passing structures cloaked in darkness.

He then saw the outline of Mitchell's Jeep parked at the curb. He slowed as gradually as his legs would allow, again leaving gashes in the pavement. Mia cut behind and held at his left shoulder. He heard her panting over his pounding heart. A sense of dread replaced his original calm. Several patrol trucks were also parked on the dark street.

Dull bass thumped from the basement of a sagging house. Grimy windows spilled out onto a rickety porch and unkempt lawn. The front door was cracked open a few inches. Avery slinked up the stairs and peeked inside. Mitchell sat slumped in a white plastic chair. His head hung against a sweat-ringed shirt. His phone face down on the floor.

Avery shouldered the narrow door open and stepped inside. The air smelled of moldy fabric and booze. Floorboards vibrated under foot. He crouched down in front of Mitchell, not paying consideration to the legion of bodies in the room.

"Hey. Mitchell - wake up. Hey." He pressed his hands squarely on both shoulders. Mitchell nodded limply, half opening his glazed eyes.

"Who the fuck are you?" a voice asked.

Avery glanced over. A group of Lafayette soldiers, three of them maybe four, postured in the middle of the room. They were red faced, uniforms untucked, cups in hand. Behind them groups of strung out civilians, observed Avery with wide eyes. A low table contained an assortment of pills, powders, and bottles of amber liquid.

"Just here to get my friend," Avery said, turning back to Mitchell who was now dropping his head in circles.

"That's not what I asked, citizen. I asked who, the fuck. are you."

"Don't worry about it."

Mitchell's eyes were open now. The soldiers stepped closer.

"See, I'm worried about it. Because, you come walking into my house. Uninvited. And now you're messing with my friend who's just getting some fresh air. I'm worried, you see that worries me." They advanced further; there were actually five soldiers.

Avery stayed crouched. Mia positioned herself across the doorway.

"I'm just here to take my friend home. I don't want any trouble." He wiggled Mitchell's knee, who jostled awake and looked over at the approaching soldiers.

In a dry voice, he forced out, "We gotta go."

Mia stood up, she growled and bared her teeth. Avery rose to his feet as the first soldier flipped open a knife and slashed. He dodged to the left and drove an elbow into a forearm. The knife clanged to the ground. Stepping back, the man threw a wide punch and another punch. He was now separated from the door and two more soldier joined.

With head and shoulders bobbing back and forth, they charged him. Avery swallowed his nerves and so went the new found energy. Confused by his internal turmoil, he lost focus for a beat. One of the soldiers spun around and landed a kick squarely on his chest, propelling him across the room and knocking him against the low table. Glass shattered. Another soldier drove his foot into the side of the Avery's knee, crumbling him to the floor.

Find yourself, damnit. The flame reignited in his chest and he sprung up, pulling both arms to a defensive posture. The soldiers now swung wildly. He'd just faced a Lancer - he could handle this. He ducked and turned away. The others in the room jeered. Mia sprung through the air and latched onto a soldier's wrist. With a howl he crashed to the floor.

Using the distraction, Avery landed a barrage of low punches, feeling ribs crack from his force. Blue smoke trailing off his arms, that was a new development. In rapid succession he sent one soldier to the floor coughing blood. A right hook shattered another's jaw and dropped him to the floor

Then came blade across his neck.

"Don't move." Alcohol wafted from the soldier's breath. They turned in toward the kitchen. Mia was locked on a bloodied and terrified soldier. The other partiers had backed into a corner. Avery saw a gun somewhere in the crowd.

"Call off that bitch of yours."

Avery was frozen. Mia growled and snapped with her paws on the man's chest.

"Do it!"

He couldn't move despite the inferno in his chest.

"I'll kill you first, then your dog. Your friend over there is already gone."

No, Mitchell wasn't going to die. Avery drove forward with all his force, grabbed ahold of an arm and flung the soldier straight through a wall like a rag doll. There was only one Able here.

The music stopped playing and the faint sound of sirens caught Avery's ear.

He jumped over to Mitchell, lifted him over his shoulder and made for the door. He whistled and Mia streaked out into the yard and straight into the back seat of the Jeep. Avery pulled Mitchell into the front seat. He ran his hands along the textured left front tire until he found the stash of keys. Limp and staggering, a silhouette appeared on the porch. Two shots ricocheted off the roll cage and a third hit a taillight. He ducked low and folded himself into the driver's seat.

With a desperate crank, the engine roared to life. He peeled away, straining around a sharp corner and into the darkness as more shots were fired.

Chapter 18

Oversized Handles

A heart monitor beeped rhythmically. Avery's eyes cracked open, his hip wedged against overstretched fabric and his neck kinked to one side. When his eyes finally focused he found himself folded on a narrow sofa at the base of a hospital bed.

Mitchell lay asleep in an oversized gown, ashen circles hung below each eye. A short nurse, with an oddly familiar wave of red hair, stood next to the bed. Her uniform was light pink and she wore brightly colored running shoes. Both hands were quickly working away on a screen near the bed; a small amount of skin shown on her back. Avery felt awkward after looking a second too long.

He twisted his stiff neck in both directions as he pushed up to a seated position. The sole of his drab running shoe squeaked against floor.

"Morning," the nurse said, tapping the screen twice and turning to face him. Her eyes kind, but dreary. A broad smile circled across her face.

"Where am I?" he asked.

"Lafayette Grace Hospital," she responded as she walked to the other side of the bed. A fresh floral smell wafted into his nose. The inside of his mouth felt hairy and he was uncomfortable with his current existence.

"You refused to leave last night...so we let you sleep on the sofa there," she said, checking the IV bag.

"I don't remember that," Avery said. "I'm sorry." His brain felt raw and scrubbed.

She straightened the sheets across Mitchell's chest. "You saved Mitch's life."

The events of the previous night came creeping back to him in bits and pieces.

"Is he gonna be alright?" he asked.

"Yeah, he'll be ok. But there were a lot of different chemicals in his system. You got Mitch here just in time to pump his stomach and get him stabilized," she said, leaning against the bed with her arms crossed, and looked him. It was the second time she had called him Mitch. Avery had never heard anyone call him that.

"I'm sorry," Avery said, looking down at the large wheels on the bed.

"Stop saying *I'm sorry*. You're making me nervous."

"Oh ok, sorr- Anyway. If you don't mind me asking a weird question," Avery said.

"Shoot."

"You've called Mitchell...Mitch. Guess I haven't known him for that long, but I know folks that have and I haven't heard anyone call him that. Do you know him?" Avery asked heightening his voice at the end.

She looked over to the window and blushed.

"I'm sorry," she said.

"Ah ah, now you're breaking the rules," Avery grinned.

"Mitchell's my brother," she said looking directly at Avery and then over at the bed.

"I had no idea. No idea he had a sister. He's never mentioned it." Avery stammered.

"Well that makes me feel very special," she continued to stare at her brother. "How much did you guys take last night anyway?"

"Me? Nothing. I'm not sure what he had," Avery said quickly.

"Yeah right."

"No, really."

She frowned.

"Honest. He called me in the middle of the night, asking for help. And we ended up here I guess. I can't remember much for some reason."

"Truth and truth?" she asked.

"Truth and truth. I thought Mitchell was cleaned up. No one knew where he was last night. Guess he found some trouble."

"Yeah," she sighed. "He's good at that. I fixed your paperwork by the way. Soldiers shouldn't be on your tail or anything."

Avery stood up and straightened his shirt. He then noticed he was wearing blue scrub pants that were a size too big and again felt like the king of Awkward Town.

"Thanks," he reached out his hand, using the other to hold onto the elastic waistband of the pants, "I'm Avery by the way."

"Good to see you again, Avery." She shook his hand. "I'm Addison." So she did remember him from the train platform! His insides flipped.

"Where's Mia?" Avery asked, suddenly realizing she was not in the room.

"Your dog?"

"Yeah. I guess I broke all the rules last night, huh?"

"Beatrice picked her up early this morning. I explained what had happened. You and Mich were asleep, she took the dog. Mia, you said? She took Mia." Addison adjusted some of the instruments along the wall.

"How do you know Bea?" she asked.

Avery rubbed his shoulder. With Mia so far away, he felt a strange distant sensation inside, "Mitchell and I live in her house together. We're roommates."

"Ahhh. Now it makes sense. He tried to get me to move into that house a few years back. In a rare case of rebellion I went out and got my own place." She swung her fist in a circle, "Anyway. Thank you." A tear snuck out of the corner of her eye, "For saving my brother's life."

She wiped the drop off her cheek with the back of her hand.

"He threw up on your paints by the way, so we gave you a pair of scrubs to wear. They're a little big."

Avery hiked them up on his hips with a smirk, "Perfect fit."

"Hey listen. I worked a double shift to stay with him last night. I usually work nights, but my schedule got flipped around...Anyway, do you drink coffee?" She asked.

Avery's head leaned back, "Coffee sounds amazing."

"They have some down the hall. And these mugs with ridiculously huge handles," Addison added, her nose crinkling into that smile.

They walked through the bright halls, a slight tension hanging in the air. Out the window, Avery noticed the skyline far in the distance. How had he known how to get here? Before now, he didn't even know there was a hospital in Lafayette. They stopped at a bank of elevators on Level Six.

"So how long have you been in the house?" she asked.

"Few months. I moved in at the beginning of June." he said.

"You've known my brother for like a month and you went out on a Stage Three Protocol by yourself to help him?" she asked.

"Mia was with me," he quipped.

She looked up at him dubiously, "You know what I mean."

"Yeah." He paused and thought about the unique bond between all his housemates, "Yeah, of course I did. He's my friend. He needed help. I guess I didn't even really think twice. He's helped me before."

The elevator chimed and the stainless steel doors opened. A short doctor with a long white coat and a stethoscope slung over his shoulders stood at the back of the compartment. The skin between his eyes was creased; he didn't seem to notice the doors open.

"Hi Dr. Yun," Addison said as they stepped inside.

"Addison. Good to see you. How are you feeling?" he asked. The expression on his face lightened.

"Tired. But good. Mitchell is stabilized. This is Avery, he brought Mitch in last night," Addison said. "Avery, Dr. Yun. Dr. Yun, Avery."

"Oh yes, I remember you," Dr. Yun said. "You saved a man's life last night, Avery."

"That's what I've been told... I'm glad I could help. Just hope Mitchell's OK."

"Indeed," the doctor said solemnly. "And Avery, how are you feeling?"

"Fine...I'm Fine." he said. "...Why?"

"Well, seeing as you are not my patient, but how should I say this...Your body was smoking when you arrived at the ER last night. Your vitals were perfectly normal. Regardless, that's a rather unique sight, even in this city."

"Yeah, I feel fine," Avery fumbled a bit. "Thanks for asking, doc."

The elevator chimed again, doors opened on level three. Addison stepped out, followed by Avery.

"Get some rest soon Addison. Doctor's orders," Dr. Yun said.

"I will. Thanks doc," she replied.

Dr. Yun looked severely at Avery. The doors closed.

She led them around the corner to a small kitchen station with three ancient coffee machines. She filled two mugs. The handles were indeed comically large, curving from the lip to the base.

They meandered slowly down the hall to a hospital soundtrack of hums and beeps playing in the background. Several nurses waved to Addison and asked about Mitchell. Some rooms were empty, stripped of all equipment and furniture; sick Lafayette residents occupied other rooms. As they walked, Avery inquired about Addison and Mitchell's story and tried not to stare at her.

She was the younger of the two Quelhursts, by almost three years. Avery did the math and that made her the same age as him. They had grown up in a quiet neighborhood on the east side of Lafayette. Their parents had both worked for Hubbard. That's how their father knew Bea. He had been terribly strict. When Mitchell was old enough, he started to rebel. She said that a group of older kids got him mixed up in all sorts of drugs.

Then their parents disappeared. No explanation. Nothing. It was a story that was starting to sound all too common. Addison said she had holed up for almost two years. Mitchell simply disappeared during that period. She hadn't really known where he was or what he was up to for a long time. One morning he was dumped on Bea's front step – she took him in and cleaned him up.

"He's so talented. If he can just keep his mind focused on the right thing - my brother can do great," she said.

"Brilliant, but flawed," Avery added.

"That's him."

"Aren't we all."

Without thinking, Avery rested his palm against her shoulder.

"People make mistakes. I'm just glad he's OK."

"Me too…" Their eyes met for a lingering second.

A ring tone then chirped from her pocket. She pulled out her phone.

"You've gotta move the Jeep, or they are going to tow it," she said.

Addison slowly guided him back through the hospital. She asked about his story in the process. How he had found himself in Lafayette. How he liked the house. He told her about Woodway and coming to the city for the Keeper job and that he liked the people and the house.

His insides felt squirmy as they walked into the lobby.

"Not the best circumstances. But nice to see you again, Addison," he said. "And thanks for the assist with the train ticket."

Addison chewed on her lip.

"You too, Mr. Jackson." She pulled out her phone. "As a hospital employee I'm required to keep up a certain Linkerage Score."

Avery urgently fumbled his device out of front pocket of the hospital MC Hammer pants. They tapped phones, providing a small bump to both their scores, exchanging contact information in the process.

"Seriously, you've gotta move the Jeep now, or they are going to tow it," she repeated, pointing out the large span of glass doors, a smile peeking out.

Avery nodded once with his own smile peeking out. He turned toward the exit holding up his pants. The automatic doors whooshed open. In a small curved parking lot outside, the Jeep sat angled across two spaces. The cabin smelled of vomit. He cautiously drove home in colorless weather, twice making abrupt turns when he saw patrol vehicles.

* * * * * *

Dr. Yun took the elevator to the hospital basement level one. Outside the staff cafeteria, he scanned his ID card at a heavy door.

When it was closed firmly behind him, the doctor walked down a featureless hallway. Near the end of the hall was his cubicle-sized office with a desk, a lamp, and not much else.

He sat down. His typical diligent focus was dulled by exhaustion. Protocol required him to report any 'unusual or suspicious activity' observed in the emergency room. He found the form on his tablet and swiftly entered information. The final section required a written report and the system required all caps, which he found tedious:

```
15:12:52 - THURSDAY AUGUST 5TH
    RESIDENT OBSERVED IN LAFAYETTE GRACE
HOSPITAL RADIATING BLUE SMOKE FROM UPPER
EXTREMITIES. MALE, 5'9", 145 LBS, CAUCASIAN,
BROWN HAIR, GREEN EYES, IDENTIFIED HIMSELF AS
AVERY. VITAL SIGNS WERE NORMAL, OTHERWISE
UNREMARKABLE AND IN EXCELLENT HEALTH. SMOKE
GENERAL PHYSIOLOGICAL MANOR ARE CHARACTERISTIC
OF AN ABLE OF PARTICULAR CAPACITY. CAPABILITIES
COULD NOT BE ASCERTAINED BY HOSPITAL STAFF
DURING BRIEF PERIOD OF EXAMINATION.
```

ARRIVED AT EMERGENCY DEPARTMENT WITH A
DRUG OVERDOSE PATIENT IN HIS CARE. FURTHER
OBSERVATION SUGGESTED.

He hit send and the report was shuttled off to a queue in the Protocol Center. By the end of the day, it would be organized into a growing case file on Lt. Quade's computer.

Chapter 19

Conference of the Somewhat Willing

"I don't have visual connection. Where's my damn visual connection?" a voice bellowed from the speakers.

On the thirty-second floor of The Tower, a cathedral like conference room sat dim and almost empty. Dark granite panels covered every surface. Mounted to the far wall, a wide monitor looked down a long black lacquered. A small diamond glowed on the screen while a faceless technician typed on a keyboard illuminated on the surface.

Through static, a hyena-like voice replied.

"Groa, cool your jets. Just give it a second."

After the technician's urgent recalibration, the three Fender glyphs appeared on the screen in a single line, and the double doors burst open.

In his neatly tailored dress uniform, Lt. Quade powered into the room. Hubbard floated in behind, phantom-like. A long cloak hung over his hunched frame.

"We must bring it up first thing," Bryce stammered.

Hubbard's hand rose, "For now, you will keep your mouth shut."

The green Lafayette rectangle illuminated.

"But-" Lt. Quade objected.

"Silence," Hubbard snarled.

Ashburn appeared in the orange glyph on the screen. He slouched in a glass-paneled room looking over Garfield. The black rectangle filled with a dimly lit chin and shoulders.

"Adjust your view ya jack off," Ashburn said.

Groa's camera shifted abruptly and a set of piercing black eyes and giant chin came into view. The black glyph illuminated.

The conference room came fully online just as the technician scurried between the swiftly closing doors.

"Mr. Hubbard, good to see you my friend," Groa said.

Bryce shifted in his chair rigidly.

"And Lieutenant Quade, to you as well," added Groa. His connection from Carrick City cracking slightly.

Bryce nodded formally. Hubbard sat uneasily next to his lieutenant.

Groa shuffled some papers and cleared his throat thunderously, "Good morning gentlemen." He said.

"Lieutenant, please keep minutes for this month's Fender Assembly."

A keyboard appeared at Bryce's seat. His entries showed on a small panel opposite the table.

```
FENDER CONFERENCE 27.95.37 TC_i
/
/
SECURE TELE CONNECTION
/
TEST 001 /\ RUNNING...CONFIRMED
/
IDENTITIES AUTHORIZED
:: GARFIELD -> ASHBURN, DELL
:: LAFAYETTE -> HUBBARD, KENYON //
     ROBERTSON-QUADE, BRYCE
:: CARRICK -> STANTON, GROA
```

"Let's get down to business, shall we? We are now in the middle of summer, a time when The Chancellery historically faces heightened levels of Protocol infractions," Groa said.

"This month alone, Fleet Command in the Outlands has reported a 50% increase in unsanctioned fence protrusions. There were also some...issues here in Carrick City last week. Nothing a few plasma shells couldn't take care of. Central Fence Command will be pushing an update to the system in two weeks. The Smoke Walkers have been more mobile this summer as well. I have a recon team investigating now. Refueling rods for the Blade are now ready. We need a two day extended layover here at Gortook Station for the changeover process and for loading of steel beams headed to Garfield."

Protruding his chin, Bryce asked, "What construction projects are underway?"

Hubbard pressed an open palm on the table.

Groa looked up, "What's that?"

Hubbard raised a single finger, "Groa, please. Continue my friend."

Groa adjusted the stack of papers and continued.

"As I was saying. Refueling should be scheduled. Sometime in the next two weeks."

Groa again glanced up, "Ashburn, my reports show that the Blade made a full speed run to the Outlands Station before returning to Garfield yesterday. Elaborate, please."

Ashburn cracked his neck and twisted his jaw.

"I needed some things. We made the run. All systems are in good shape. The first gen Fenders built that train to use. You guys remember that, right?"

The wheels of Hubbard's chair echoed in the hall.

"What was the cargo?" he asked.

"It's on the manifest."

"It reads here: *A Gaggle of Bitches*," Groa said plainly.

"There you have it."

"A higher level of discretion would behoove you, Dell Ashburn," Hubbard added.

"I'll show you..."

Groa cut him off, "Let's move on. Dell, please provide us with an update."

"Summer is treating Garfield well. A fun season in my city, as always. But, I digress. Wells are down 12% from last year. There's some concern about this downward trend in water supply. If there is any chance of it effecting supply to your cities, I will inform the group. K?" He took a long swing from a stout, wide rimmed glass.

"Hubbard," Groa moved on. "Interesting rumors from your neck of the woods. Please Report. "

Hubbard's voice rolled slowly, "Bandit activity to the south is up. And there was a minor intrusion into our dedicated transport system. Similar to Groa, I have additional units in the field to ensure things return to normal. We should know more by the time shut down comes in a few months."

Groa drew out his next words dramatically, "And what about within the city walls?"

Hubbard paused, pressed his fingers together. "A Forerunner was detected several days ago."

Sounds of surprise came from Garfield and Carrick City.

"Our Record Holder is notoriously...close to the vest as you all know. But our system detected high level activity around 2:00 AM on Thursday," Hubbard added.

Groa puffed out his chest, "You should have reported this immediately." Sounding a bit taken aback.

"Who?" Ashburn asked.

"No details are confirmed yet," Hubbard responded.

And Bryce interjected, "That is precisely why we are conducting a rigorous search effort to draw out the new Forerunner and determine their level of -"

A loud slap broke his sentence.

Hubbard faced the screen directly, "We are monitoring the situation. All available resources are on high alert."

Bryce's face was purple, his shoulders rigid.

Groa inquired, "When is the last time we encountered a Forerunner that we couldn't control"

"Ashburn?" Hubbard asked.

"Six and a half years ago. Kid drank himself to death, so who cares."

"He happened to be your kid brother," Groa said.

He emptied his glass, "Yeah, whatever."

Groa continued authoritatively, "Hubbard, you know the severity of this matter. If the connection between Forerunner and key is allowed to fully mature, that is a serious security risk to The Chancellery."

"Understood."

"All right. I have a lunch arrangement. Other than our little new Forerunner and minor water supply issues - Nothing that cannot be addressed individually, right?" He pounded the table, "Right?"

Agreement rumbled in from the other cities.

"Meeting adjourned."

The screen went blank. Hubbard rose gradually, leaving Bryce to finish his record-keeping task. In the time spent walking to the door, a sharp image unexpectedly solidified in his mind's eye. He saw his queen Jaron - wings spread, calling savagely. The image disappeared in a flash.

A hand found the ribbon in his pocket, his ability now at full power. He scanned the thoughtscape again, searching for his bird, but found nothing but an oddly shaped box. He was accustomed to full control - of his own thoughts, and those of others around him. With patience, his mind billowed across the foreign box sitting in the cross hairs of his mind. He detected memories and emotions locked safely behind iron walls and thick padlocks. He quickly withdrew his conscience back to the physical world.

He knew of very few people capable of building such a memory chest in their own headspace. One of them currently shared the room with him. With that he released the ribbon to coil neatly in his pocket and proceeded to the door, his vision churning with red rage. For a brief second, he glared back at Lt. Quade, whose face was now devoid of color. This was an issue that would be dealt with swiftly.

Chapter 20

Do Over.

Avery and Bronwyn sat on the front porch. Avery's leg ached where he had been kicked. The neighborhood kids played a game of tag in the street that boarded on full-blown chaos. The air was heavy and throbbed with a chorus of crickets and tree frogs.

Paolo's truck lumbered down Forest Avenue and turned into the driveway. Mitchell slouched in the passenger seat.

Avery stood and leaned against the banister. Sensing the tension, Mia paced next to him. A clear loop of energy now flowed imperfectly between them - transforming slightly when the distance increased.

Mitchell then appeared, walking slowly. He kicked the pavement as he approached. Silence was all that was needed.

Bronwyn grabbed Mitchell's hand and pulled him in for a big hug and welcomed him home.

Mitchell turned and stared at the center of Avery's chest. He let out a breath and then pulled Avery in tight. He smelled of hospital.

"Thank you," he said under his breath. "Thank you."

Avery's vocal cords twisted around in circles and tears welled in his eyes. He blinked rapidly several times and slapped Mitchell between the shoulder blades.

"Glad you're alright," Avery whispered.

Mitchell held on for an extra second and walked inside without saying anymore. The door to Bea's study creaked open and closed. Paolo had held back and was just now approaching the porch. He simply walked into the house, pounding fists with Avery as he passed. The door closed with a solid thud, making the air around them seem to change states.

Before Avery could sit back down on the step, Bea's voice erupted through the front window.

"There it is," Bronwyn said.

Avery hung his head and tried not to listen.

"Whadya think's gonna happen?" he asked.

"Good question," Bronwyn said.

"This isn't Mitchell's first strike," she added.

Avery rubbed his head with both hands.

"I dunno." He said, not able to think clearly.

What were you thinking?! They both heard from inside.

"What happened before?" Avery asked.

"He finds his way back to the pills. He's come back here all strung out more than once. Luckily I've been able to catch him before Bea or Flow saw. But this is a whole 'nother ball game."

"That was a long time ago, sounds like," Avery said.

"Yeah, but it still happened."

"I dunno," Avery repeated.

The study door squeaked and then feet scuffed on the stairs.

They sat there for a while. The kids across the street continued to run in circles. One of them stopped abruptly and slouched his shoulders and protest: *Hey guys, do over! Do over, I wasn't ready!*

Chapter 21

We're the Helpers

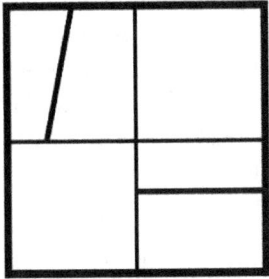

The Argus Bureau

Stillness settled on the 1400 block of Forest Ave., the children had returned home and the two housemates headed inside. Cracked open a few inches, Bea's office watched the hallway. Bronwyn stepped into the kitchen.

"Avery." Bea's voice reached out, as if she could see him through the door.

He stepped inside apprehensively. Sitting behind her broad desk amplified Bea's presence.

"Close the door, please," she said.

He gingerly rolled the doorknob into place.

"Hi," he said, sitting down in the same wooden chair where he had discussed moving in only a few months ago.

"So."

"Are you going to kick Mitchell out of the house?" Avery asked.

"We will discuss him shortly," Bea said calmly. "But first, there are a few other items that we need to discuss. Hmmm?"

"Ok."

"First of all. You acted very courageously going after Mitchell. And you saved his life. He is like a son to me, and for that I'm very grateful."

He again found his emotions tied around his throat.

"Secondly," Bea looked straight into his eyes, "Avery, I am sure you are now well aware...you found your key last night. You are an Able."

"Yeah," he said, uncoiling his voice, "What's that mean exactly?"

"It means you unlocked your power, a power that has been stored inside you since the day you were born. In the presence of your key, you will be able to call upon that power. It lives in you and it lives in your key."

"But my key is Mia," Avery said.

"Yes."

"Is that ok?" he asked.

Bea laughed full heartedly, "I am certainly not offended."

"That's good," Avery said. "I was kinda worried about it actually. And, well, there's like a million other things that are confusing right now." He couldn't help but think of home, and Jim's phone call he overheard, and Addison.

"Of course," Bea said. "It will all take time to sort out. And don't worry. Things will sort out. You'll become more comfortable with your powers as you use them more. The connection between yourself and Mia will grow stronger."

"I have been craving dog food, is that bad?" Avery joked.

"Perfectly normal. Part of the process," Bea countered. "But Avery, allow me to give you some advice. Being an Able is not to be taken lightly. You are now the steward of something very powerful. And you alone decide how that power gets used - what direction you guide the flow of energy. Also know there are many eyes in many places - here in Lafayette and beyond. Our world simply is not a place where being an Able is a secret easily kept."

"Am I in danger?" Avery asked. "Am I putting you all in danger?"

"Do you feel in danger?"

"Well. You don't need to feel safe to feel unafraid."

"So true," she said.

"Are you?" he asked. "Are you an Able?"

Bea blinked twice, "Yes Avery, I am. There's beauty in paying attention, so fellow Able, pay attention. It's an uphill climb until you find that full connection. How long that takes, depends on the Able. For me, it took years. But when you do, when you find that, it will feel like you can see all the pieces."

"Sounds like a case for world domination," Avery poked.

"Ha! Look at my advice crumbling into pieces." Bea said.

Avery was blunt, "What's your power, Bea?""

She sat silently for several minutes. In time, she stood up and pulled a leather bound notebook from the bookshelf and walked around the desk.

"I must admit that your abilities were no secret to me. When you came into the city, I knew you were an Able and I knew what was locked inside. It was just a matter of you and your key finding each other."

"How's that possible?" Avery asked.

"Well, that's my power. I can read and understand the energy held within each one of us. I am what is often called the Record Holder," Bea said.

She handed him the notebook, "Open it."

He hesitated.

"Please," Bea urged.

Each page had two neatly hand written columns, the text in beautiful script. The first was a long string of numbers. The second was a description of some sorts.

19845773   *Shell, collect during visit to beach.*
14845774   *Fountain pen.*

The list continued page after page. On one of the last pages was an entry with a triple star.

16745895   *Shepherd dog****

"That's me," Avery said. "But why is my entry starred?"

"You're different, that's why."

Avery flipped through the pages and saw that the handwriting changed as he went farther back and only a few other entries were similarly marked.

Bea continued, "No one knows what creates the bond between a key and its holder. As you can see, it can be almost anything. A rock, a shoelace even. But if someone's key is another living thing, it makes that connection even stronger. It makes the individual's powers even stronger. You, Mr. Jackson, are a Forerunner."

"A what?" Avery asked, his head spinning. "And how did you..."

Bea held up her hand. Helicopter rotors clapped in the distance, sending a chill down his spine.

"There is always only one Record Holder. For many years it has been me. No one has found their key without me knowing. To the people I am close with, I can see potential powers. In strangers, it's not so easy. But with you, your potential was like looking at a high definition photograph."

"But you didn't know what my key was," Avery said.

"There's no way of knowing, even for me. But the bond between you and Mia is more powerful than any I have seen before. It will only get stronger. I tell you this now, Avery, because there may be turbulent times ahead and I need you to understand," she said.

Avery closed the book slowly

"Just remember there are times for strength and there are times for kindness," Bea said.

"Is something going to happen?"

"The world is ever changing kiddo."

"Well I know that."

"But understanding change and accepting change are very different."

"Can I ask you a question then?"

"Of course."

"When I did the assessments in Briarcamp. The old man who ran this hostel in town seemed to know so much about things.

He mentioned something called the Argus Bureau." At this she shifted, "And that came in handy along the way."

"Russell."

"You know him?"

"Very well. An old friend."

"How so?" Avery asked.

"We started the Argus Bureau together."

"What? Really?"

"Yeah. Really."

"Like catacombs and guarding an ancient treasure?"

Bea snored, "Well, no catacombs. But a passcode or two AND maybe we are guarding an ancient treasure."

"What is it?" Avery asked anxiously.

"Our humanity."

That took some of the wind out of his sails, but he was still urgently curious.

"How do you mean?"

"The Fenders do so much for us, but they also starve us of what makes people, people. Freedom, Friendship - that's stripped away in the name of security, Linkerage, and whatever else." She continued, "Common edges. Connections. Balance. That's what the Argus Bureau is about. The Fenders want to pull us apart into separate silos, standing alone at a distance from our neighbors."

"How does that work?" he asked. "No offense meant there. But I didn't know the Bureau existed until two minutes ago. Why not just go after them, fight the good fight."

"They're a powerful lot, those three. Standing up to them isn't an easy task," Bea said. "And standing strong doesn't always mean standing rigid. We work in the background, mostly. Helping Ables and Grove Keepers, providing information." After a beat, she added, "Having secret meetings."

"And since you know who all the Ables are. You can help protect them," Avery said.

"We're the helpers." She folded her hands together. The helicopters grew louder.

"What does this mean for Mitchell?" Avery asked.

Bea collected the Record Book and deposited it back on the bookshelf.

"Mr. Quelhurst. He has yet to discover his key." Bea's face showed intense frustration, "At his current rate, he may not be alive to find it."

"Are you kicking him out?" Avery asked again.

"We are not kicking him out."

The guilt that had coagulated around his heart started to dissipate.

"But I've made arrangements. He needs help beyond what Florence and I can provide. I was arrogant, I thought I could provide all the help and support he needed." Bea said, "But I was wrong. Mitchell needs someone who can help break open that locked trunk of issues. All we've been able to do was throw stones at it since he's joined the house."

"So someone's gonna help him get better?" Avery asked.

"We're all going to help him get better," Bea responded. "But right now, we need some extra fire power. I know a gentleman who specializes in this thing. The two of them are locked up in the library for twenty-five days. Mitchell is probably hating my guts at the moment, but tough shit."

Avery continued asking questions about keys and Ables and addiction. Bea answered them the best she could until commotion on the side of the house pulled them away from the conversation.

Muffled yelling first caught their attention.

Then a heavy car door slammed out by the street.

Arguing now, a group of voices. Avery recognized Paolo's tone and ran to the front door. Paolo was face to face with a pair of soldiers near the end of the driveway. Avery pulled open the door with Bea and Mia right behind.

"You think you can just come in here like this?" Paolo shoved one of the soldiers, sending him back a pace.

"Get off our property."

The other soldier snapped open a retractable baton and swung at Paolo who was built like a brick wall. The baton struck his forearm. Paolo grabbed the weapon, twisted, and flipped the soldier on his back as his partner reached for his weapon.

Avery felt the new energy churn inside his rib cage. He ran out to Paolo.

"Hey, hey. What's going on here guys."

He positioned himself between Paolo and soldier. And now had a gun pointed at his check. Holy shit. *Ok, back up.*

"Stand down citizen."

"There must have just been a misunderstanding," Avery said, and glanced back at Paolo who was seething.

When he looked back, the unarmed soldier was upon him.

"He said stand down."

The first strike caught Avery off guard. It sent stars into his vision and dropped him to one knee. Paolo vaulted over him and tackled the armed soldier. A shot fired into the air, Avery flinched on the ground. His vision cleared and found the second soldier had rearmed himself with the baton.

Avery could break the guy in half; he wasn't even worried about it. But how was he going to get Paolo out of this? Just as the soldier rose to strike a citizen he surely didn't know was a Forerunner, Flow's voice boomed from the front porch.

"Gentlemen," she called the soldiers both by first and last name. They both retreated from their attacks. Paolo was still going, Avery had to pull him off. Flow strolled out to them like she didn't have a care in the world, a ceramic tortoise sat in his breast pocket and Avery couldn't quite describe it... but she looked more pink and on fire than usual.

The soldiers retreated, abandoning their weapons on the pavement. Avery still held Paolo across the shoulders as she quietly talked with the two soldiers curbside at their patrol vehicle. After a few minutes, he felt awkward bear hugging his roommate and gradually let go.

Paolo cursed under his breath.

"Protocol enforcement, my ass," he rasped.

Bea walked up and put a hand on Paolo's forearm.

"You need to learn to let them be," she said calmly.

"They got no right coming here and poking around," Paolo said, still breathing hard.

Bea nodded, "But it's their job."

The patrol truck started with a hiss and was gone in a flash.

Flow came over to the group, smacked Paolo across the back of his head, "Stop it." She looked like she'd just been on an amusement park ride.

"Now let's all get some sleep."

They headed into the house.

"Thanks, Flow," Avery said quietly.

She waved him off and they all retired into their rooms.

Avery sat quietly for a while, letting the overwhelming information settle. He hoped Addison was safe. He pulled up her contact information on his phone - but decided to wait. Mia was snoring on his bed.

Unbeknownst to them, a special surveillance team had been deployed to the neighborhood. A telescopic lens was trained on the garden. Motion and heat sensors were positioned at regular intervals along the block. And a mobile command post was parked in an empty parking lot around the corner. But strict orders now kept any soldier from entering Bea and Flow's property.

Miles away, in a windowless office, Bryce simmered. High above him, Hubbard had broken into the mysterious mind box that he had spent years concealing and was sorting through the contents. Things were unraveling.

Chapter 22

#imnewhere

Hi Addison.

avery, hi!
how are you?

Currently sweating uncontrollably,
But good. you?

good. just got home from
work, peanut butter and jelly time.

And a baseball bat.

what?

Nothing

Ok...
talked to Mitchell at all?

No ...doesn't like to
pick up his phone...

kids these days

seriously

how's Mia dog?!

Panting up a storm at my feet
but generally loving life.

good, good

Can I defend your brother
for a second

bro code

Yea
Bea's gotten him some help.

                                selection in the library with some guy
                                     that's helping clean him up.
                                               seclusion*

K
if it can get him clean for good...
anyway

                                     He's doing something, just thought
                                             you should know.

                                     Can I awkwardly transition
please

                                Would you like to hang out sometime?
                                     ya know - not in the hospital?
id like that

                                                         Awesome
what did you have in mind?

                                          hmmm, I hadn't gotten that far
:/
;)
get back to me when you've
thought of something?

                                                         For sure

Chapter 23

Friendship Maintenance

Avery and Mia padded out a narrow crack in the sliding back door. Energy hummed between them.

In long strides with Mia marching alongside, Avery rounded the corner of Forest and turned south onto Woodward. The city was still and grey in the early Saturday morning. Small wisps of blue smoke hovered close to his skin. He did not notice the high elevation drone pinging the location of his phone and monitored his energy level. Or the patrol vehicle parked two blocks down.

Bea had been right: it still felt foreign to think of himself as an Able. It was as though he manned someone else's rocket ship with half of the controls missing. He needed to put in work toward connecting himself fully to his abilities - making them one in the same. And he needed a safe place to practice.

Bea had offered to help with training and had left for The Shoulder on an ancient three-speed bike a half hour before him. Despite the head start, they arrived together, converging from different sides of the grove.

Behind the towering front gate of the Shoulder, his sentinels stood in a mask of fog. Avery operated the complex set of locks and waited for them rotate open. Once they were both inside and done engaging in morning small talk, he took an extra minute and stood with his toes in the beginnings of the undergrowth. He had grown accustomed to his new grove, but it was his first time being there without Jim or Wallace.

Mia curiously pushed into the turf, eager to find something more interesting to chase than stationary trees. Her snout sniffed and puffed through the dense clumps of vegetation.

Avery slipped over to the main driveway with the bottled energy feeling as though it could burst from his heart. He adjusted the knots on both shoes, straightened.

"Alright, let's start simple," Bea said, walking up to the path clutching a coffee mug. "Try to ease into the energy."

Avery let loose and burst down the forest corridor. Mia's bark echoed and she surged to follow. He called back that feeling of limitlessness, though it came in fits and starts. So much for easing into it.

His step faltered as the last line of trees approached. Before he could adjust his right foot caught the loose gravel. Damnit. At speed he flung forward, crashing belly first into the end of the drive and sliding across the northern lawn, leaving a dirty gash in the turf.

The impact punched the air from his lungs. Mia overshot and playfully looped back as he collected himself. The last of the gravel had scraped his elbow. He wiped off a small trail of blood and kicked some of the turf chunks back into place.

He got to his feet and jogged to far side of the clearing. Bea ambled into the lawn on her bike.

"Gradually, dummy, gradually," she said, circling him.

"Got it."

This time he started...gradually, allowing himself to adjust the power, the feeling, the connection. He still miscalculated the stopping distance and was forced to cut hard left. He slammed into one of the brick fence columns, pitching it askew upon impact. Mia whined as he bent over his knees. He had succeeded in breaking some shit already.

"Again," Bea called from the other end.

Avery flew back across the field, better understanding when to adjust the power. He slowed at an even pace. Still driving chunks out of the grass, but not bulldozing the fence post.

"Good. Again."

Five passes later and he had a solid command of straight lines.

Bea watched closely and said little. Just making keen little adjustments as he progressed.

The next hour was full of routes of various velocities, directions, and levels of difficulty. Twice more he crashed into the fence and scraped up both forearms. In small steps he began to calibrate his pace and dexterity. His power was like a coiled spring. It built with speed and distance and could be released in bursts as he learned control.

By noon he could blaze a twisting diagonal route through the sentinels. At full speed he cut and redirected with a new found confidence, more restraint than reaction. He even tried leaving the ground. In a bound he could elevate high enough to grab hold of a lower branch, but again misjudged the trajectory and landed hard. *Crap.*

Mia never missed a beat. Their hearts pounded, lungs filling with sweet air. They would occasionally peel apart as they traced between the behemoths, but she would soon find the same slipstream of shared fluid energy. Each pass further set the connection between Forerunner and key.

Both mentally and physically spent, Avery lined up for one last practice run across the diagonal trial. He accelerated with clean, driving strides. Cogs of a complex puzzle fell into place with each step. He hurtled forward, feeling light and powerful. When he passed the barn a strange energy washed across him. A toxic sense of frustration invaded his mind. It was there and then gone. He slowed and looked back to see nothing but the sagging panels and darkened windows. What was that?

Feeling frazzled, he returned to the office to drink from the hose before filling his hand for Mia. Bea stood near the gate with a wide grin. His phone buzzed. It was Paolo.

"A," Paolo said.

"Hey, what's up?"

"Where you at?"

"I'm at the, ah, I'm at the Shoulder."

"It's Saturday, you good?"

"Just had something's to take care of."

"Whatever. Hey, we're stopping by the library. See how that Mitchell kid is doing. You in?"

"Yeah, for sure. What time?"

"Now."

"Meet you there."

Avery turned to Bea, "They're going to visit Mitchell at the library."

"Uh ha."

"I was gonna...you want to come with?" Avery asked.

"No, no. You go." She said.

"You sure?"

"Oh yeah," Bea climbed on her bike. "He probably doesn't want to see me right now anyway. Good that you kids are going to see him." She pushed off, "Good training today kiddo, tomorrow I'll take you out to the island. There's good space out there." And she winked and pedaled off, "Be safe!"

No one had spoken to Mitchell since the overdose and quick retreat from their house. It would be good to see him, do some friendship maintenance. Avery checked the fence at the points where he had collided, locked the main gate, and headed toward downtown at an easy trot. The monitoring drone had broken from its pre-programmed route and tracked him until he crossed the threshold into the downtown district.

Balanced on a wedge of a block, the library was rounded and stepped in at each corner. Other than being topped with a pleated copper roof, the plain facade disappeared between the surrounding structures of towering concrete and glass. The first floor sat mothballed for decades. Officially, the stacks contained archived records reaching back to the first generation of Fenders and their claiming of the city. Other than Mitchell, no one had as much as opened the door in years.

His housemates were clustered on the front steps. Bronwyn was on her phone. Paolo pressed his nose against the revolving door. Addison waved and jogged over when she saw him.

"Hey hey."

There was a light, awkward hug where neither knew how far to go in.

"Hi," Avery said. "So this was totally my plan. A date to see your brother in rehab," He said, kicking the pavement.

"Oh, so you were asking me on a date, huh?" Addison blushed. "How about dinner next week?"

"Deal," Avery said, unable to subdue an ear-to-ear smile.

Addison touched him on the elbow and turned to the others.

Bronwyn pulled the phone from her ear.

"He won't listen to me," she said.

"Dip shit," Paolo chided.

"Let me talk to him," Addison said.

Bronwyn looked at her with a twisted jaw and handed over the phone.

"Hey Mitch, it's me. Hey."

...

"No, we came here to see how you were doing."

...

"Why do that."

...

"Cuz that's what friends do for each other," Addison said.

...

"Please."

From around the block a pair of armored patrol vehicles, the size of buses, surged past. Black smoke belched from their exhaust pipes. Then another pair rounded the corner. And then a third pair. The smell and vibration jarred the group standing on the sidewalk. Avery instinctively stepped back and shifted into a defensive stance. Would they need to fight again? Soldiers riding shotgun leered at them. But all six vehicles turned toward the Tower.

Ok, maybe not.

"Patrols are a getting a little nuts. Please, open the door."

Addison handed the phone back to Bronwyn despondently.

"He hung up."

Then a deadbolt clunked open. A short sage of a man motioned for them to entre. He wore circular, thick-rimmed glasses, with silver hair swept over the top of his head and a neatly trimmed beard of the same color. One by one they pushed through the weighty revolving door into a foyer of dual marble stairways wrapped in a black railing and lit by tall windows bordering an ancient reading room. A distant dripping echoed throughout the space.

"How quaint," Bronwyn said.

"Hello all," the man said, holding his hands properly behind his back. "My name is Francis. I am Mitchell's rehabilitation advisor." He shook each of their hands curtly.

Francis pointed up the stairs, "Our work space is up here." He said.

A narrow hallway led them to the back of the library. The walls were beige with water stains and dark wood trim muted by decades of dust. Francis led them to the end room where a door stood slightly ajar.

"Mitchell?" Paolo asked.

No response.

They walked closer. The shuffling grew louder, hard breathing.

Paolo pushed opened the door. Sweat soaked, Mitchell was completing jumping jacks in the middle of a long office overflowing with things. Floor to ceiling maps mounted on layered wheeled panels lined one wall.

"Hey," he said nonchalantly, finishing a set.

"There he is!"

"Mitchell!"

"Hey buddy."

The tribe entered and greeted Mitchell overwhelmingly. Paolo pulled him in tight, followed by Addison. Avery held back, hands in pockets. Bronwyn bustled by, pinched his ear, and immediately started to survey the office. Large bottles of water were lined up along the wall. A wide drafting table stretched under windows opposite the wall of maps. Boxes of fruit, bread, acorn butter, and green and yellow liquids, were stacked next to the table. Addison shuffled through a pile of clothes in the corner, looking for holes to fix and buttons to reattach. Paolo inquired about the workout.

"Yeah. Good. I guess. Alive. An hour and a half a day of this stuff. Helps sweat out the toxic dump in my body."

"Alive is good. We're all happy about that," Bronwyn said.

They walked through the different exercises, Paolo showing him different push up variations. Francis watched with amusement. When they were finished, he confirmed that the physical activity wasn't the only part of the rehabilitation. They were working through a transcendental meditation sequence, concocting individualized herbal teas to target different organ systems, and rigorous journaling.

Mitchell rolled his eyes and came over to Avery as the others milled about the space and chatted.

"So, you wanna talk about what happened at all?" Avery asked, not knowing how to properly position himself in the thrum of activity.

"Whadya mean?"

"Like, you know, what happened that night," Avery said.

"It doesn't matter." Mitchell receded a bit.

"It does matter," Francis said from the other side of the room.

"I fucked up. That's what happened," Mitchell said, his words dropping with a heavy weight.

"Put some words together, then," Avery said.

They were all there to carry some of that weight. They were stronger as a group.

Unwilling at first, Mitchell slowly got to recounting how a year ago he had slipped back to the pills and the booze - it had happened, but it wouldn't happen again. During that night a big Lafayette kingpin had cornered him at a bar just inside the wall and made a proposition: move some product and he could get Mitchell a cache of old utility maps for the city. All he had to do was make runs between the OD and Lafayette, six trips to be exact. It was stupid. He did it anyway. He wanted those maps. But what he really wanted was the rush, the excitement of outsmarting the border guards.

On the last delivery, the Outer Domain dealer slipped him three little white pills as a thank-you - or an easy way to take care of a problem. And he couldn't throw them out, just couldn't do it.

Mitchell tugged on the base of his beard, leaned hard against the windowsill.

"You're not alone in this now," Addison said

"You got an army standing with you," Bronwyn stated, walking over and resting her hands on his neck. They held together with Mitchell and he apologized to each of them. Gradually, they all went back to the tasks they were more comfortable doing. Paolo found the leaking pipe and fixed it. Addison reattached two top buttons and fixed holes in every single shirt. Bronwyn organized his food stash and made sure he had enough water.

This still left Avery feeling out of place. He looked down at a stack of old newspapers. He scanned headlines from hundreds of years ago. A report of a shiny new model sports cross-over vehicle with adjustable hybrid technology, a review of a snazzy new restaurant serving free range beef, gossip of a pop starlet having an affair with a hip-hop artist. Mitchell came back around to Avery after talking a long while with Addison and Francis. He didn't smell of hospital this time and for that Avery was glad. It was easier to see him here in his element, with his people around him.

"How's it feel, Mr. Forerunner?" Mitchell asked.

"Weird as hell." It was Avery's turn to be red faced. "You try walking around knowing you have jet packs attached to your legs."

"Yeah, I don't see the problem with that."

"Fair point."

Mia pressed against Mitchell, wanting him to scratch her ears. It was actually starting to feel more normal, but there were still times when Avery felt like he was at the helm of a runaway train.

"Did they say anything to you at the hospital?" he asked.

"How do you mean?"

"People there, did they ask you questions."

"No."

"Good."

Avery swallowed. The elevator, Dr. Yun, the blue smoke.

"That's not true," he corrected.

"What?"

"There was one thing actually. I was with Addison and we ran into this doctor. He asked about how I felt. That's it, I guess."

"My sister, huh," Mitchell inspected Avery.

"She got me coffee. That's all."

"K...and a doctor asked about stuff."

"Yeah."

"K."

Chapter 24

A New Record Holder

Bronwyn packed just enough to fit in a single overstuffed bag. Avery helped her maximize what fit inside. *The art of rolling your underwear,* he called it.

A seat was reserved on the eastbound Blade leaving Lafayette Central Station at 6:00 PM.

Thick clouds blanketed the city. The housemates, minus Mitchell, all milled about in the front yard while Paolo checked every moving component on his bike. Bronwyn refused a ride to the station. So they made plans for him to fetch the ten-speed during his next material stop.

"You know mister, I've ridden a bike at least four million times," she chided while hefting the pack's waistband onto her hips.

"The breaks might be kinda sticky," Paolo said, smearing grease onto his pant leg.

"I'm sure I'll manage. Thanks lil' bro."

They embraced.

Bronwyn then grinned at Addison, "I got some of that shampoo you suggested. City girl's gotta survive somehow. Don't tell anyone."

Addison giggled; holding back tears, and pecked her on the cheek, "Secret's safe with me," she said.

Avery then tightened the strap on the top of her bag.

"See you around," she said squeezing him tight.

"You bet. Stay out of trouble, ok?"

Avery backed away with tightened lips. He had only been a part of this tribe for a short period. But losing one hit somewhere deep.

Bea, maintained a calm exterior and looked solidly at Bronwyn.

"Are you set?" she asked.

"Yep."

Bea inspected, as she always did.

"I'm all set. Good to go – promise," Bronwyn proclaimed.

"Ok. Be safe. Be strong."

"I'll miss you so much Bea."

They hugged tight. Bea whispered something in her ear. They had talked in private for a long while in her office that morning. An object of great value was packed tightly in the bottom of her bag.

Flow stood wrapping a hand on the bike seat.

"Remember to plant in a straight line on that mountain side. Ya filthy pirate hooker."

Bronwyn screwed up her face and sashayed across the lawn, "You should worry about that filthy mouth."

Flow stuck out her tongue then planted a big kiss on Bronwyn's cheek and relinquished the cycle for departure.

With that, she was on the bike and away. At the end of the driveway she swiveled around with a mischievous smile, "Ta ta!"

They all waved and expelled well wishes.

When she disappeared around the corner, each housemate peeled off into the house, Addison had a shift to start in a half hour and made for the streetcar. Their mood was melancholy with the departure of one of their own.

Bringing up the rear, Bea clutched Flow's arm tightly.

In a hushed tone, Flow asked, "How's she doing?"

"It takes time," Bea said in a contemplative timbre. "But she is handling the responsibility way better than yours truly at this stage."

"But dammit you were cute back then," Flow said proudly.

Bea yanked her arm in protest as she followed her into the bedroom for the night.

Chapter 25

A Long Brewed Storm

"Good morning Mister." Flow and Bea sat together on the back porch when Avery walked outside the next morning. Flow leaned back in her chair.

"Morning ladies," Avery said with a throaty voice. He walked out into the garden, picking the occasional weed and looked up at the morning sky. Heavy rain clouds lurked just over the treetops.

"When you get a chance, check the charge on the roadster?" Bea asked. "She hasn't been driven in ages - The keys are on my desk."

"Can I get them?" Avery felt compelled to ask. It was not a steadfast rule, but no one entered Bea's office without her permission.

"Of course," she said.

He walked back inside and pulled open one of the office doors, slipping inside. The keys sat on the neat desk. What he didn't know is that the Record Book was no longer in the house.

Back upstairs, he quickly dressed, scrubbed his teeth, and pulled on his running shoes. When he returned to the first floor, Bea and Flow were laughing together. He paused in the kitchen to observe. How they loved was how he wanted to love.

"I can wait on getting the car ready, " he said, poking his head out the door. Flow sighed with laughter lingering on her breath.

"Don't worry kiddo. I'll be ready soon." Bea replied.

He headed to the garage. The smell of stale oil and aged timbers always made him think of home. His fingers ran along the roadster's swooping fender. He searched for the hood release through an open window, finding a round knob and pulling with some effort until he heard a heavy thud.

Beneath the hood he found an immaculately preserved electric motor with chrome framing on each end. The wide cylinder of an engine ran into a transfer case, batteries held along a compact tray under the frame, and a simple bracket carried a small control computer.

With a tap, the computer came to life. The simple display showed two readings. *Oil Pressure: Green. Total Battery Life: 65%.* He eased the roadster out onto the driveway and Bea walked up.

"What do you think. Leave the top up?" Avery asked.

Bea looked toward the clouds threatening from the west, "Leave it up, my hair hates the rain."

They both climbed in. Avery was about to close his door when Mia jumped into his lap.

"I almost forgot," Avery said, feeling a touch of embarrassment.

"C'mon get in." Mia vaulted off his lap and landed in the narrow backseat, looking victorious.

They eased out onto the neighborhood. Then moved smoothly toward downtown as he gained control of the sensitive pedals. The Lafayette monitoring team marked their departure in detail.

About a mile down Woodward Avenue, they rolled to red light.

"Oh - turn here," Bea said, pointing across the windshield. Avery cranked into the turn lane as the streetcar bumbled passed. With a green light they found themselves crawling through a deserted industrial park with cracked asphalt parking lots.

"There's no stops along here," Bea said like a mischievous teenager. "It'll spit us out right by the island bridge. Give it some go."

Avery eased into the throttle, the engine responded instantly, and pulled through the first curve.

"You baby. Give it some power," Bea slapped his leg and rolled down the window.

He stepped on the accelerator, the gearbox adjusted slightly. They blasted along the wide-open road. 80 mph. 90 mph. 115 mph.

"There ya go," Bea said. With a hand resting on the open windowsill, she grinned at the rain scented air rushing against her face. Clouds of different blues started to mix together.

Avery respected the silence and concentrated on the road. The tight suspension kept them glued to the pavement. He used the wide road to cut broad arcs as they flew through the vacant industrial park. The speed felt similar to his own power, smooth and exhilarating.

Several large raindrops thumped on the windshield as they exited the industrial area and pulled between tall apartment buildings. Narrow slivers of the river poked between other mauve structures. He let the car coast to a stoplight. As if she was stepping back from her thoughts, Bea looked at him calmly.

"Turn left here. The bridge access road isn't far."

They turned onto the riverside avenue. Mia poked her head between the seats and licked Bea's shoulder.

"You come out here a lot?" Avery asked. He saw a sign for the island up ahead.

"Gosh, it's been awhile. Flow and I used to visit almost every weekend. Those were fun times. She was a little miffed at yours truly for not inviting her on this trip. But - business is business," she said.

Avery turned onto the bridge feeling anxious to test his abilities once more. A soldier stepped out of a narrow booth and motioned for them to stop.

"Under the visor is my pass," she said quietly.

Without a word, Avery handed him a small laminated card with a reflective green glyph in the corner. It was scanned and returned.

"You're all set," the soldier said.

The island, which Hubbard called Cabrio Isle, was almost three miles end to end and no more than a half-mile wide. The river front property had been subdivided many decades ago. Large parcels facing Lafayette were sold off to the wealthiest city patrons, with more modest lots along the opposite edges of the island. Shallow streams and narrow paths meandered through a densely forested center.

Bea and Flow's cottage sat on the modest side. A narrow road wrapped along the back of grand estates guarded by stone walls and elaborate gates. Gusts of wind blew against the car. The frustrated summer weather quarreled between blazing bursts of sunshine and sulking rainclouds.

After getting blown around for several meandering miles, Bea directed him onto a half hidden gravel driveway. A small, square cottage with grey timber siding and moss covered shingles sat behind a row of overgrown trees. The front door and two large windows faced a narrow patch of grass that sloped down to the river's edge.

The lot was sheltered from the turbulent weather, but the river chopped with white caps. Bea quickly excited the roadster and unlocked the front door. The inside was spare and stagnant. Just a simple sitting room, side tables covered in books, and a narrow cabinet. A small eating area with a narrow legged table and kitchen sat at the back. Off to the side was a hall leading to the bathroom and a single bedroom.

Avery was looking at a framed picture hanging on the wall. A younger Bea and Flow. They were sitting on the porch of the cottage, holding hands, Flow making a face.

"The water valve is under the sink in the kitchen. Be a gem and crank that thing open?" Bea asked.

Avery ducked under the counter and pried open the rust caked valve. He let the faucet run, clearing out orange water.

"Why is it, ah - never mind." Avery stopped. Mia was agitated and he felt it in his bones.

"So nice and quiet here, isn't it? " Bea said, washing her hands once the rust had cleared. They were shaking and he saw this. She scrubbed three extra times then put a teapot on the stove.

"The view out to the water sure is something," she said, regaining her composure.

"How are things at the Shoulder?" she asked.

"Quiet actually," Avery said tentatively. "Not a lot to do right now. And Jim's got things so locked down. I'm getting really good at mowing…Sorry, I shouldn't complain. I'm lucky to spend time there everyday."

Bea said, "Perhaps things will change soon." She walked into the sitting room and opened the cabinet. From inside she pulled out a heavy wood paneled radio with a single speaker and cluster of knobs on the front. Avery recognized it, Jasper had a similar machine in his kitchen. She carefully placed the radio on the table. Rain started tapping on the roof and windows.

"You think so?" Avery asked. "Feels like he's got something against me."

"Are your trees healthy?" Bea asked.

She returned to cabinet to retrieve one more item: A square tea box.

Avery pushed his hands into his pockets.

Bea glared at him as she did.

"Mostly. There's an unhappy tree over on the east side of the grove. If it were up to me, we would cut it down . But Jim insists that he has it under control. I dunno," Avery said.

"This concerns you," Bea observed.

"Yeah," Avery said, picturing the sickly tree standing next to the barn. He watched as Bea dusted the radio. First wiping clean the flat surfaces, then each of the many knobs. Her easy manner had returned.

"Water's about to boil," she said. And with that, the teapot began to whistle.

Avery returned to the narrow kitchen. "What's the radio for?" He asked, filling two mugs with steaming water.

"A rather important piece of machinery as a matter of fact."

"That thing?"

She then pulled open the tea box. The Argus Bureau branch-like emblem was inlaid in the wood.

"My uncle has one just like it." He scooted closer to the table.

"Yes he does."

She filled two strainers with loose green tea and plopped them into the mugs.

"It's how us Bureau members talk to each other."

Avery looked in disbelief.

Bea continued, "The Fenders monitor just about everything. Cell phones, email, travel. You name it and they have a Protocol officer assigned. But what they have completely forgotten about is the radio waves."

"So you just turn it on and talk to people?"

"Well, there are codes and such. Remember we are a secret society after all." She pulled a top rack out of the tea box to reveal a hidden compartment that contained notecards with specific numbers and call signals.

"And this one is now yours." She turned the box around and slid it across the table. Avery was flabbergasted. Every edge was perfectly beveled. The tops and sides were of varnished cherry and each knob was matte steel.

"Bea. I can't accept this. It's yours - for one. And two, I'm not qualified or anything."

"Remember what we talked about kiddo?"

"Yeah."

"Then this is more important to you then to some ol' hag on her way out," she said with a warm smile.

"What do you mean?"

Bea waved it off.

"Give it try."

Carefully, he pulled the machine closer and inspected the interface carefully.

"Power and scanning are on the right side."

The knobs turned with a heavy smoothness and the speaker soon crackled with static.

"Try the left three knobs to 3, 1, 3," Bea said.

Once the last knob rolled over, the static dropped and seemed to connect to another radio.

"This is Sparrow. Please confirm." He knew that voice.

Avery swallowed and scanned the instruments for non-existent information.

"This is Sparrow. Please confirm."

Bea slid over a card.

"Sparrow, this is Greyhound. Confirmation code is....616589."

There was a long pause.

"Avery? Avery is that you?"

"Jasper!" Avery exclaimed.

"How are you boy? Are you safe?" Jasper asked.

"Yeah, I'm good. Here in Lafayette, with Be-" Bea cut him off.

"Hi Sparrow, this is Westie," she said.

"It's been a long time," Jasper said.

"Yes, yes it has."

"If you'll excuse me, but I have someone that may want to talk to our newest code member." There was the creaking of a chair on the other side.

"Avery?" his mother's voice pulled the floor from under him.

"Mom, yeah it's me," he brushed the tear from his cheek.

Mia padded out of the room, he felt the strain in their connection.

"Oh honey. I've been worried sick and been emailing and bugging Quincy and sending letters. It's so good to hear from you."

"I'm doing good. Just been busy. But I'm good."

There was a pause.

"Avery, how are - "

Then there was a crack outside and the house exploded in a ball of flame. Wood shards and glass flew in every direction. The shock wave blew Avery into the kitchen. His head smashed into the plaster wall. Cabinets ripped from their mountings, landing on his chest, stealing the air from his lungs. Debris filled everything, or was that his vision just going blurry? His senses faded. There were rapid footsteps. He could not see, he could not move. He heard shuffling and muffled commands being called out.

"Secure her." he heard.

Smoke filled his lungs. He panicked. Footsteps now retreated through the debris. He fought to clear his mind - find some oxygen. His mind connected with Mia and energy rushed in. With two kicks, he was on his feet. He threw the remains of the kitchen clear as if it were a dollhouse.

Piles of burning timber covered the area where the front of the house had been. Rain now poured inside sizzling against fire.

"Bea!" Avery screamed. "Bea!" He pushed the remains of the table out of the way. Nothing. Then he heard the helicopters. Vaulting the house in one bond, he landed violently. In stride he was through the vegetation. Two tactical copters were already airborne and gaining speed. He blitzed forward, calling up every ounce of everything in his body. Mia followed three steps behind. They caught up to the second machine and he flung himself into the air, cutting against the violent torrent of air and smashing both fists into the side panel.

The helicopter veered to the side as he dropped back to the road. Without built up speed he couldn't reach the altitude for a second attack. After righting its course, the pilot rotated to strafe the Forerunner. A line of bullets spat from an open hatch, tearing through pavement at his toes. He dove for cover, Mia bounding for the other side of the road. The helicopter hovered and the gunman aimed into the brush, mowing a line of fire across Avery's shoulder. He pressed to the earth, not daring to look up.

Abruptly, the gunfire stopped and the helicopter blades changed timber and faded quickly. He searched for the connection with Mia for a beat and propelled himself back to the road. He'd punch every bullet out of the air; rip the blades one by one from their sprockets. The helicopter was gone.

He flew, throttle wide open. Ignoring bends, fences, anything in his path. When he reached the tip of the island, there was only rain lashing on stormy water. She was gone.

Avery collapsed to his knees.

"No."

"No, no."

Tears streamed down his trembling face.

"No. I'm sorry."

He closed his eyes, wanting to rewind the clock.

Mia stood guard, rain drenched, ears held against her head. The pain in her eyes was indescribable. For several long minutes, he knelt there. Rain insulting his face, waves beat against the low, rocky shore.

He then called Paolo.

Avery struggled to make words come out of his mouth, "Come out to the island," he said.

"Was' that?" Paolo asked.

"Just come out to the island. Something's happened," Avery choked out.

"A. What's goin' on man?" Paolo asked again.

"Damnit, just get here! Bea's gone!" he screamed.

The line went dead.

Avery stumbled back to the house. He found the radio smashed into bits. The tea box charred, but intact. Bea was gone. He collapsed against the trunk of a tall pine tree. Rage flickered in his mind. He was responsible.

Section 3

The Exposed Nest.

Chapter 26

We Stick Together

Paolo's truck peeled into the gravel driveway and skidded into deep ruts. He ran to the smoldering house and then charged at Avery, slamming him hard against a tree with both arms.

"What hell happened?" Paolo hissed. He crushed Avery against the jagged bark, breaking the skin and causing bloody streaks.

"Answer me!" Paolo's eyes were two inches away from his face, "Some sort of set up. You filthy piece of trash."

The bark dug deeper.

Mia whimpered behind them. Energy built up in Avery's arms. He let it drain away. Leaving himself exposed to the pain.

"Talk, you coward," Paolo demanded.

"We were sitting inside. On the radio. And then the house just exploded. I chased them." Avery struggled to breath under Paolo's force, "But..."

Paolo threw Avery to the ground. Mud sloshing across his face.

Seething, Paolo knelt near the front of the debris. His hand pressed against the mud, eyes tracking around the wreckage before marching back to Avery who was standing up.

"What did you see?" Paolo asked right up in Avery's face.

"The explosion knocked me out," Avery said in half panic, half despair. "I heard foot steps. Then voices. By the time I got out from under the rubble, they were back into the helicopters." He looked down at his bloodied knuckles. "I couldn't stop them. I tried....I tried."

Paolo picked up a shard of the destroyed radio. It made Avery's mind rush to Woodway and the panic his family must be enduring.

"Thought you were a Forerunner." he said, throwing the piece into the flames. "They came for her. What for?"

Inappropriately sunlight slowly replaced the rain. For Avery, the next several hours faded into a blur. Mitchell showed up for a short period. And somehow they all made it home. If he drove, or how he got there he could not recall.

When they returned, he walked immediately into the garden holding the surviving tea box. The rain had simply materialized into an oppressive humidity. He moved through the syrupy air, still only vaguely aware of his surroundings and how he his legs were working.

Flow sat between rows of tomato plants, facing away from the house and away from him. Her wide brimmed hat drooped over her shoulders. The garden hose was abandoned on the ground. Water streamed silently out into a now flooded patch, mulch floating in the pool.

He sat down behind Flow in her garden row. The weight of his heart almost too much to bare, but his mind demanded that he show himself to her. Expose himself, unguarded to the reality. The hose gurgled and soaked Avery's pant legs.

"She called them Perfect Times," Flow said eventually, not moving or looking over.

Any tone was inappropriate, but he tried to channel the calm, deep tone of his uncle, "What's that?" he asked.

"Beatrice. She called them Perfect Times." Flow turned her head. He could see just the tip of her nose.

"They were just little moments between us. When we were moving in symphony. Simple things. When I forgot my keys and she came up behind me and slipped them in my pocket. Or a favorite song came on the radio when the temperature was just right to have the windows open and we would dance together." Flow stopped.

Avery felt her recalling those moments, like someone looking through old photographs.

"And she kept a list of them. This little notebook with a pink leather cover." Flow reached out her hand and rolled a leaf between her fingers.

"Perfect Times. Like the poetry of our lives. She would always say." Flow's hand dropped, "We had one this morning. She made breakfast and it was finished right as I was done reading the paper. We talked about some old friends and drank coffee that was just the right temperature. It was a splendid little time together. She wrote it down before you left." Her voice wavered, "And she kissed me ever so softly before she left. The kind that makes your back tingle."

Avery could not think of any words. So he just sat with Flow. He kinked the hose and sat next to her. Sometimes that's all we can do, just be there physically for someone.

Flow straightened after a while. Her shoulder rolled back, she cleared her throat, and pushed to her feet. Avery jumped up. Flow pulled off her hat, face like stone, and grabbed the tea box.

"Not your fault Keeper. This was a long time coming."

With that, she walked into the house.

Not knowing what to do, Avery turned off the hose and coiled it near the shed door. He realized that Mia was laying, head on paws, on the back porch. Her eyes followed him with the same sadness that he had seen this morning.

She followed him into the kitchen. The air felt cooler inside. On the table sat his phone. How it had ended up there, he was not sure. When he turned on the screen, he found ten missed calls from Addison and numerous text messages. The last reading: *I'm coming over, don't go anywhere.* Four new Linkerage requests insultingly blinked for his approval.

Less than a minute later, Addison rounded the house.

"I've been calling you for hours!" she sobbed.

Avery held up his phone, "I just saw."

She wrapped her arms around him. He felt a biting urge to just disappear and remove the burden he had become.

"What happened?" she asked, her cheek pressed against his chest.

"Someone attacked us." The words pushed out tears that he desperately tried to hold back. "It's all my fault. None of this would have happened if I weren't here. I should have saved her."

Addison pulled away slightly, seeming to sense something of tremendous power surging under the surface.

"Flow will know what to do next. Just stay here," she said, reaching for his hand, calming him.

Mitchell's Jeep soon crashed into the driveway. He bustled passed, clutching a stack of loose papers to his chest.

"Oh, so this is a thing," he flat panned and marched inside.

Avery released her in embarrassment. She blushed and scowled at her brother. The door slammed closed.

"He can be such a jackass," she said. The space between them persisted. "But, I have to go to work."

"K."

"Be safe."

"I will."

She unexpectedly placed a light kiss on his cheek. Then she climbed on her bike and pedaled away with a wave. Avery stayed put at the back door. Flow and Mitchell argued boisterously inside. Counteracting emotions swirled through his insides. He needed a second, a few breaths, maybe an escape hatch of some kind.

Paolo returned to the house in similarly violent fashion. His truck slammed into the driveway. He rushed through the door, ignoring Avery. Less than a moment later, Flow stuck out her head

"Come inside."

She pulled a chair away from the table. The script A that had been stenciled into the back panel was been intricately carved into the wood.

"In this house. We stick together," she said and squeezed him around the middle, "And we need you in here."

And in the kitchen, under dim light, hunched over maps and an old laptop, they made plans.

* * * * * *

  Perched in the surrounding trees and crouched by windows across the street, the monitoring team recorded these movements. The arrival of a new face and the frenzied commotion of vehicles triggered a direct report to their commanding office. The message never reached him.

Chapter 27

Across the City

Flow and Paolo trundled through snarled thicket blocks that flirted with the north city limits. The sunken highway that formed the city's North edge was a treacherous place. Heaps of debris and busted bridges cluttered the border, and a free-for-all of scrappers, illegal border hoppers, and border patrol officers roamed freely. Paolo first demanded that Flow stay safe at the house. But she flatly refused, climbing into the truck, arguing that he could cover more ground with her help. And she was right.

Through the mess of vegetation, a low concrete wall running along highway's rim came into view. They proceeded carefully into the open.

"It's just up here. Go slow," Flow said. The morning sun radiated off the hard surfaces and scorched the truck cabin. Only two bridges still reached across the man made channel. They were coming up on Bridge B. It was strangely empty. Rows of jagged metal barriers sat haphazardly across the span. No guards visible.

Paolo made a sweeping turn at the base of the bridge to point the truck outward then jumped out and proceeded to the guard station. Empty. He stepped over to the barricades and looked down at the ribbon of squalor below. Nothing. It was an unsettling scene, border security was of absolute importance to the Fenders.

Paolo returned to the guard station and pushed open the door. On a narrow desk he found a tablet manifest. The last recorded departure:

```
14:37 - 3 TA VEHICLES - DEPARTURE FOR TAC.
NORTH \\ CONFIRMATION CODE: DIAMOND
```

He returned to the truck.

"Weird," he said. They wheeled back onto the access lane and headed east, "I don't like this."

The evening prior, the house had laid out plans to put their tribe back together. A quiet search plan meant to cover as many of the secreted corners of Lafayette, the places of Hubbard, without drawing suspicion. They hoped.

Paolo had helped reinforce some of failing walls along the highway, he knew the command officers well. This was their angle, but they did not expect to find nothing.

Two miles down from Bridge B, a service tunnel ran up to the sunken highway and connected to abandoned sewer lines beyond the city limits. The bulkhead had been sealed to keep out flooding, but last Mitchell had heard - bandits had busted it open. This was their second stop.

They covered the distance with no signs of anyone, soldier or civilian, and navigated down a narrow entrance ramp tapering to the roadway below. They were more than twenty feet down. A skeleton of concrete piers and tangled web of iron girders stuck out from the wall. Remnants of a bygone age were piled on the road. The hatch they were looking for was a thick metal panel depressed into the far wall. Leaving the truck idling, they both got out to investigate. Signs of a crowbar marked the lip of the hatch. Paolo tapped, tested, pulled and turned, but it obviously hadn't been opened in ages. Flow checked the surrounding piles of debris.

As they searched cautiously, the whir of a drone invaded their position. The four-rotor machine surged over the wall. Sun glinted off a gun package mounted to the undercarriage.

"Get down!" Paolo yelled, propelling himself over the truck. A rotary of gun exploded. Paolo pulled Flow to the ground as bullets pinged off a charred car frame. They skidded to a stop on the gritty pavement.

"What the?" Flow stammered.

"You ok?" he asked.

"I'm fine!"

"You sure."

"Just do something," Flow said. She was without her key. The tortoise sat in the glove compartment of the truck.

Paolo shifted his weight onto his arms, covering Flow. His systems churned in overdrive. What the hell had they been thinking? He snapped up to check the surroundings. Another round of bullets ran through the pile of concrete overhead. Not good, not good.

The drone's meddlesome scanning grew louder. Paolo pushed around to the front fender, keeping metal in between them and danger.

The distance to the truck was impossible. And a large pile of tires blocked any escape in the other direction. They were pinned. He whispered a prayer under his breath. Without access to her powers, which Paolo knew were formidable, Flow was frozen with fear. Adjustments to propulsion sounded off the high walls as the deadly machine glided closer.

"Not good." Flow slunk below the frame.

The drone swept above of the car, overshooting by just a foot. It was enough. Paolo drove upward with all his force. He grabbed ahold of the gun housing and swung downward with astonishing force.

The drone smashed into pavement. He pounced, ripping the red-hot weaponry from the frame. Sparks flew from entangled wiring. He pulled off a propeller as it attempted to spin to full power. Dust stung his eyes.

A small panel flipped open, shooting out a short antenna. He clasped both fists overhead and beat down on the top of the enclosure. The lightweight frame crumpled under the power of his fists. Circuit boards busted and sprung from their housings, the propellers stopped. He flung the decrepit frame against the wall, fracturing it into pieces.

He returned to find Flow wedged near the wheel well. He scooped her up and made for the truck. Just as they reached the cover of the thicket blocks, another pair of drones flew across the site, dropping high explosives and sending the section of sunken highway into a ball of flame. What went unnoticed were the wisps of white smoke trailing from Paolo's arms and shoulders.

From the echo of a tall corridor, Mitchell, Avery and Mia exited the Lafayette Art Institute. The museum had been Mitchell's first guess as to where Hubbard would hold Bea. He had bribed their way in. Slipping a role of cash to a shadowy character posted at the rear load docking, nose stuck on a phone screen. The museum was supposed to be a safe holding place in Lafayette, even for those with a diamond on their lapel. But no well-dressed soldiers appeared to be stationed there.

Beyond the grand entrance hall and galleries depicting a victorious Chancellery, the art museum was a labyrinth of shadowy halls and converted galleries. They had swept through the complex of tall galleries shrouded in half light. Mitchell kept tabs on their progress in a shabby spiral bound. Avery searched the high and far flung spaces. All they found were room filled with weapons stockpiles, others only containing ruined art still hanging from the walls.

As they exited down the decaying loading dock stairs, the watchman, looking more bug eyed, held a phone to his ear.

"Get in," Mitchell urged.

Avery could move faster than the Jeep. All he needed was to flick an internal switch and he was gone. But they were a team, and that was more important. A map with several hand written marks, sat on their dash. Mitchell didn't really need them; he knew where they were going. They weaved, fast and loose, across the city.

"Where're we headed?" Avery asked. He kept a watchful eye on the rearview mirror and the sky.

"Police station."

"What, we're just gonna stroll in and ask?"

At speed, Mitchell cranked hard.

"Yes."

Avery concentrated on his breathing, pushing back on the weight of sleeplessness that tried to consume him. His paperwork was tucked in his breast pocket. Though if they got stopped, he didn't think checking their papers would be their first concern. Mia seemed wonderfully entertained in the back seat. Her tongue wagged freely.

They crossed into a small patch of half occupied blocks, then down a slender alley. Collapsing garages and overturned dumpsters lined a corridor just wide enough for the Jeep. Mitchell did not reduce his speed. Branches scraped the doors and snapped in their faces. What a stupid idea, Avery thought.

"You've been here before?" he asked.

No response.

The alley opened to a castle-like structure folded against a wide intersection. A vaulted entrance opened up to the back, with turrets and spires at the corners and arched windows on the second floor.

"What is this place?" Avery asked.

"Precinct Number Eight." Mitchell responded. "Grab the stuff in there." He pointed to the glove box.

Avery pulled open the glove box to find three plastic bags tightly wrapped around white powder. No, this wasn't what they were doing.

"It's not for me."

Avery's hands stayed put.

"It's to get us in the door."

"What about cash."

"It won't work."

"Why not?"

"Because it just won't. Ok? Now give me damn bags and let's go find Bea."

With the powder-filled bags tucked in his palm and Avery following cautiously, they approached the rear entrance. After several long moments, the doors swung open onto a velvet-covered lobby. They stepped inside. A spiral stair curved up through the middle of the room and fat men sat in overstuffed furniture and puffing thick cigars.

"Mr. Quelhurst," a voice called from a side room mostly enclosed with thick curtains.

"Stay here," Mitchell whispered.

Here with these guys? Remember your powers, you idiot.

Mitchell entered the curtained room. While he was inside, two Lafayette soldiers arrived at the back entrance. When the door opened, the blaze of hot sun temporarily blinded Avery. They inspected the room, nodding to one of the fat men and then marched into the space where Mitchell had just joined the voice.

It didn't add up. Police precinct? My ass. The energy in his gut swelled. His arms tingled. Mia repositioned herself at his far side - her demeanor now razor sharp. At the count of ten they were joining the conversation. Mischievously laughter came from the room that seemed to be getting smaller. Was that movement on the stairs? Where would Mitchell be standing? He hadn't gotten a good look at the soldiers' collars. They could be Lancers.

At the count of nine and eleven fifteenths, he took a determined step forward only to be brushed aside by the soldiers charging out. Again they scanned the room and departed. Mitchell followed shortly after.

"Go upstairs, check all the rooms," Mitchell said and disappeared down a dim corridor.

"Yep, ok. I'll do that," Avery said. He marched up the stairs, diverting any eye contact with his fellow guests. Upstairs was more spartan. Rough wood covered the floor, simple lights hung from walls of peeling wall paper. There were five doors, all closed. The first two were empty apart from a trashcan and broomstick. In the third, he then found a man counting money under the light of a single desk lamp.

"Excuse me, but have you seen an silver haired lady around lately?" he asked. The man shook his head side to side very slowly.

"Thanks." Avery closed the door and kept moving. The next was filled with cell phones of various makes and sizes stacked neatly on three tables, but no one inside. The final door opened to a luxurious bedroom built inside one of the round corner turrets. Candles flickered, jazz music danced from a cylindrical speaker.

"Scott is that you?" a voice called.

A woman wearing no more than a towel over her shoulders stepped out of the bathroom. Her artificial proportions and bright blonde hair was familiar.

"Avery?" Crystal asked.

"Hi."

"You know my boyfri -, my friend Scott?" She didn't seem bashful of her mostly nakedness.

"I ah, no." Avery tried to scan the room without looking directly at her bare skin.

"Ok...."

"Any pleasant old ladies hanging out with you up here?" Avery asked. Mia nosed him in the knee.

"Nooo, not that I know of."

"Ok, that's great. Have a good day." He went to close the door.

"Avery." He paused.

"Yeah?"

Her arms were crossed now.

"Have you looked in the natatorium?"

"The where?" he asked. Nipples were visible, this was a challenge.

"The city pool. Just a suggestion."

"Got it. Thanks Crystal."

The door slammed harder than he wanted. He ran downstairs. Mitchell waited on the last step.

"Nothing," Avery said.

"No dice in the basement. Let's go."

They were back in the Jeep and reversing back up the alley in no time.

"Hey, I saw someone I knew upstairs."

"A, I don't wanna know, I really don't," Mitchell ducked from an errant branch.

"No, not like that."

"Then, speak."

"She asked if we had checked the natatorium."

Mitchell slammed on the brakes.

"She said what?"

"Crystal, she was one of my Pre Loads. Asked if we had looked in the...city pool. I dunno what that means. But it's what she said. Also her boobs were perfect circles."

"I should have thought of that," Mitchell muttered. They careened out of the alley and were on their way.

A looping route took them north past a lone, gritty tower. Avery took in the massive structure from the open roof of the Jeep.

"Don't look too close," Mitchell joked as they veered past a sign reading *Protocol Center*.

Several exits beyond they peeled onto a steep exit ramp and slammed to a stop an open lot. Set far back from the road, a broad rectangle of a building squatted almost out of sight. It was plain, with tall windows along the front. A thick tangle of vines clung to the outside. At the center of the building, double doors crested with an ancient looking symbol of a seated man, balancing objects in outstretched hands. Mitchell simply pushed them open.

"That easy?" Avery asked.

"This city is weird," Mitchell stated.

A shallow entry court opened into an unlit natatorium. The glassy pool deck was lined with white tiles. A scent of dust and chlorine lingered. Mitchell paused for a beat. Avery felt it too - a strange and sinister energy. Sick and desperate. They circled the pool with cautious steps, Mia's nails clicked on the tile. Mitchell led them to a chlorine eaten door. It screeched open to reveal stairs dropping into a shadow-draped dungeon of a place.

They made it to the last step before seeing the soldiers, three of them. A pair advanced. Standard issue: tall and angular and wielding batons. The third held back. He was fresh faced, too young for the double stripes of a Lancer on his collar.

"Stand down citizen," The first duo commanded. From his back pocket, Mitchell flipped open a narrow blade.

"No need for that chief," Avery said.

He sprinted past, catching the first baton strike, twisting and flipping the soldier to his back. The second soldier landed a blow to Avery's flank. With another yank, Avery was yielding the fallen soldiers blunt weapon. Faster than either soldier could react. He bludgeoned both in the stomach and knocked them out cold with a blow each to the head.

"Show off," Mitchell muttered.

The young Lancer then sprang into action, disappearing for a flash then reappearing right before landing a blow on Avery's jaw. Avery's jaw stung, but he was only stunned. He followed only a step behind. The Lancer dissolved again, then materialized to kick behind Avery's right knee. This sent him crashing into a freakish kitchen. Stainless steel contraptions clanged as he fumbled to a stop.

Toward Mitchell, the Lancer commanded, "Stay where you are."

Mia barked defiantly.

"Alright, alright," Mitchell said.

Avery grabbed a pot and swung blindly over his shoulder. He missed the kid Lancer but gave himself an opening to push back into the action. He charged, then noticing a bloodied prisoner chained to the wall. Was he the only one here?

In a flash the Lancer attacked again and vanished. He had only struck from the right, Avery noticed. He was too new with his powers. Avery lunged at empty space in which the soldier then appeared. They collided into the wall. The Lancer's strength could not match a Keeper and a Forerunner.

"You don't have to do this," Avery said, grabbing fist fulls of the Lancer's uniform.

Terror flickered across the young Lancer's face. He tried to compose himself in the rigid soldier way.

"Attacking a Lafayette soldier is a Protocol Infraction punishable by death." His voice hadn't even dropped yet.

Avery smashed his head against the stone wall. Knocked out cold, the boy folded to the floor. Even if it was necessary, it still felt wrong to use his powers this way. They were companions in more ways than they were different. Mitchell unceremoniously tied the three soldiers hands together with an extension cord.

"You good?" he asked Mitchell.

"Bea's not down here. But I'm fine," Mitchell responded and nodded over to the wall.

The prisoner hung limply from arm chains, seemingly unconscious. Dried blood covered swollen cheeks. Avery crouched down and touched the prisoner's shoulder. The man convulsed violently.

"Who? Wha?"

"Shhh, shh shh," Avery calmed.

"Huh?" His eyes barely open.

"What's your name?"

"Hen, heen," his voice rasped like desert sand. The features of a wide and kind man who had helped him at the Lafayette gates and The Tower clicked in Avery's memory. Henry.

At the end of the corridor, Avery found a sink and some filthy dishes. He returned and raised a cup of water to the prisoner's lips, who gulped with fatal urgency.

"Henry. I don't know if you remember, but we came into Lafayette together. Back in June."

Henry looked at Avery very cautiously, "Motorcycle." His energy faded in and out. "Is this some sort of trick?" he asked.

Avery steadied him with a hand.

"Where did you come from?" Avery asked.

Tears sat so close to the surface, "I didn't do anything wrong. I promise. I don't know anything"

"I know you didn't," Avery said.

"Garfield," Henry's head sagged. "I'm a data analyst from The City of Garfield. I don't know anything about any Ables. I promise."

He was thinking of the Ambassador flags he had seen some many times from The Shoulder.

Avery stepped back to Mitchell who was positioned at the stairs.

"We gotta help him," Avery said. He was thinking of the Ambassador flags he had seen some many times from The Shoulder.

Mitchell looked over at Henry, then up the stairs, then to his watch.

"This is not our problem."

"It is now," Avery said.

"This city is filled with shit, Mr. Forerunner."

"Just help me get him to the Ambassador's house. Then it stops being our problem."

"The Ambassador of what?"

"Garfield."

"Are you crazy?"

Avery put a clenched fist over his heart, said no more. Mitchell scanned the scene, his face locked in a conflicted frown.

"Ok," he conceded.

Channeling his power, he pulled the chains straight from their moorings. Dust scattered on the floor. Mitchell walked over, handed him a hacksaw. He didn't want to think about its previous uses, but it took care of the chains. All that remained were the shackles. The soldiers started to stir. They needed to move.

Henry was too stiff to move on his own. Avery cautiously raised him to his shoulder and they climbed out of the chamber without looking back. Dusk had arrived.

They weaved cautiously across the spine of downtown, slowly working toward the river. Henry, barely conscious, huddled low in the back seat. Luckily they passed no patrols.

When the Ambassador flags came into view, Mitchell slowed. Topped with an orange banner, the first compound was surrounded by an impressive wall. However, the front gate sat ajar and looked onto an unkempt lawn. Avery carried Henry like he would carry a sack of potatoes. Mia dipped her nose to the ground and circled.

He knocked twice and waited. Helicopter noise rose in the distance. Energy trembled between he and Mia. Henry raised a heavy hand and touched his cheek as if to see if he was still alive.

Avery knocked twice more.

"Alright!" A voice boomed from inside.

The door swung open violently.

"What the fuck."

The Ambassador stood tall, with a thick beard, piercing eyes.

"He needs your help," Avery said, looking down at the wounded man in his arms. "He's from Garfield."

"I know who he is," the Ambassador snapped.

Henry turned his head painfully with a half moan, half smile.

"Where did you find him?" the Ambassador asked.

Avery hesitated.

"Can you help him?" he asked again.

The Ambassador looked passed Avery, seeing the Jeep just outside.

"Bring him in."

They walked into a tall parlor room. A long sofa sat below a picture window. Appearing near the back was the crazy attendant who had checked Avery's passport when he first arrived in Lafayette.

"Here." The Garfield Ambassador pointed.

Avery laid Henry down with care.

"Now you need to get out of here."

Avery looked right into him now. He was not afraid.

"Go, now," said the Ambassador. The attendant moved forward a few steps. He pointed to the door with a nod

Henry pulled a thumbs up and mouthed, "Thank you."

At the front of the house, Avery took some extra seconds closing the door. His ears perked, mirroring Mia. In that lingering moment, he could hear rushing feet and a door slamming.

"Jesus. What happened? Who did this?" asked the Ambassador. "Get the bandages from the upstairs bathroom," he yelled.

Henry was safe.

With that, Avery eased the door closed. A sludge of sorrow and guilt had been cleansed in some way. But the night was uneasy. The sounds of aerial vehicles were all around.

"One more place to check tonight. You game?" Mitchell asked when he returned to the Jeep.

"Let's go" he said confidently.

They pulled away from the compound. The Shoulder drew closer, her calm darkness looked out as they drove along the fence. Avery maintained a forced mental distance until they approached the west gate. The gate that was never opened. But in this strange hour, on this strange evening, it sat glaringly ajar.

"Hold up," he said. He was standing on the seat when the Jeep came to a stop.

"That's not good," Mitchell said.

Avery listened. He scanned. His jaw tightened.

"Something's not right," he sat back down gradually. "It's gonna have to wait until tomorrow."

"You're kidding, right?" asked Mitchell.

"You said one more spot. I'm not leaving the search."

"This is your grove, you gotta do your thing. I'll be fine. Lone wolf, that's how I roll anyway."

Avery felt like he had been hit with a fire hose. He sat, torn. His mind raced, jumping to the blast, the fire, then back home to his mother and Jasper. He opened the Jeep door.

Chapter 28

Queen

Avery stepped from the chaos of the city into the strange silence of his grove. Mitchell revved the engine, then sped away. Avery's heart pulsated in his temples with Mia guarding rigidly as he pushed and latched the gates. They swiftly moved toward the station, around Susan B. Anthony and arching toward the station.

"Are you fucking kidding me!" Jim exhaled. The station door slammed open. His eyes were red and the skin on his face blotchy. He marched into the grove. Avery pressed against a Sentinel trunk while Mia crouched in the underbrush.

When Jim disappeared he sped to the station. The only sound inside was a keyboard.

"Wallace?" he asked at the open door.

"Avery?"

With two long strides he was inside. Several of the desk chairs were flipped on the floor. Wallace looked bedraggled. There were hand print stains on his shirt where it looked like someone had grabbed him.

"What's goin' on?" Avery asked.

"There's been an incident."

"What are you talking about?"

"The barn."

"What do you mean the barn? I thought that was just harvesting equipment."

Wallace shook his head. He rolled back to his computer. Avery was right behind. Wallace zoomed into northeast quadrant. Tree 327 blinked orange, then red, then orange. Two alerts scrolled across the of the screen:

CRITICAL SENTINEL DAMAGE DETECTED - CODE 12
FENCE BREACHED - CODE 32.4

"I discovered it late last night," Wallace said, "The monitoring system pushes critical notifications to my phone. Sometimes there are false alarms. I check 'em out anyway. The northern gate was breached too. This was no false alarm. I called Jim, but he was already here..." Wallace hesitated, "He's frickin' deranged. I couldn't even get him to talk to me."

"Wallace. What's in that barn?" Avery asked calmly.

"He's never let me inside. I haven't had a chance to analyze the damage data." His eyes zig zagging around the screen.

Wallace looked clutched by internal conflict, and kept silent. Avery had no time for this, he needed to get to the barn.

He sprinted out of the station, flew up the central drive, then cut into the grove at an angle. Bounding through the tall grass, he dialed up his power with Mia right beside him. When he neared the barn a stench hit him like a wall. Doors rattled on their hinges with puffs of dust.

"No! No! No!" Jim's voice, but distorted and fraudulent.

Avery rushed around the side of the barn. The smell physically drove him back. Jim paced back and forth in the underbrush. His pants now smeared with blood. The barn seethed and shook.

"Jim," Avery called and continued to circle wide, keeping both the barn and Jim in his sight. Mia held back anxiously.

Jim looked over. It was like he was looking straight through Avery. The muscles in his arms tensed.

"Jim," Avery repeated as he shifted several more steps. "Talk to me." He broke his direct focus and scanned the Shoulder. There was something unsound happening in the air.

Then quick footsteps - Jim charged, leading with his head. Avery spun and back paddled. Jim careened past and out of the clearing. He sputtered to a stop before facing Avery who was now had the barn to his back.

"Yooouuu. You did this," he said with a bloody voice. "It was you."

"Jim you gotta tell me what happened. We're Keepers, we can fix this." Avery held out his hands.

CRITICAL SENTINEL DAMAGE DETECTED - CODE 12 blinked in his bead.

"You told Hubbard she was here." Jim stumbled into a tree trunk. "It was you," he said again.

"Told him what?"

"Don't play dumb with me kid. I know your story! You would have been killed if it were up to me! My hands were tied. And now looked at this. Ruined!"

"What are you talking about? Who's SHE?" Avery asked.

"The QUEEN! She was my ticket. You filthy coward!"

Jim lowered his head and charged again. Avery stepped away easily, shifting his weight and droving Jim into the barn wall. Several of the thin boards cracked under his weight. A screech that chilled Avery's soul expelled from the barn. The walls shook.

"You'll pay for this." Jim didn't looked up, just stayed hunched in the dirt.

"We have to fix this," Avery said looking down at his boss.

"There is no fixing this," Jim growled.

Avery noticed his arms tense again. Jim's bloodied fingers dug into the dirt. Avery stepped back. Jim reared up, swinging both fists wildly. He seemed possessed, out of his own body.

Jim then froze and cocked his head to the side. Helicopters. He ran. Jim disappeared toward the western edge of the grove and Avery followed closely. There was no way Jim could outrun him, but the alarms again jumped into his mind. Keeper, first. He turned back to the clearing.

As he arrived, a tactical helicopter cut over the clearing. Branches pushed away from the clapping rotors. Avery whistled to Mia and they catapulted behind the nearest tree. He peaked around the massive trunk to face the clearing.

A team of soldiers and a taller, skinny, Lancer fast-roped into the grove. They wore lightweight armor and grey helmets. The soldiers carried compact assault rifles and moved in expert formation – their sole focus was the barn. The Lancer held back, moving coyly away from the action.

A larger soldier placed explosive charges against one of the barn walls. Precision blasts vaporized nearly half of the structure. Out of the dust charged the vilest creature Avery had ever seen. Scale-like black feathers covered a massive black bird. Her wings opened high, more than twenty feet across, chest as wide as two men. Matte black eyes moved mechanically with pulses of deep red. Thick yellow liquid dripped from her claws.

She lunged at one of the soldiers, snapping his spine in a single bite. The remainder of the assault team retreated to a safe distance. The creature spat out her victim and lunged to the limit of the coil of chains.

"Hold your fire!"

"Hold your fire!" they yelled.

Now the Lancer approached, holding both hands out calmly. Two more soldiers readied an acetylene torch strapped on a shoulder harness.

Citing strange noises, the Lancer drew near to the queen Jaron. This seemed to calm her. She clicked her beak as if controlled by a rusty gear set, but settled into a submissive stance. The assault team held their ground, keeping their weapons trained on this freak thing. The Lancer soon gave a signal, and the two soldiers advanced cautiously. Sparks flew as they cut through the chain. She screamed like a jet engine crashing into an organ. Avery covered his ears in pain.

One chain link gave way, then a second. The queen crouched down low and then took flight with another deafening call. She wobbled at the tree line, talons snagging on high branches, then swooping toward The Tower. After she had gone, the helicopter returned. With the clearing awash, the team applied a blue liquid across the barn remains and collected their fallen comrade. They then banded together under the helicopter. Thin wires shot from their shoulder packs and drew them up to an open compartment. When the last soldier closed the hatch, the helicopter climbed and a strange beam of piercing light expelled from the nose. When it touched the blue liquid, the barn ignited. Flames lapped as the craft turned skyward.

The dry wood burned in aggressive fits, snapping and coughing into the evening sky. The heat pressed to Avery's face. In short order, the roof collapsed, carrying three of the walls with it. The plume of ash and sparks belched higher. Mia shifted uncomfortably with the invasion of that putrid smell.

Avery could do nothing about the raging fire and moved cautiously for the path, cutting back to the main drive where he saw Jim's bloodied shirt strewn on the ground.

"Jim?" He called out into the open. "You there?"

They continued to the western gate, which was again thrown open. The grove gave off an uncalm aura. The stench of the queen lingered in his nose. He again, closed and locked the gate and returned to the station.

As Avery raced into the office, Walled kicked at a narrow door in the hallway.

"What's happening?" Avery asked.

"A much bigger problem." Wallace said.

```
CRITICAL PATHOGEN DETECTED
CONDITION - CODE T-07-X - QUARANTINE ADVISED
```

Chapter 29

DR 60

"A virus has completely overtaken tree 327," Wallace said, coming back into the room carrying a large bag and a sledgehammer. Avery saw Drop Spikes. Narrow carbon fiber tubes filled with a lethal set of chemicals separated by a thick plastic tab in middle. Driven into a trunk, they could kill the healthiest Sentinel. He had never before used them.

"The monitor on 327 threw a pathogen code. Surrounding Oaks are showing stress, but none have pushed a positive reading yet...Where's Jim?"

"I don't know," Avery said, his mind reeling.

"You don't know?" Wallace asked.

"He attacked me and then ran off. As far as I know he's gone. Then a group of soldiers dropped in and busted some fucking monster out of the barn. Jim called it the Queen. You know about that?" Avery squinted.

"Soldiers here? In the Shoulder?" Wallace asked.

Avery nodded as he surveyed the equipment in an effort to dissipate his anger. How had Wallace let this happen? How could he? No matter the circumstance of the Jaron's presence in the Shoulder, a quarantine demanded full attention from them both. They had a perilous fight ahead.

"Hubbard's men don't come here," Wallace said.

"Well I saw it with my own eyes. And they burned down the barn on the way out. What do you think is causing this?" Avery asked. He thought of the yellow goo that dripped from the queen's talons.

Avery scanned a book that that lay open on Jim's desk.

"Do we know that this is the virus?" He asked.

"Whatever it is, there was some connection between the tree and the queen. It weakened her until she was free."

"That means the tree's been infected for years," Avery said while he continued rapidly grabbing sentence fragments at the beginning and end of each paragraph.

The computer started emitting various warnings.

Avery's eye then caught on the last paragraph:

DR 60 Characteristics:

Rare mutation of DR 59-B. Pathogen discovered in remote grove in Carrick City. Aggressive pattern of growth within entire Quercus cell structure following what is believed to be a prolonged gestation period - potentially years in length - before highly contagious outbreak. Containment is essential to grove survival. Unique ability to cross to fauna, sedative qualities. Gestation period in secondary candidates was not studied based on the severity of viral outbreak within original study population.

That was it, that's what Jim was using.

He ripped the thin page from the binding, "Come on, we have a job to do." He handed the passage to his fellow Keeper.

"I'll get the saw," Wallace said.

Loaded down with gear, they moved out. Drones hummed in the distance.

"We need to contain the spread as soon as possible," Avery said.

"I haven't seen the infection. You're sure it's DRC 60?" Wallace held up the crumpled piece of paper.

The smoldering barn soon appeared in the distance, along with the rancid odor. This answered Wallace's question. Mia circled wide around the clearing. The energy between them simmered. Avery gritted his teeth to stay focused and shifted the hammer and spikes over his opposite shoulder. The flames had died down, leaving a smoldering pile. Sentinel 327 was now yellowing and sallow liquid oozed from its charred trunk.

"So, first steps," Wallace said, keeping his eyes moving. "One, We need to drop a kill dose. Two, we need to find a containment line."

Avery nodded again. He realized he had never been in the field with Wallace, who was now moving like an expert. This was his grove, he was of Keeper of the Shoulder despite being held down by Jim's will for so many years.

"Let's go to work," Avery said.

Wallace set his gear down and started securing a green harness around his waist. He unhinged the chainsaw's brittle plastic case. Keepers rarely used motorized tools - they preferred the direct contact and control of a well-crafted hand tool. But this situation called for all means necessary. Mia guarded for any movement in the grove.

Avery pushed the heavy bag off his shoulder. The spikes clang together ominously. Each spike had a sharpened tip that was covered by a plastic cap. On the opposite end, a small lever could be flipped open to break the seal between the two chemical constituents. He methodically popped off the caps, turned the knob and shook up the toxic cocktail. Acid stung his nose.

Wallace walked over, "Here." He said handing him a pair of thick gloves, safety glasses and dust mask with yellow elastic straps. "And take one of these. You're a Keeper." Wallace then handed him a hatchet from his harness. The handle was tapered hickory with a leather blade cover.

"Thanks," he said quietly.

"I'm gonna find the edge of the infection at ground level. Then start clearing branch connections between our sick tree and healthy sentinels," Wallace said.

The nodded to each other and started.

Wallace pushed out into the underbrush, slicing away foliage with another razor sharp hatchet.

Avery pulled on the protective gear and walked to the base of 327. The earth steamed under his feet. The monitoring device now blinked dark red above him. Yellow pus oozed like an infected wound being squeezed from the inside.

Metal struck metal with a clang. The spike sliced into the wood about a third of the length. He swung hard again. The spike smoked. The smell becoming more repugnant, like a mixture of rotten flesh and industrial sanitizer. A third blow drove the spike flush with the base of the tree.

He rotated ninety degrees, reset and drove the next spike into infected wood. At the third spike, his first swing reverberated harshly and the spike bent in the middle. A numb stinging crawled up both of his arms. It was then that he noticed a small, corroded pipe curving up from the ground and running up into the trunk.

With the hatchet, he cleared away soil. No more than three inches below the surface, the pike turned and ran away from the tree. He grabbed tight and shook angrily. A narrow band of earth loosened in a straight line toward where the barn once stood. Just inside the pile of smoking debris, was a small spigot. Thick yellow goo dripped from the spout. Avery felt his mouth dry.

He forced himself to return to the tree. He straightened out the bent spike with the blunt end of the hatchet and pummeled the rusted pipe into mangled scraps at the base. Ignoring the fatigue in his shoulders, he drove in the final two spikes.

When he finished, the hammer thudded to the ground and he pulled away the dusk mask. Fresh air stung his sweat-covered cheeks. The Drop Spikes simmered behind him.

Yellowing leaves now rained down from tree 327. Adding to the pile of burned remains. The battle for their grove was not over.

Wallace appeared at the near side of the clearing.

"What do we got?" Avery asked as he approached.

"Come take a look," Wallace motioned.

There was a two-foot wide band of vegetation cleared in a rough ring around their known infection zone. Wallace knelt down and ran his fingers along the forest floor. It was dusty and dry.

"See that?" Wallace asked.

The soil was tinged with a yellow hue.

"Yeah…" Avery brushed off his check with the back of his wrist.

"It's the same way all the way around the southern edge. But nothing to the north," he said looking up at Avery, soil particles running through his fingers. "How many spikes do you have left?" he asked.

"Six." Avery said

"You can see leaves starting to drop along here," Avery said, pointing to branches around 327.

"We gotta break any connection before they get infected." Wallace cleared his smoky voice. "I'll start giving the neighbors a haircut. Drop those spikes around the perimeter of 327. If we're lucky, that'll catch it," Wallace said. Mia caught Avery's eye. She was sitting safely on the other side of the clearing.

Avery prepared the next batch of spikes. Wallace fueled the chainsaw. The engine coughed, coughed and fired. They both went back to work.

His heart weighed heavy as he drove in spikes at even intervals between 327 and the next layer of Sentinels. It was as if the virus was leaching the moisture out of the ground. Two swings and the spikes were driven fully into the dry earth. It was only time before the spikes started to kill everything in a wide radius, and hopefully take the pathogen too.

Wallace had started to slice a clean break in the branches that crossed the containment line. Thick strands of wood popped and crackled as they fell to the ground from their once lofty heights.

Pulling on his own harness, Avery started on the opposite side of the break line. With his power dialed in, but not at full strength, he clipped off small branches in single, blue streaked swings. The process felt like shucking corn. He moved from the outer edges and worked backward until the area was clear. Blisters formed on his sweaty palms and after an hour of solid work, the last connected branches of trees 412 and 413 floated to the ground. He snapped on the blade guard and slid the handle into his harness.

By the time Avery met Wallace in the clearing, he was resting a foot against a large downed branch and taking long drags from a cigarette.

"I remember the day they brought her here," he said with a long exhale. "Jim and some tall lieutenant had her chained to the back of a truck, they came in that west gate and drove right here. Those big black eyes - couldn't tell where she was lookin'. I never went inside. Not once. All he told me was that he soaked her food in that yellow shit."

For Avery, it took a minute for the reality to sink in.

"You remember what that lieutenant looked like?" Avery asked.

"Tall, light skinned dude, eyes like ice," Wallace said. "And no, never saw him around again."

"Jim said the queen was holding everything together. Maybe a weird symbiosis thing between her and the virus," Avery thought.

"Maybe."

There was a tense quiet between them. The squawk of Jaron's now mixed with the buzz of helicopters and drones in the distance. Avery's mind went to his tribe and their search for Bea. He had to stay focused and tried to push it from his mind. If they could contain this problem, he would go back to the search.

They walked over to 327. Nearly all the leaves had fallen in a yellow pile. The entire tree drooped.

"Gotta keep moving," Wallace said and pulled the chainsaw back to life.

Avery's phone then rang. He didn't recognize the number and answered tentatively - half expecting an emotionless Protocol officer on the line.

"Hello?" he asked.

"Avery Jackson, we're gonna need this gate unlocked in a jiffy." Flow's voice was unmistakable.

"Flow, what are you doing here?"

"Talk later. Get here now. Kisses." The line went dead.

Wallace looked at Avery with an annoyed smirk.

"I um, I gotta go do a thing," he said and turned toward the south end of the grove.

"Go on."

The chainsaw yelled to life.

When Avery arrived at the gate, he peered nervously in both directions. Confused and terrified, he didn't see anything at first. Then the red roadster screamed down the road and stopped outside the gate. Mia's tale fluttered against his knee. She barked and pawed the ground.

Flow piloted the little car with Paolo riding shotgun with a lap full of wooden boxes and computer equipment. Bullet holes riddled the grill and pierced the windscreen in several places.

He heaved open the gate. In the distance, Jarons flocked recklessly around the towers of downtown.

Stunned and tattered, they unfolded from the vehicle. Paolo's face and forearms were all scratched up. Flow limped on a bum ankle.

"Come inside," Avery said.

"What the hell happened?" he asked Flow as she eased into Wallace's desk chair with a wince.

"Hubbard's cronies attacked the house," she said.

"They came here too," said Avery.

Flow rubbed her temples, "That sack of shit."

"How'd you guys get out of there?" Avery asked.

Flow gave a sly grin, "Paolo knocked out the first two as they came in the front door. I polished off the second pair." She tapped the small ceramic turtle poking out of a breast pocket.

Avery still didn't know what powers her key unlocked. She seemed confident and now was not the time to inquire. Paolo jostled into the office with the first-aid kit from the supply room perched on top of the boxes he'd brought from the car.

Flinching as Flow cleaned his scrapped cheek, "They shot at us from the neighbor's yard. With some luck, we got out to the garage somehow."

Avery could taste his rage.

"Hubbard normally wouldn't touch us with a ten foot pole," Flow said.

"We sure it was Hubbard?" Avery asked.

"Course it was Hubbard, who the hell else could do this?" Flow asked.

Avery shifted over to the window anxiously. His concern jumped to Addison. Was she safe? He sent a quick sequence of text messages.

"Lt. Quade," Paolo said in a low voice.

"That twit," Flow said.

"Why would they attack us like that?" Avery asked. "They already have Bea."

Paolo pointed firmly at Avery's chest. It was like an arrow piercing through his heart. He had been there on the island, right next to her. Why hadn't they taken him too?

Flow looked hawk-eyed out the window. Her fingers wrapped on the desk for a long while. Her expression was that of her wife's calm precision. Now an extra flame flickered in her eyes. She did not share Bea's capacity for restraint.

Wallace's computer alarmed.

Flow wheeled away, "Wasn't me."

"What's good A?" Paolo asked.

"Pathogen outbreak," he said, pulling up the monitoring program. 327 was now completely missing from the system.

Flow tried to stand but her bum ankle buckled under her. Avery rushed over, but she waved him off and leaned on the desk.

Gears started to turn.

"Avery, go back to your job," she directed. "Paolo, check the perimeter."

Flow opened the square tea box then looked up at the room.

Paolo asked about the fence and gate system before breaking off to check their perimeter. Avery and Mia rushed back to the clearing.

Mia ran ahead. When he broke into the clearing Wallace hung from tree 328, cigarette hanging loosely from his mouth as he cleared the last adjacent branches.

"You should quit smoking," Avery called up.

"This damn place is gonna kill me anyway," Wallace jabbed, pulling a long drag, "Everything ok topside?" Smoke curled around his cheeks.

"Yeah," Avery chirped. "I'll give you the details later."

While Avery was gone, Wallace had finished the break line. He dropped back to the ground. The soil underneath their boots was now an unnatural red where each Drop Spike deposited their poison. Though none of the surrounding trees showed major signs of stress.

After a brief conference, they agreed that 327 needed to come down. Covered in tree bits and visually drained, Wallace handed over the chainsaw to Avery. He went about stamping down the last glowing embers of the barn and cleared straight lines away from the dying tree for safety.

Avery started with a clean slice to the trunk facing the barn - the direction of the fall. The powerful chainsaw ripped through desiccated wood too easily. Congealed yellow residue came flying away in large chunks.

Then he pushed a cut through the center of the trunk with the engine straining. To release pressure, he clipped a notch out of the back face. He then whistled and pointed for Wallace to stand clear and finished the front cut in a roar.

327 fell in slow motion.

The clearing where the barn once stood was now filled with the felled giant. The inner rings, which should have been iron strong Oak, were disintegrating globs around the wrecked tube that had for too long filled the noble tree with disease.

Avery gnawed the thick truck into manageable slices. Wallace worked around him and rolled logs into an organized pile.

When the chainsaw finally went silent, the night had dimmed further. Both Keepers moved to inspect their Sentinels. Thankfully, only signs of stress from the fire - browned leaves and flame kissed bark. But no monitoring spikes showed infection and the soil was returning to a normal color.

Sweat soaked and exhausted to the core, they returned to the station where the Lafayette branch of the Argus Bureau was coming to life.

Chapter 30

Lavender Scented Brontosaurus

Addison was dreary from a hectic shift. She had just received a page from the front desk to come collect a patient from the lobby - a rather unusual request. The hospital guards controlled lobby entrants, but she was too drowsy to think much of it. Her eyelids ached as she walked to the elevator.

Usually the mid-day hours were quiet. An easy ten hours tending to sprained ankles and heat exhaustion. This day was different. She had quietly been inquiring about reports of other prominent people gone missing. If she could help find a pattern, maybe she could help find Bea. And the ER had been swamped with patients with surprisingly brutal injuries and curious stories.

Injured soldiers rarely received treatment at the hospital. They were taken to a military ward along the river. But, three were brought to the ER entrance in unmarked cars. She had been shocked to treat an old Outer Domain Surveillance officer with blood mysteriously dripping from his nose and mouth. His eyes were vacant, frozen with a stunned look. They were able to stabilize his condition. Though a CT scan showed massive brain hemorrhaging. He likely would not survive nightfall.

Elevator three opened with a chime and she wedged in with a janitor and his cleaning cart.

"Lobby, please," she said sweetly. They dropped another floor, and the doors opened. Dr. Yun stepped on; his arms crossed tight, an extra-surly expression smeared across his face.

Her phone buzzed. A message from Avery made her heart pater. Clumsily, the phone slipped from her hand and clattered under the cleaning cart. Shoot.

"Gotta stop in Cardiology. Sorry doc," the janitor said. She tried to push back against the cart

"Cardiology is on one," the doctor said dryly.

"I mean Radiology," the janitor said. "Radiology, yeah that's it."

Addison crouched and reached urgently. The bleach on the cart stung her nostrils.

"Excuse me," she squeaked.

She was only free to grab the phone when the janitor shuffled onto floor two, muttering under his breath. Emergency lights now flurried outside the main entrance. Dr. Yun was half turned. The waiting area was empty, not a single patient or family member sat in the cluster of sofas and chairs. The strange day kept getting stranger, she thought, jamming her phone back in her pocket not looking at the message.

She exited with the doctor and when she turned the corner, a squad of six soldiers rushed into the lobby. Their grey uniforms and assault rifles a stark contrast to the sterling surfaces. A commanding officer, fatter than the rest, walked up to the doctor. It was only when she heard her name did her quizzical attitude turn into dread.

"Miss Quelhurst, step this way."

Her heartbeat hastened. There must have been an incident outside the hospital. She hadn't collected the patient fast enough. She hoped no one had gotten hurt.

Dr. Yun advanced smoothly, his shoes clicking on the tile.

"Addison," he said

"Dr. Yun what's this all about?" she asked. "I got a page about a patient in the lobby. I didn't know there was any trouble."

He pulled the ID tag from the tail of her shirt without warning, and scanned it.

Suddenly she found it hard to breath.

"Target secured," the commanding officer said into a shoulder-mounted radio.

She stepped back, only to be driven forward with the butt of a rifle. A heavy gloved hand held her shoulder and pulled one of her wrists tight behind her back. The soldier smelled of car exhaust and cheap cologne.

"Wait," she pleaded. "What is this about? I didn't do anything. I've been at work all day. Ask any of the - " Her mouth dried. "Ask any of the nurses in the ER."

The zip tie tightened around her right wrist. She squirmed away from the soldier and pressed to Dr. Yun.

"My protocol record is spotless!" she pleaded.

The doctor held up a single, boney finger.

"Aiding and abetting a rogue Able is a serious offense, Addison. I cannot tolerate such actions in my hospital."

She tripped on a soldier's boot and fell to the floor, her panicked brain misfiring. Backpedaling on hands and knees, she was pulled to her feet, pleading with the two soldiers now holding her.

Just then, a round bellied tattoo-covered man pushed through the revolving door. Sunglasses covered his eyes. He moved confidently, wearing a loose fitting floral shirt and baggy shorts. His name was Bulldog. He'd been one of Avery's first Linkerage connections; he'd been there in the thicket blocks. How he was here.

Six different gun barrels trained on his chest until he started to speak.

"Roger that, flexible flamingo in a parrot suite." His arms swaggering, he came up to the group. An amused confusion started clouding Addison's head. She felt the soldier grip on her arms slacken. Bulldog continued.

"You know we're eight, nine on the two-five."

Dr. Yun shook his head.

"Who are you?" he asked in a puzzled voice.

"Patrick."

"What was that?" Dr. Yun asked again.

"Persimmon."

With his chubby arm, Bulldog guided Addison's captors back a few paces. The soldiers' guns now hung benignly at their sides. When he turned back, he continued addressing Dr. Yun.

"You know doc. I've got this thing on my shoulder. Think it might be a busted corpuscle."

Dr. Yun now looked like a sleepwalker.

"No? Didn't think so either."

Bulldog whistled to the two soldiers standing near the door.

"Hey guys. Jumping Jacks. Pronto."

One soldier started to raise both arms sheepishly before his partner swatted them down.

"Lavender scented brontosaurus."

They both sat down with legs crossed. Addison barely held in a giggle. She was delighted beyond imagine, flowers danced in her vision.

The commanding soldier rubbed his eyes and inquired with a heavy tongue, "Who are you..."

"Pocahontas," Bulldog said. "Gentlemen, I apologize for the confusion. I will ensure Ms. Quelhurst attend to the taco palpitations - over on the poop deck."

"Whatsss the protocol command number?" the head soldier asked, rubbing his belly.

"One, one, six, cucumber."

"Dumbledore," the soldier responded.

"That's my man." Bulldog nodded toward the door. The depths of Addison's mind screamed back into action, but her limbs would not respond. Bulldog waved two fingers. The fuzziness lifted ever so slightly and she followed him with jittering footsteps. Bulldog fist bumped a seated soldier. As they circled out the door, cut off the zip tie and handed a stick of gum to Addison.

"Chew on this." he guided her to Paolo's large truck waiting outside. She half flung herself in into the passenger seat. The peppermint gum tingled in her mouth and in her head. The euphoric, floral feeling dissipated.

They thundered past a group of unassuming hospital workers, around the two patrol vehicles parked precisely in the drop off lane, and disappeared into the thicket blocks all before anyone in the lobby could even remember their own name.

Chapter 31

I'll Do It

MRAP – Mine Resistant Ambush-Protected Vehicle,
gross weight: 43,500 lbs.

Avery and Wallace returned to a transformed office,
Paolo shortly after. Flow had managed to clear two of the desks
and push them together in the center of the room. A large map of
the city spread across one half. Stacks of binders and reference
books blocked out both windows. A hundred year-old faded
plastic phone was plugged into the wall. Flow sat with her ear
pressed to the receiver and turned the knobs on her Argus Bureau
radio.

They all stood in awkward silence as she finished a
hushed conversation. When she hung up the phone, her eyes met
Wallace.

"Good to see you Colt," she said.

He grinned pleasantly, "Tortoise. It's been a long time."

Avery's head snapped from his fellow Keeper to Flow and
back. Was Wallace a member?

They hugged.

"You all smell like crap," Flow stated.

Wallace then checked the monitoring system. 327 was
gone. A hole ripped into the geometric fabric of the Shoulder. But
the other three hundred and ninety-nine sentinels showed no
additional signs of the virus. The quarantine was successful.

Wallace faded back to the doorway with cigarette in hand
and pointed for the search effort to continue unimpeded.

"Has anyone heard from the Quelhursts?" Avery asked
quietly. The distraction of saving the grove faded fast.

"Addison's safe," Flow said confidently. "Bulldog scooped
her from the hospital a half hour ago. No word from Mitchell."

A bit of relief washed over Avery. Mitchell was made of piss and vinegar - he'd been fine. Paolo shifted uncomfortably near the barricaded window, rolling a rosary across his fingers.

"So what's new?" he asked.

Wallace returned and flipped to a screen on his computer that Avery had never seen. It showed a complex cascade of code, white text on blue background, next to a routing diagram that updated every second or so, "A few years back I was able to tap my monitoring program directly into the city-wide server network, thanks to the Shoulder's connectivity to Protocol headquarters. They got no idea I've been in here."

Damn, Wallace. He really was part of this Argus Bureau thing.

"The city is broken down into security wards," he continued, pointing to the faded map on the table, "Each one has Security and Protocol office that is the node for essentially all communication within that ward. Radio communication, burst transmission, military orders - even civilian phone calls and emails are routed through Protocol Command at these offices. And that's where my little piece of magic sneaks in."

The program cloned each communication without being detected. It used a massive cache, the Shoulder's station server, to collect the information as it passed through each node. With no real interruption to the data stream, the Lafayette system had no reason to look for an intruder. Once the data was skimmed, the filter went into action, cleaning up the noise.

"And I've got eyes on the Ambassador Bridge," Flow said.

"The Blade pulled into Central Station at 8:30 this morning, but nothing's left all day," Wallace said.

"He wouldn't use the train," Flow commented. "That's not his style."

"You sure?" Avery asked.

"He likes to keep things on the down low. Sneak something out, under the noses of his own men. He's always been like that," Flow argued. "Keep an eye on that station, but my gut says he doesn't take Bea through there - not unless he has no other choice."

"If I'm Hubbard, I don't need to sneak around my own city," Avery said. "Why do we think she's getting moved outside the walls in the first place?"

"He's right," Paolo said.

The phone rang. Flow grabbed the receiver.

The room was motionless. Wallace's computer then alarmed. The monitoring program threw an urgent window.

```
10:50:56 CENTRAL COMMAND - MESSAGE RECEIVED.
//
EL0096:SD56R - FIRE / TT: GH340 - FIRE
```

"Not good," Wallace said despondently.

Flow hung up the phone with force. A tear sneaked down her cheek. She hastily wiped it away.

"They're burning the house," she took a deep breath and reset her focus. "The library's on fire too. And where the HELL is Mitchell?" She threw a binder across the room.

"Bait," Paolo said flatly. "It's bait."

Heated debate about their next move broke out. Avery stood near the door, the smoke of Wallace's cigarette sitting in his nose. A calm precision building as he looked straight at the skyline through a crack in the door.

"She's in there," He said in a low voice. It took a second for the words to catch the entire room.

Flow swiveled in her chair and he had all eyes in the room.

"What's that kiddo?"

"Bea. She's in the Tower."

"We don't know that," Paolo said. "And even if we did, getting in the joint is crazy town."

"I'll do it," said Avery.

Stunned stillness.

"No. I won't allow it," Flow said finally.

"I'll get her back."

Wallace quashed the cigarette but under his boot. Then it all fell apart.

A blank green screen and a simple alarm on each of their phones was the only warning before the attack began. The front gate crashed open and rain of bullets blew in all the windows. Avery dove behind a desk as bullets ate through the back wall. They should have seen this coming. It was too easy, Hubbard had been tracking them through Linkerage this whole time.

The strange blue light that had come from the tactical helicopter dropped from the sky and underbrush a flame all around the station. Over the calamity, Avery heard Flow.

"Run boys!"

Mia was right next to him. Paolo crouched on the other side of the desk.

"You hit?" he called over.

"I'm good!" Paolo yelled back.

Avery called up his strength. In a pause in the gunfire, he burst up and made for the back door. The other three followed. They made it out of the station as another explosion ripped through the door.

Tactical soldiers rushed at Avery and Paolo, commanding them to the ground. That wasn't going to happen. *Understand and Execute*. Avery charged the soldiers at full speed. They could not react fast enough. He steamrolled through their tactical formation, snapping weapons, breaking arms, and landing kicks as he went. Sentinels blazed overhead, dropping burning branches all around him.

When Avery dropped the last soldier and turned, Flow was standing in the madness, ankle braced, looking unfazed. Wallace knelt low to the earth, holding a double-barreled shotgun. Where had that come from?

White smoke curled from Paolo's arms.

"Go," Flow stated. "Colt and I have this handled."

The next round of soldiers streamed through the gate as Avery and Paolo hesitantly withdrew into the darkness of the grove. A massive ball of purple flame burst from Flow's hands like she was Mega Man and Wallace fired his gun in double bursts. They drove back the front line with remarkable force.

Avery, Mia, and Paolo made for the west gate. Drones zipped over the grove, blasting the fence and surrounding houses at random. They moved around the flames and made it through the gate as one of the massive armored vehicles came to a hissing stop in their path. The tall headlights blinded them.

"You ready for this?" Paolo asked. Avery could feel Paolo's newfound energy and massive strength.

"Of course."

The door slammed open, "Hey, Losers. I got a new toy."

It was Mitchell. Avery sprang through the gate and hugged a reluctant Mitchell. They clamored inside the MRAP and rumbled away. The Shoulder burned.

Mitchell would not give any details other than that he was fine, he had checked a few more of the Lafayette's holes, no signs of Bea. And assured them he asked before borrowing the MRAP. But Paolo had to restrain him when Avery broke the news about the library fire.

In a giant stolen war machine, they made for The Tower.

Chapter 32

Doing Brave

The air was oily and heavy inside the back of the MRAP. Outside, which started to resemble that of downtown, was deadened by nearly an inch of reinforced steel and ballistic glass. Rows of seats faced inward. Avery held Mia into the seat next to him, she panted curiously. He had a hatchet and a coil of rope. Mitchell piloted with Paolo riding shotgun.

The plan seemed simple, and the plan seemed impossible. With the attack vehicle, they could drive into the city's heart without question. Maybe. Avery found Lafayette uniforms neatly folded in an under-seat compartment, along with a loaded assault rifle. They all now wore the uniforms.

Frantic flashing green lights fluttered ahead. Mia peaked around through the windshield. Avery now felt her apprehension.

"Check point ahead," Mitchell said.

"You two should get down," Paolo called back. The engine whirred and spat as they slowed.

A pack of soldiers were stationed at the next intersection. They stood in the back of assault trucks and in the road. Guns pulled across their chests. A master sergeant held up a hand to stop their approach.

Avery and Mia ducked low against the seat rails.

The MRAP stuttered to a stop. The sergeant came up and knocked on the window.

"Access number," he commanded.

Mitchell was frozen.

"Solider, I need your access code."

"Check under the visor," Avery whispered.

"Where?"

"Over your head. Check up there."

Mitchell evaded all eye contact and pulled a small card from the plastic flap above the smeared windshield. He opened the door and handed it to the checkman.

"Sorry. Ahhh, was waiting on radio confirmation. Orders keep changing tonight. Ya know?" said Mitchell.

"Please Hold," the master sergeant stated

Sirens and Jarons wailed through the partially opened door.

Plastered to the armored floor, sweat stinging his eyes, Avery realized this whole perimeter wasn't about Bea. This was about him. The rush from place to place, disaster to disaster, had kept him from realizing that he was the target. He hardened himself to that reality.

The sergeant returned.

"Cargo?" he asked.

"None. Sir." Mitchell replied.

"Confirm your mission again."

"Logistic support and...Pancake tactical response." Mitchell responded.

"Parallel tactical response." The soldier sounded annoyed. "Fuel level."

"Three quarters," Mitchell lied, the gauge was near empty.

"Proceed."

Mitchell saluted and drove onward.

Avery and Mia climbed off the floor.

"Where'd you pull that from?" Avery asked as he pulled himself up.

"Was reading off his tablet."

Inside the perimeter, soldiers were everywhere. Not a single civilian was in sight. Teams were stationed at major intersections, Green and white vehicles slowly patrolling the empty streets. The MRAP plodded through.

In painstaking time, they circled around the tangle of streets. They then turned onto the library block - now collapsed, flames lapping high into the night air. Not a soul tending or fighting the flames. Mitchell knuckles whitened on the steering wheel. Paolo placed a hand on his shoulder.

"I'm sorry my friend."

Across the street was a shuttered station for the old elevated rail line. Mitchell backed into an empty service dock. Heat from the inferno radiated through the vehicle. Avery had had enough of fires for one day. Blocked by the mass of the MRAP, the back stairway was as dark a place as any in downtown.

"My shifts up in a minute. You're gonna need to get out here," Mitchell said.

"Don't forget the drive," Paolo called back. He was referring to the small thumb drive Wallace had given Avery. It contained a virus.

"Do a job," Mitchell said.

Avery shook each of their hands as hard as he could, "Be safe."

"Start with floor twelve," Mitchell reminded him.

And with that, Avery and Mia were out the back hatch with the rope coiled over his shoulder and the hatchet tucked in his uniform belt. A single heel kick, timed with MRAP belching out of the driveway, and the rusted door lock burst. Up two flights of stairs, and the old station sat in waiting. Screens hung from broken hinges. Copper parts scavenged from their innards long ago.

The Jarons, they were gone. He walked to the track edge. Clear sky. He listened. Only the sounds of soldiers and amplified commands.

The elevated line took him up and away from the burning library at first. He passed over and through narrow streets, and then circled back toward the river. With the invisible river shoreline at a distance and no buildings close to him, he felt exposed. This is where Mitchell had warned him to watch for orbiting scanners. His ears perked at the faintest electric buzz. In his periphery he saw motion and dropped flat to his chest onto the track. Mia crouched next to him with a paw on his arm. Their energy now ignited, but he forced himself to stay motionless.

In a burst of high frequency sound, a basketball sized contraption whizzed over him. It clicked and shifted before shooting north. He waited a beat, listened. Remembering that drones always seemed to travel in pairs, he raised his head only an inch. Nothing.

Go, his body told him.

His legs churned. He and Mia sprang up together and in two steps were at full speed. Feet and paws dodged and landed among the clutter on the track.

Just ahead, the track kinked back into the tight city blocks. Behind him he felt an approaching object. This time he had no option but to keep moving forward. As his training with Bea in The Shoulder had taught him, he demanded more from his legs. Together they surged around the curve and away from the river as the second orbiter scuttled passed.

A half second's glance behind him sent his foot driving into a loose junction box. *Fuck.*

The brittle enclosure clanged angrily along the track before coming to a teetering stop on the ledge. He pulled it back to safety and crouched down to recompose. Steady. Stop being stupid. You're being stupid, he told himself. He listened.

After several deep breaths he found a more gradual pace. Along the route were several more boarded up platforms. Domed security cameras hung from the roof as expected; they were cracked open and wiring splayed out.

Another curve, then another, and then a long straight away reached out. At the fringe of the darkness, The Tower stood like a century. Amazing and Terrifying. Narrow bands of light sliced up the brick shell.

His skin tingled. He felt strange moving intentionally toward the structure. A hundred steps did not seem to get him any closer, until suddenly a bank of windows and massive flagpole mounted to the brick looked him straight in the face.

The railway ran surprisingly close to the Tower and with no notable surveillance. Thirty feet stood between track's edge and third floor windows. But it was thirty feet of gaping nothingness that could take him barreling to the pavement below with any misstep.

Blue smoke flickered from his arms. He eyed his rope.

He fastened a looping knot with a healthy amount of slack. Judged the distance again. Probably thirty-four feet. And the flagpole was about as tall, and as thick as his leg.

He tossed the rope overhead. The loop grazed the Lafayette flag and fell back to the track. A second try and it caught just at the knobbed end and fell. A third throw and it dropped over and pulled tight. He then picked up Mia. She looked at him dubiously. Then seemed to understand. You got this, he said to himself. You're doing brave.

With a running start he leaped through a path of blue smoke. Feet first, he missiled through the air and connected with the heavy glass. It shattered inward. Avery released the rope and tumbled into a darkened room full of featureless cubicles. The stillness was eerie. He released Mia and moved toward the workstation furthest from the window and he plugged in the USB drive into a workstation. Wallace's program went into action.

With that task completed, they advanced into the heart of Hubbard's fortress.

At the end of empty desks and chairs, was a bank of four elevators. Behind the closed metal doors, the cars clunked up and down. Pushing the buttons did nothing. And on second consideration, taking the elevator was a completely stupid plan.

Just around the corner was a musty stairwell. He climbed. The stillness was now terrifying. Each floor was marked with a simple placard:

4 - Maintenance
5 – Coordination
6 – Accounting
7 - Protocol Division 1
8 - Protocol Division 2
9 - Monitoring Transaction Control
10 - Protocol Division 3
11 - Material Handling

And then:

12 - Protocol Division D - Holding and Command

The metal door, which should have been locked, swung open with the turn of the handle. A cellblock occupied the entire floor. Long, low, lined with cold light and off-white doors a hundred-times repainted. At the end of the hallway stood the massive, Viking-like Lancer Avery had encountered in the lobby months before. He held a long chain, each link thick and dangerous.

Avery moved beyond the threshold and pulled out his hatchet.

"You took a prisoner of ours," The Lancer's voice echoed.

"Henry didn't do anything."

"You don't know that."

Avery didn't respond.

"He said you'd come," The Lancer let slip a fraction of a smile. "And here you are."

"Where's Bea?" Avery asked.

"Not on this floor with the common filth." Chains clinked between the Lancer's fingers. That meant she was in The Tower.

Avery did not wait. He marshaled everything he had into motion. Cell windows blurred. Still wrangling with his power, he was upon the Lancer before he could ready himself to strike and glanced off the giant man's torso and slid to the floor. The hatchet clanged away.

The Lancer repositioned himself between Avery and the exit. The door closed by an invisible hand. The confined space worked against Avery now. The Lancer's expression was devoid of emotion; he took up most of the hallway.

Panic crept into Avery's chest. He needed to compose himself. Find an angle, find the Lancer's weakness. He needed to get the hell off this floor. The chain continued spinning, drawing closer and closer.

Avery dove, this time he hit true, but it was like running square into a granite slab. He no longer had power, but he still had speed. His fists railed against the Lancer. Landing blows against jaw and cheek and eye socket. The punches seemed to have little effect other than to draw a low growl from his opponent.

The Lancer caught Avery's arm and flung him onto the floor. He sprung back immediately, but he'd forgotten about the chains. They wrapped around, his ribs, and removed every square inch of air from his lungs.

Mia lashed at the Lancer's ankles, ripping fabric and drawing blood. The Lancer kicked her down the hall with a yelp. Avery writhed. The chains twisted. Mia lay motionless on the floor. Then an awesome strength whipped him against the wall. Blackness.

* * * * * *

The MRAP blended into the madness. Patrols now looked to be moving without designated routes and ran headlong into each other. Wearing uniforms with the right colors and markings was what Mitchell and Paolo hoped would get them through.

The radio also provided useful information. Additional units were being called to the nests, to deal with unwieldy flocks of Jarons who had left the city center. Reports of citizen attacks were being reported on the west side, the work of Wallace and Flow. Mitchell eased up on the accelerator, trying to keep the thirsty engine from running dry before they could refuel. Paolo kept a keen eye on their flank. As they rounded a tall corner, neither noticed the checkpoint reaching across the narrow street. Mitchell had to mash the brakes once he saw the line of soldiers.

Led by a checkpoint sergeant, a squad of heavily armed uniforms encircled the vehicle.

Mitchell whispered and repeated to himself, "Parallel tactical response. Parallel tactical response."

His mind went to the assault rifle positioned under the seat. He opened the door and handed over the control card.

"Code," said the agent.

Mitchell recited the seven-digit number.

"Cargo."

"Empty. Waiting on new orders... And." He lowered his brow, "We need fuel."

The agent's tablet beeped. Then double beeped.

"Last check said you were at three quarters."

"Gauge error," Mitchell said quickly.

"We need to check the hold. Put the vehicle in park and release the back hatch."

All the labels had worn off a wide panel of switches. Mitchell flicked them all. The rear hatch did release, followed by the floodlights blazing, the front winch cranking, an alarm sounding in the hold, and the engine jumping an octave - burning more fuel.

"Shit." One by one he flipped down the controls until the MRAP returned to normal behavior.

Two soldiers stepped inside. Ironically, they had nothing to hide. Nevertheless, his heel found the butt of the gun. Paolo looked as though he was ready to break someone's face.

More beeps. Some muffled discussion. The hatch closed, but did not latch properly. The sergeant reappeared.

"Proceed. Orders are..." A rare hesitation. "Orders are...are in process."

"Roger that." Mitchell slammed his door.

Tension eased as they put distance between them and the checkpoint. The street lights ahead were half working, leaving dark splotches in their path. When they reach the end of the block, their headlights were the only illumination in the darkness.

The first strike thudded against the roof.

Mitchell didn't look up. He thought he'd run into something and wasn't about to admit the mistake. Paolo looked up but said nothing.

The second strike - a violent screech, denting the roof panel and tossed the twenty-ton vehicle sideways. There was a temporary weightlessness until they came crashing back down, flinging both of them around, grasping and cursing.

Paolo landed in Mitchell's lap.

"What was that?" he exclaimed.

"Get off me," Mitchell rasped.

Then there was the scream. The ear splitting, soul shaking scream. Talons blacker than the night lashed against the windshield. The queen's screams mixed with metal on concrete. The rear hatch flew open. Tires and hoses burst, glass crunched. They huddled against the passenger seat. Mitchell grabbed the weapon, though it was no good inside.

Her face appeared at the rear hatch. The black orb of an eye focused on them. Her beak chattered open and closed, ooze seeping from the jawline. Then sweeping filled the air until she came crashing on the front fender. Swoop, then crash. Swoop, then crash. Her terrible weight splintered the glass.

"So this is tactical response," Mitchell said.

The driver side door flung open and the giant beak grabbed him.

"Mitchell!" Paolo called as he was yanked violently from the cabin.

Paolo surged out to find Mitchell clutched perilously in the Queen's beak. Legs kicking, cursing like a sailor. The queen twisted to get a better hold and somehow Mitchell was able let loose a stream of bullets from the assault rifle. She dropped him.

Paolo looked down at his hands. The rosary sat coiled in his hand.

The queen screamed out again. More shots until the machine gun clicked on empty. Paolo stood. A raw, muscled energy pulsed through his veins. He stepped over to a large rectangular mailbox, tore it from the ground and threw it at the queen. The box clipped her wing hard. Her head snapped up. Come at me, he thought. That's right, come at me.

White smoke now flowed from him. He ripped a light pole from the pavement, rotated it overhead and flung it at the queen as she lunged airborne. It hit her in the chest, dropping her to ground behind the overturned MRAP. There were sounds of agony from the queen. Mitchell clambered to his feet and made for safety. She stumbled. Wings folded and unfolded. Then she took to the sky and disappeared in a hobbled rage.

Bullets from approaching soldiers began to ping against the overturned MRAP. Mitchell and Paolo took to an alley and disappeared.

"You OK?" Paolo asked.

"Never been better," Mitchell said.

* * * * * *

On the 3rd floor of the Tower, a small executable file finished installing and illuminated a simple command line on Wallace's computer.

* * * * * *

When Avery came to, his arms and legs were shackled. His head was foggy and his ears rang. Mia sat in his lap. Her jaw was taped shut and she looked up at him desperately.

They were just inside the cellblock. The gigantic Lancer stood several paces away, tapping urgently on his phone. Avery's legs were numb. He shifted as best he could, sending the leg chains clanging. The Lancer looked over and pocketed the phone.

"Get up," he said. Avery struggled with tingling legs and a blurry mind. It must have taken him several minutes to stand. He kept Mia in his arms. Motionless, the Lancer watched.

"Out the door," Was the next command. Eyes appeared behind the cell doors now. Wide and leering expressions. Avery turned away and the Lancer drew closer, pointing up the stairs. And so they went. He was forced to concentrate on every step due to the awkward sway of the shackles. The Lancer kept an even distance behind. His weaponized chains hung at the ready.

The procession continued up and up. Avery forced his original desperation out of his mind and with each flight he resolved to gather as much information as he could.

Echos came from the lower floors. Security cameras, positioned at each landing and at each door, trailed their every move. The Lancer limped from the wounds Mia had inflicted. It was clear he was in pain even if he was trying to hide it. Avery gave Mia a reassuring squeeze. The air was getting colder. They approached floor thirty-two.

"Stop here," the Lancer walked forward, produced a key card from his left pocket and scanned it.

They stepped into a grand corridor of smooth marble and tall doors. Avery followed the Lancer and struggled with the magnitude of where they were. The key card went back into the Lancer's left pocket. Cool air circulated about the floor, curling into locked rooms of mystery.

The Lancer approached the pair of polished green doors at the end of the room.

"She stays here." The Lancer nodded at Mia. Avery did not move. He could refuse, but he knew that would end poorly. He could obey and the Lancer could kill her. Mia growled behind the tape. It's just one room, I'll know if he's doing anything, Avery thought.

He lowered her to the floor. She positioned herself defiantly between Avery and the door. Whatever had happened before, Mia showed no fear of the Lancer.

"It's ok girl." With shackled hands he flattened the fir on her head. "Stay here," he whispered. Then he stood. The Lancer stepped forward and removed the hand shackles. Avery hoped for both sets, but his legs remained bound.

"He's waiting. Don't do anything stupid."

And with that, the Lancer pushed open the door.

The conference hall was hard and institutional, and hung in sour light. Avery moved forward several paces and paused. The blackened windows flitted with green light from the street below, then the end chair swung around. Slouched over, hand pressed against his temple, Hubbard glared across the chamber.

"Good evening Mr. Jackson," he said with a smoky voice, "I don't believe we've had the pleasure."

"No. I don't think so," Avery said mechanically.

"Fitting that you decided to stop by my conference hall. Rather splendid isn't it? I can't take all the credit. The original tenant was a fat faced banker with more money than brain cells."

Avery rocked back on his heels, eyes locked on Hubbard.

"There is a broken window on the third floor that has my security team rather flummoxed. Have any ideas?" Hubbard asked.

"Maybe," Avery said.

"Of course."

Anger rose like a building wave, Avery's shoulders tightened, "Taking an innocent old woman is an act of a coward."

Hubbard gave Avery an acrid look.

"A tragic oversight on my part," Hubbard stated. "I was in a bit of a quandary. First, I had a lieutenant who was getting a little...overzealous in his pursuits."

Hubbard nodded to the other side of the table. Avery inched closer and peeked across. Crumpled on the floor lay Bryce's dead body. His head was kinked at an unnatural degree and blood oozed out of his nose and eyes.

"You see in my old age I may have gotten a touch complacent." His eyes ignited. "Lt. Quade was grasping at power, desperate for an edge on me. The fool was trying to get the record book. He didn't even know the book was gone. I needed a way to draw him back in."

Avery stayed frozen.

"He was getting sloppy. Couldn't see the whole board." Hubbard's eyes trailed off as he scrolled a ribbon through his fingers.

"And to think he had my queen this whole time," he said more to himself.

Avery scanned the conference room. Nothing but darkness and chairs.

Avery said looking down at the floor, "I'm one of your Keepers," Avery felt the words skid out of his mouth.

Hubbard's chair adjusted minutely.

"Oh yes," he said. "Yes. I know all about you. I'm the one who brought you here."

A wide screen on the opposite wall flashed to an image of Avery smashing through the window eighteen floors below. It flipped to an information card stamped the day he entered Lafayette. Then to his test scores, to a bird's eye view of him pulling away from Woodway and finally him passing over the 7A double bridge.

"You see. I have eyes in places you can't imagine," Hubbard said.

A grainy video then stuttered through several frames before showing a blurred figure streak up from the road below. His face came into view for two frames before disappearing. It was from the drone he'd tried to destroy the night he'd found his key.

"How luck would have it that the very Forerunner I've been searching for would play into the same traps as that fool of a lieutenant. It's amazing what people will do for friendship."

Avery struggled to maintain his footing, when the sensation started. Gradual at first, like smoke drifting down from the ceiling. A cloud settled over his mind, seeping into the folds. In response, the connection with Mia repelled some of the cloud as it thickened.

"I don't want any trouble," he said. A blue cast shimmered around him.

"Ahh, but you are trouble Mr. Jackson. You present serious trouble for me, for the city, for The Chancellery. You and your key, starred in the Record Book for good measure."

The cloud solidified into tentacles that probed deeper, pulling at parts of his mind. Avery pushed back as if his mind had two arms.

"There are others who would push you to use your powers against The Chancellery," Hubbard continued. "And your own power would call you to action eventually."

"Where's Bea?" Avery asked.

"It's all about individual control. My city. My problems. A little insect like you needs squashing." The sensation was a flood now. Avery writhed in place.

"Where's Bea!" Avery demanded.

"Where I take my prisoner is of no matter to you, young man!" The voice did not come from the room, but thundered inside Avery's head.

Avery thawed into liquid motion in that moment. He blocked the swinging tentacles lashing at his thoughts and propelled his body toward the doors. In one long stride, he snapped the leg chain and crashed straight through the doors. Wood exploded outward and he crashed square into the guarding Lancer who stumbled to the side.

Chains then lashed down on Avery's back, cracking several ribs. He dropped to the floor, spun painfully, grabbed a long sliver of the door and blocked the next attack. Metal snapped against the old wood panel. The Lancer shifted angrily, swung again. Avery tracked the chain, grabbing the final links and yanking backward. Without distance, his force was no match for the Lancer, but it provided him an opening for a counter blow. He drove the sharp sliver into the Lancer's abdomen. The huge man yelled in agony.

Avery left the ground, shifted, and drove a knee into his opponent's leg. The Lancer grunted angrily. Avery landed and drove his boot into the wound Mia had left earlier. This crumpled the Lancer. Avery drove a savage knee to his throat. With all his force he dropped his elbow to the back of his neck.

He then grabbed the key from the Lancer's left pocket before ripping the tape from Mia's snout. She licked him on the face and together they disappeared in a blue blur.

Dropping down the stairs at a blinding pace, Avery felt Hubbard's mind clawing to find him again. Doors flung open, and urgent voices bounce off the walls. Blood dripped from his back and shoulder.

At the bottom of the stairs he allowed himself only enough rest to draw one long breath. With footsteps pounding down overhead, he flung open the final door and stepped into the vaulted lobby. Only two soldiers stood between him and the revolving doors - a tall female Lancer, with narrow, drooping shoulders and a stocky man lacking a neck. What was this? The stairwell racket stopped, replaced by his mother's voice.

"Avery, please. It's time to stop this."

He spun around, expecting to see her standing at the guard counter.

"Honey. Take it easy. The Tower's a safe place."

These weren't this mother's words. Something snagged Avery's eye. The female Lancer held a ballpoint pen in her hand as if the flimsy plastic was a lightsaber and her eyes gleamed in strange pulses.

"Won't you stay with me for awhile?" Now Bea's voice pleaded.

Mia snarled.

And just as she did, the stocky Lancer curled into a contorted ball and spun into an attack. Avery jumped, knees to chest, landing on the counter just as the soldier punched a depression into the stone.

Addison's voice pleaded, *"Avery, please!"*

The bowling ball thing was just getting up.

"Avery." This was Bea, actually Bea.

The two Lancers retreated and Avery turned slowly. At the bottom of the processional stairs were Bea and Hubbard. She was graceful as always, despite an uncharacteristic disheveledness. Hubbard stood close, as if holding on to some invisible restraint. Avery could strike. It didn't matter how strong Hubbard was, Avery was faster. He could get her out of this place.

Commotion outside the front entrance escalated in volume. With a horrible grinding and a smash, a jagged hole appeared in the wall. Through a plume of dust Paolo and Mitchell appeared. Paolo expelling white smoke, Mitchell wielding the assault rifle. They were breathing heavy.

There was a moment of bewilderment.

"How touching," Hubbard called over. Mitchell advanced, his finger floating over the trigger. Avery raised his hand for him to stop. He stood in front of his housemates, his friends.

"Let her go," he said with calm resolve. "You can have me."

Hubbard began to chuckle - low and poisonous.

"You think I don't already have you, Mr. Jackson?" he asked. "You think there is a deal to be had? A compromise to spare her life and the lives of your silly tribe?"

Paolo and Mitchell moved to stand shoulder to shoulder with Avery.

"I am your problem. Not them," Avery said. Bea stood calmly with a smile.

The rage reignited in Hubbard's face, "She lied to ME. See, locked in there were lies. Lies on top of lies! That is my problem. The Argus Bureau is my problem. Nobody does that to me!"

Blue smoke blazed on Avery's skin. What Hubbard did not see was the matching response in Mia. The same blue wisps now drifted from her fir. Their connection was now complete.

"Avery, be smart," Bea said.

"Shut up!" He struck her down. As she rose from the floor she caught eyes with Mia. In her proudest moment, Bea held a fist across her heart. To Avery, time slowed. And then, with a silent and deadly strike of his mind, Hubbard made the final blow.

Bea's neck snapped. She fell.

At a speed only matched by his key, Avery hurdled at the Fender of Lafayette. Lancers crashed into the room but could do nothing to stop his attack. Avery struck Hubbard's square in the face. There was almost no weight to the man but Avery punched with his whole being against a weighty darkness that he could not see.

Hubbard flew backwards but twisted unnaturally in the air and landed too softly. A hand went to his pocket. To his flank Paolo locked mightily with the now bloodied blonde Lancer. Mitchell dropped to Bea's still body.

The next second Avery's vision began to cloud with black splotches his ears filled with the sound of crackling wood. He ran toward where Hubbard was standing only to be met be a violent strike from the wrecking ball Lancer. The darkness was complete now, the fire raged so close to his ears he thought he could taste the ash.

Mia snarled angrily through the mental smoke, her vision was black too. Cold hands wrapped around his neck. He yanked free, stumbling blindly. A fizz and a pop, a narrow body struck him from behind. Damn this blackness. Pain flashed across his back where the chain had lashed against. Paolo's voice called out.

Avery fumbled to his feet. Another strike from the rolling body. Rapid blows on his left then his right. He stumbled, swinging blindly and connected with a something, someone. His ribs seared in pain.

Gunshots erupted in rapid bursts.

There was a way out of this. He focused on the brightness . Morning grove walks with his uncle. His mother's voice across the bureau radio. Addison's smile. His vision slowly began to clear. Hubbard had gone, replaced by a violent frenzy all around. The wrecking ball Lancer was dead on the floor. Paolo still battled the blonde one, heavy punches landing against armored muscles. Mitchell fought back advancing soldiers with the assault rifle, throwing empty clips to the floor one after they other.

The young Lancer from the natatorium stood at the top of the stairs, Avery drove up the stairs with Mia by his side. He collided with the lightweight Lancer and nearly drove him through a granite column. The strikes, drenched in blue smoke and anger, came furiously. He pummeled the Lancer's face. When more soldiers advanced, Avery picked him up and threw him headlong into them.

A fleshy smack came from behind Avery and he heard the chains fall to the floor.

"A, we gotta go!" Paolo called from a distance

The young Lancer, blooded and maimed, rose to his feet and called off the soldiers. Avery was poised to end this fight when the boy raised a clenched fist across his heart.

There were no words to be had.

Avery turned and ran. He collected Bea's body. Lifting her as a lead weight descended on his heart. What waited for them outside was a sight that would have made her smile.

Chapter 33

The 12:00 PM to Garfield

They climbed through the Paolo-formed hole in the Tower wall. Avery expected to be met with a full battalion of Lafayette's soldiers. What they found instead were the streets ablaze with the chaos of curious and astonishing happenings. Argus Bureau members, streaked in different colors, were stationed all around.

The Jarons had returned in full force. Fireworks exploded from a purple tinted man on a roof across the way. A pair of attack vehicles surged forward as Avery, Mitchell, and Paolo departed from the Tower. A slender woman with raven colored hair stepped out and lobbed tennis balls bathed in pink. On each bounce they flashed in spectacular fashion until exploding between the advancing units. She pointed them toward the wide boulevard.

A tall man, who easily could have passed for a soldier, met them at the corner. He and Paolo embraced. No individual could have held back the Lafayette army. But together, they held them back in spectacular fashion.

Soldiers clashed against colorful defenses all around them. Sparks, and force fields, billowing bubbles against bullets. Screams from the air, broken glass. Their guide was able to smell the dangers and moved them through.

From a laptop, Wallace did his part. Streetlights turned on and off. Doors opened. False commands rang from loud speakers. Steam even blasted from vents in front of approaching soldiers. He toggled the controls of the city in concert with the trapeze act of the Argus Bureau.

Once away from the Tower and the main boulevard, Avery's group stayed to the alleys and narrow passes. Paolo lifted cars and bent dumpsters to block their progress. Mitchell shot down pursuing Jarons, grabbing ammunition from fallen soldiers.

Avery's back ached; he could feel blood collecting along his spine. Hubbard's presence still stuck between his temples. They trudged onward, eventually finding themselves mercifully outside the containment perimeter and in a district of featureless warehouses. The melee was replaced with an oddly discomforting nothingness, Paolo offered to hold Avery's burden. He refused.

Now the night seemed to crawl around them.

"Something's up. My senses aren't working," their guide said, looking around for Mitchell who had disappeared. Paolo ran up and back along the warehouse row, whispering his name. Avery was about to start in on the search when a whistle cracked the tension. Mitchell's head stuck from a narrow access panel in the far warehouse.

He led them through the hatch and down a dark hallway and into a cavernous space. The back half was stuffed with shelves. Flow came out from the shadows. She approached Paolo first, checking a scrape on his chin and slapping him proudly on the chest. She hugged Mitchell, holding him tight to whisper in his ear. Then to Avery. At first she did not look at the lifeless body in his arms, only straight into his eyes.

"I'm sorry," Avery said.

She looked down at Bea. Calm on her face.

"I-" Tears invaded Avery's eyes. "I wasn't fast enough."

Flow ran a hand across Bea's hair. A tear escaped.

"This wouldn't have happened if I hadn't come into your lives," Avery said.

"No," Flow said. "No, Avery. That's not true."

Addison appeared holding a white hospital sheet. They rested Bea on the floor and covered her. He now noticed the others standing in the warehouse. Wallace and the round man with tattooed arms, who threw up a peace sign when their eyes met. And Francis stood near the shadows, watching silently.

"I knew this would happen one day, Avery. We live in a wild and ragged world. We had our good run together, but this pot's been simmering for years. It was time." She cleared her throat, "Chin up, Forerunner. Those folks out there - They don't really know what they got themselves into by making this old dyke mad."

Avery steeled himself and met Flow's gaze.

"Still plenty of work to do," Flow said and returned to a cluster now formed around Wallace.

Addison peeled off and came over to him.

"You look like hell," she said. Avery was dizzy now, his face pale and clammy.

"I'm fine."

Addison found the source of blood staining his shirt.

"You're not fine," she said as she turned him.

"It's just a scrape."

The fabric pulled away and Avery nearly fainted in pain. Addison guided him to a folding chair. Mia licked his hand.

"Someone find me a first aid kit. Something. Anything."

Mitchell ran into the warehouse and came back with a big red zipper package. With the contents spread on the floor, Addison went to work. She cut the uniform from his back. A long, open chain-shaped gash ran across Avery's back from shoulder blade to shoulder blade. Using all the gauze available she cleaned the wound. Then prepared needle and thread.

"This isn't going to feel good," she said, resting a gloved hand on his neck.

"I still think you're pretty," he said through clenched teeth.

"Good god," Mitchell snorted.

In even stitches, Addison pulled closed the folds and dressed the wound with what was left in the first aid kit. Paolo found a box of shirts in the back of the warehouse. Avery painfully pulled on a *Class of 2095 - Phoenix Pride* t-shirt.

"Over here," Flow barked. A jittery energy washed over the group as they circled around the pile of pallets she was crouched on, "Time to get you three out of the city," she said while Wallace showed them a command message he had just intercepted:

```
CENTRAL COMMAND - IMMEDIATE
\
WANTED PERSONS, CITY WIDE SEARCH IN EFFECT
STAGE 2* PROTOCOL
\
AVERY JACKSON
PAOLO HATCH
MITCHELL QUELHURST
\
ACTION: CONTROL, DETAIN.
ACTION: BORDER MISSION PACKAGE C
```

"According to my sources." She pointed to Wallace. "They're in a special stage two protocol. Hubbard has his queen back. He wants to reestablish the nests, show he's in control. He needs to get his soldiers back in order...and who knows what condition he's in."

Avery recalled the punch, like he had been striking a man made of tar.

"The Blade leaves for Garfield at midnight," Wallace said.

"There's no way he'll let that train scoot out of here," Bulldog said from against the wall.

"Hubbard doesn't want to tip off the other Fenders that something's wrong," Addison said.

"Exactly," said Wallace. "He's got to let it leave and on time..."

"I used to babysit the conductor," Flow stated. "After some convincing, he's going find you space. Not first class, but it's a ticket out of here. Just need to get into the station. And we're still working on accommodations in Garfield. The AB will figure something out."

Flow made the call, "You leave in five minutes."

Avery and Addison walked away few steps.

"You need to change these bandages at least once a day," she said.

"Yes ma'am."

"I'm serious. An infection is the worst thing that could happen."

"Once a day, I will."

"I'm scared," she whispered.

He was scared too, but tried to hold that deep down, "Don't be," he said.

"What's going to happen?"

"I'm not sure."

"Are you OK with that?"

"No, not really. But it's the only choice we have."

"So is this goodbye."

"No, I promise. I still owe you dinner."

She then grabbed his arms and kissed him softly.

A tense buzz soon filled the warehouse. Wallace had determined that a full battalion was positioned at the train station. Guards were posted each platform and roving scouts throughout.

Paolo's sternness held strong, but glimpses of shear terror flashed on his face.

Avery had briefly pulled him aside and they talked keys. He talked him through the importance of controlling the initial spark, and how he would learn over time to release it in a more deliberate way. For Avery is was speed and momentum. For Paolo, brute force.

As the time arrived, Mitchell started drawing a map of Garfield on the floor with a marker, reviewing landmarks and road names with Bulldog and Wallace.

"Ok, kids. Time to go. Remember to stay together." Flow's face trembled.

She hugged and kissed each one of them and sent them to the access hatch.

11:41

Avery met eyes with Addison one last time.

Wallace peeled back the hatch. Avery and Mia climbed out, Paolo and Mitchell following close behind. Their names were now on bounty. Avery anticipated an onslaught of terror. In the current calm, he just felt numb.

Lafayette still sounded like a war zone. An omnipresent hum was broken by gunfire and the screaming of aerial vehicles. The Argus Bureau was still causing mischief. Technicolored lights flickered in the night sky.

Addison poked her head out, tears streaming down her cheeks.

She couldn't look at them directly.

"Be safe you guys," she whispered and then ducked back into the warehouse.

Bulldog appeared.

"Train Party!" he whooped. Then he was gone. Francis appeared, called Mitchell over and pulled him close. They exchanged some hushed words. And then it was time to move.

The nameless industrial drive ended onto a large vacant field. Beyond that, several blocks of sad houses dotted the street before the tall and wide train station stood. They made swift progress, crossing the field at a diagonal.

They shuffled between two darkened houses. A horrified woman peeked out a side window right as Avery passed. They caught eyes and Avery held a finger up to his lips.

In the shadows at the front of the house they scanned the open road. There was no cover between them and the side street that would take them to the back of the train station. The station's entrance drive swarmed with all manner of military vehicles.

A guard truck with a gun turret mounted in the bed zoomed past. Then another. And another.

"Avery, can you outrun bullets?" Mitchell asked.

"Look, they're headed away from the station. We're all good," Paolo said. They then turned back toward the station.

"Damnit," Mitchell said under his breath.

A window over their heads opened. The lady who had seen Avery threw a grenade out of the window and toward the guarding soldiers. Her range and aim were spot on. It hopped and skipped and exploded right by the first assault truck.

Soldiers sprang into action, circling into a defensive position pointing toward the explosion. The distraction they need.

"Run you idiots," she called down.

The four ran in the other direction. No looking back now.

11:48

The rear of the station sloped down against a hulking wall. A dark tunnel punched through and under the station and that's where they were headed. It was the type of darkness that their eyes couldn't adjust to. The terror was for real now. They held against the wall then advanced into the tunnel.

Half way in and they ran straight into a soldier stationed in the blackness. Shocked by the sudden appearance of bodies, he only had a chance to half raise his weapon before Avery flipped him onto the ground and knocked him cold with two punches. Then several times over he smashed the neutralized soldier into the pavement – rage and confusion burning off his mind with each meaningless strike.

"Avery." Paolo pulled him up. "Stop."

Mitchell stepped in between them, "We're good, man, we're good." Avery let go and slumped against the wall.

Mitchell used the soldier's own handcuffs, bound him to a pillar and tied a ripped shirtsleeve around his mouth.

11:52

They arrive at the designated emergency fire vent. It was constructed of louvers that seemed impenetrable. But, Paolo got a firm grip on the middle panel and pulled it back like an aluminum can. White light jabbed out into the darkness.

Avery went first with Mia in his arms. Then Paolo and then Mitchell.

Paolo pushed the vent roughly back into a position. If someone were to look closely, they would see handprints in the metal. The station thrummed with voices, and horns, and deep chested engines. Hunched down in sharp gravel, they looked like ants staring up at The Blade with her smooth panels glinting under harsh lights. They pushed as close to the train as possible and made for the front of the car. A greasy aroma came from the massive wheel trucks.

11:55

When the group neared the front of the train Avery felt the familiar sensation of someone pulling on his mind.

"Get down."

He dropped to the gravel and rolled under the low-slung body panel with Mia. Mitchell and Paolo jumped into the space between the cars, clinging to the cabling.

Not two seconds later a flock of Jarons flew across the train's roof. Several smashed into the outer wall, while the rest of the pack swooped toward the back of the station. The downed animals recovered, twisting wings and legs like someone was winding up a doll. They hadn't noticed three bodies under the train and took to the air once again.

11:57.

Mitchell snapped his fingers and Avery rolled out into the open. They moved up to the last passenger compartment. Steam hissed out of the mammoth locomotive. They were stuck now, waiting on the trust of the conductor.

11:58.

A narrow door sprung open. The conductor, slender and wearing a shallow brimmed cap and tailored suite, motioned urgently. Nearly on top of each other, they jumped inside. A rush and thump followed with the door sliding into place.

Inside the cabin, narrow running lights ringed the sloped roof. The air was crisp and almost sweet. Rows of stainless steel cases lined one side, strapped to the floor with wide bands. Three compartments stacked against the outside wall, each equipped with windowless doors. The last was open.

"You four are my personal luggage. Get into number three." He pointed to the open door.

There was a single low bench, next to a small portal window. It was otherwise bare, just wide enough for Mia to sit at Avery's feet.

The conductor pushed a canteen into Mitchell's lap.

"Complements of the Conductor. I'm locking you in now. And don't dare make a sound." With that, they were sealed inside.

At 12:00:02 the Blade pulled away from Platform One. She gained speed in elegantly, slicing through the night-veiled city.

From his window position, Avery watched tensely. There was nothing they could do now. Lafayette pulled away. He felt as though he was being pulled away from this new life.

From station to city wall would take sixteen minutes, based on Wallace's memory. When they cut passed fourteen minutes, Avery saw something that drew a lump in his throat.

A pair of fully armed drones hovered above the tracks. Various lights and sensors blinked from their undercarriage.

"Mitchell. Do the drones have anything that can detect Ables?" he croaked.

"That's the rumor. Why?" Mitchell whispered before leaning over and looking out the window.

"Oh god."

"What's out there? What going on?" Paolo pushed to see.

"Hold your breath," Mitchell said.

"What's that gonna do?" Paolo hissed.

"I don't know. Got any better ideas?"

The drones came into better view as the tracks pointed toward the boundary wall. That was it. They could only get so far under Hubbard's net. Avery held his breath.

Something strange then happened. Two rockets ripped up into the sky, peeled apart in separate trajectories, and collided with the drones. Explosions rocked the train.

"What the?"

Unguarded, the Blade flew through the boundary gates and out into the Outer Domain.

"Guess you got an army standing with us," said Mitchell.

Back inside the city walls, among the anonymous thicket blocks, the Garfield Ambassador slung a double-barreled rocket launcher over his shoulder and stepped onto his motorcycle. Before any alert even went out, he was gone.

And not far outside downtown, patrolling soldiers found an unregistered red convertible roadster a flame in the middle of the street.

Chapter 34

Deep Roots

The sky wore her best crystal blue apparel for the morning. And the streets stood empty. In a quiet bosque of trees in the corner of the cemetery, Flow clutched the square tea box against her chest and held a simple bouquet of wildflowers - lights purples mixed with splashes of bright yellow and bright green. The tall man that had helped Avery, Mitchell, and Paolo out of the Tower stood behind her, sweating in a suit coat and watching the road anxiously. His name was Jeffery.

Francis was also with them. His thick-rimmed spectacles replaced wide sunglasses. He wore a simple black suit over a crisp white shirt, a gold chain peaking out from under the collar.

His fingertips rested together at chest level.

In a controlled, soft tone he spoke.

"We are here today to remember Beatrice Ferndale. Since words may do little justice to her tenacity and many of those who may wish her farewell could not be here this morning - I will be brief."

Flow's face cracked, tears streamed. Jeffery supported her.

Francis continued, "We come to remember a woman who stood strong and stood strong with so many. I want to share one story, from ages ago, but a true testament to the caliber of woman she was. When we were very young, we used to play in the same park. One day I had just lost my basketball to a group of much older, much bigger kids and was sitting under a tree crying into my knees. When all of sudden - *wapp* - I get walloped so good that it nearly knocked me over. Bea had punched me right in the shoulder. *Get up.* She commanded. I stood up, blubbering and stammering. She then gave me a big hug and whispered in my ear, *I don't know how to play basketball. So you gotta teach me.* And with that. she handed me the newly reclaimed ball."

Francis straightened his jacket.

"It has been said that when the root is deep, there is no reason to fear the wind. Bea's roots ran ever so deep, and they were built with of her connection to each and everyone of us. So while we may mourn the passing of one of our greatest, remember that we must never fear the wind blowing her memory away. We will hold her strong in our hearts and in our actions."

He raised his right hand, closed it in a fist, and pressed it against his heart, "To Bea."

Flow mirrored the gesture, and then crumpled against Jeffery's shoulder.

Francis collected a small potted plant. Fans of long, oval shaped leaves sat in a tuft above the terra cotta container. A shovel leaned against his hip.

Flow collected herself and accepted the pot from him. And Jeffery took the shovel. At a cleared spot in the shade of a smooth barked Maple, he removed his jacket, rolled up shirtsleeves and dug a narrow hole. Dark soil piled neatly at his feet.

Bea's ashes, held in the ornate tea box, were laid to rest here. They all said their goodbyes. The Sweet Woodruff, planted above her, guarding her with delicate white flowers.

Francis pulled Flow aside for the briefest of moments when they had finished.

"Are you ready for what's next?" he asked.

With a tear still glinting in her eye, Florence just smiled. The ceramic tortoise rotated in her pocket.